Valen's Pack
Run with the Moon
Exodus

The Vamp for Me
My Life Without Garlic
Don't Stake My Life on It
Sunshine is Overrated
Don't Drink the Holy Water
The Trouble with Mirrors
That's One Cross Vamp

City Shifters
Bearly There
Harey Situation

What's his Passion?
Unexpected Places
Unexpected Moments

Anthologies
Racing Hearts: The Lonely Ones

CITY SHIFTERS
Volume One

Bearly There

Harey Situation

BAILEY BRADFORD

City Shifters Volume One
ISBN # 978-1-78686-063-7
©Copyright Bailey Bradford 2016
Cover Art by Posh Gosh ©Copyright October 2016
Interior text design by Claire Siemaszkiewicz
Pride Publishing

Published in 2016 by Pride Publishing, Newland House, The Point, Weaver Road, Lincoln, LN6 3QN, United Kingdom.

BEARLY THERE

Dedication

Remember to laugh every day.

To my friends and family, I love you all.

Chapter One

It was going to be another one of *those* days. So far, 2015 had been filled with them.

"Jagger, the Montemayor case is on the line. They hate the ad campaign idea. *Hate it.*" Debbie growled the last two words out as she tossed the file on his desk. "Assholes. Screw professionalism here. They're just being jerks because they want a high-quality ad at a bargain-bin price."

Jagger picked up the file and opened it. It was a brilliant ad campaign he'd planned, if he did think so himself. He was good at his job, though more and more, he found himself disillusioned about it. *Crap like this doesn't help at all.*

"What is it, specifically, that they hate about it?" he asked, glancing up at Debbie. With her blade-sharp cheekbones and Nordic good looks, she could have been a model. Would have, but according to her, she was too heavy and she wouldn't starve herself for anyone. Jagger didn't get the too heavy part, but he was aware that society had warped visions of both male and female beauty.

And he was glad he had Debbie on his team, because she was one tough, smart person.

"The cost, of course," she seethed. "They don't want to pay three million for a successful and innovative campaign. They want something similar to this but for less than half the cost."

Jagger wanted to throw the whole damned file away. "Well, that's gratitude for all our hard work, huh?"

"Yeah," Debbie scoffed. "After you brought them back from the brink of bankruptcy and doom three years ago and Sonny Montemayor swore he'd be indebted to you and your brilliance forever. Asshat."

"It's business." And Jagger hated it. "What *is* an asshat, anyway?"

"Don't give me any shit, Jag," Debbie warned. "I know you're even more pissed off than I am over this."

Jagger didn't bother to deny it. Debbie had worked with him for seven years and she knew him well. "Have we tried reaching Sonny?"

Debbie snorted. "Oh yeah, several times. He's miraculously out of the office every time, and his cell goes to voicemail. Cowardly bastard hasn't returned any of our calls directly. He's had his assistant pass along messages. It's like he's reverted to a fourth-grader."

"Seen it before when someone becomes successful *and* wealthy." Jagger used a finger to trace a path down the numbers for the ad's costs. "There's no way to do this any cheaper. If he wants a whole different campaign for his organics, then it'll be equal to what he's willing to spend. We're not carrying the costs for this."

"Renner won't be happy," Debbie pointed out. "He just about shit a pony over the cruise ship campaign. As if we could have predicted that whole debacle. Then with the Fortuna company dropping us for that new ad agency? Yeah, Renner will not be happy if we lose this client."

"He won't be happy if we eat the cost on it, either," Jagger muttered. "God damn it. I need to talk to Sonny, or someone who can sit down and go over other options. That's not going to be his assistant."

"You might have to go all stalker-like on him and hunt him down in person." Debbie sat in the chair across from him and took a pen out of her suit pocket. "Hand me some paper."

Debbie preferred to work the art for her ideas out by hand first before moving on to the more complicated techniques. Jagger passed her a notepad he had in the top drawer. "Have at it. I'm just going—" Movement outside his office window caught his attention and he frowned. There were definitely people approaching his office.

Shit, he'd hoped no one would remember. As stressful as the office atmosphere had been lately, there was more to think on than Jagger's birthday.

But maybe he was wrong, and whatever was going on had nothing to do with his birthday.

Debbie looked up at him, then twisted around to peer over her shoulder. Her smile in profile warned Jagger that he was about to be embarrassed at the very least.

"Come on in!" Debbie called out.

"Don't—" Jagger started, but the door was flung open and his jaw dropped as he stared at the blond-haired man wearing a pink bunny costume.

"Just be glad we only paid for the singing telegram and not the strip-o-gram," Debbie said as the blond stepped right into the office.

"Well now," the bunny man drawled as he cast his hazel gaze on Jagger and smirked. "Is this the birthday boy? No one told me he was so handsome."

Jagger snapped his mouth shut and leaned back in his seat. He was probably a nice, bright shade of red, but he'd be damned if he'd let himself be any more embarrassed than he already was. He crossed his arms over his chest. "Debbie, maybe you could move to one side so you're not blocking the view."

Snickers and outright laughter came from the people gathered in and beyond the doorway. It was their amused and happy faces that made Jagger determined to at least appear to enjoy this…bunny. It hadn't been just him who'd had a shit time so far this year.

Bunny Boy kept that smirk in place as he waved his fluffy pink boa. He was wearing miniscule, shiny pink shorts and a glittery pink tank top. Jagger noted the promising bulge those shorts covered but didn't let himself stare. He had more control than that.

Strangely enough, though, the man turned him on. Jagger was stunned by that. He preferred his lovers to be more like himself — bulky, rough-looking —

"So birthday boy here is how old?" the bunny asked.

"Thirty-three," Jagger answered, aware that when he did so, Bunny Boy shivered ever so slightly. He stopped himself from remarking on that, or asking if the man wasn't supposed to be singing.

"Oh ho, double treys," Bunny Boy crooned. "That's gotta be a lucky sign. For you, at least. You don't look a day over thirty."

Jagger doubted it, but he wasn't opposed to a cute guy flattering him, even if it was said guy's job.

On closer inspection, Jagger could see the palest of bruising under his left eye, and… He squinted. Yes, there under his left cheek was another bruise. Jagger suspected makeup was involved in the cover-up of both of those places.

Bunny Boy plastered on a smile that looked pretty damned fake to Jagger, and he began playing with that boa as the music started. Not the traditional birthday music, oh no, that wouldn't have done for him. This sounded like banjos and inbreeding had been involved in the conception of the song.

And Bunny Boy started singing along to lyrics that had everyone but Jagger laughing. Jagger didn't take them personally—it wasn't as if the song had been written just for him, and he understood that everyone in the office could use a little enjoyment and release from the pressures at work.

But Bunny Boy turned around and shook his pink-covered ass, and Jagger's dick demanded all the blood from upstairs at the sight of that bubble butt. Jagger was trying his best not to drool, trying instead to keep an amused look on his face when he was thinking filthy thoughts about what he'd like to do to Bunny Boy's ass.

Not that he'd do any such thing. It'd just been a while since he'd gotten laid. Jagger forced his gaze up Bunny Boy's lean body just as he turned around. Jagger noted the way his nipples pressed against the thin tank top. When he made it up to Bunny Boy's face, there was a sardonic smile pulling at those full lips.

Jagger squashed down his arousal as irritation spiked through him. He got the distinct feeling he was being laughed at then, and he didn't care for it at all.

Chapter Two

Oops.

Kevin Kelly didn't have to work at ditching his amusement once he was aware that the handsome guy across the desk had taken it wrong. For a short few moments, Kevin had been happy and flattered because he'd thought the man—*Jagger, oh my God, his name is Jagger!* — had been giving him an appreciative look.

It'd been a long damn time since an attractive guy had showed any interest in him. And when Kevin was dressed in pink and shorts that would make a Hooters' girl blush? Well, he was already feeling like a moron.

So he'd thought, just going by the way Jagger had ogled him, that maybe Jagger was interested. For a few seconds, anyway, until Kevin's attempt at a flirtatious smile failed.

But it didn't matter, because Jagger the Stud was now glaring like he was ready to swat Kevin upside the head. Having had just such an experience the day before, Kevin wasn't eager for a repeat. He plastered on a smile he hoped was obviously fake and benign. Then he tried not to let his sudden nervousness make him botch the song and dance routine.

It'd be easier if he was a naturally talented guy, at least in the singing and dancing department. As it was, he could barely carry a tune in a bucket, and he had to use the same single dance for every delivery he made, including the strip-o-grams. That damned dance was going to stay in his repertoire forever—he'd practiced until his feet had bled. His one, solitary dance.

God, he hated his job.

His bunny ears kept slipping. He had the wedgie to end all wedgies.

Jagger still looked like he wanted to smack Kevin.

Kevin wiggled his butt and shook his bunny tail, then turned and bent over so that Jagger got an eyeful of pert ass and white fluff. If that didn't wipe away some of that irritation, then Kevin was surely not going to get a tip.

Kevin might not know how to dance except for his one routine, but he sure knew how to shake his ass. He did so then, peering back over his shoulder to see that Jagger's gaze was right where he wanted it.

Kevin just hoped it wasn't because he had a hole in his shorts. That'd be his luck.

He spread his legs a little more and did a gyrating move guaranteed to bring any cock to life. Jagger's gasp might have been too soft for anyone else to hear it, but Kevin did. He was only the space of the desk and a step away from the guy. The woman who'd been in the chair had moved, taking the chair with her.

Kevin felt a devilish urge to screw with Jagger, just because the man seemed so... Whatever he was. Handsome, snarly, horny, judgy—Kevin didn't know him, didn't know what had made him get that look on his face earlier, but Kevin wanted to poke. *Just like a moron poking at a rattlesnake with a toothpick. Yup, I'm that kinda stupid today.*

He'd blame it on the lack of food. Kevin turned slowly, making sure he had some good hip movement going on. He pursed his lips at Jagger and lowered his eyelids until he could barely see. Hopefully, it was a sexy look. If not, well, there wasn't much help for it.

Jagger didn't seem to be laughing at him. Instead, those hot, honey-colored eyes were focused on him with an intensity that threatened to give Kevin a boner. Not a good thing to have happen in the tiny shorts he had on.

Kevin concentrated on Jagger, refusing to think about his own body lest he wind up with his pecker poking out for everyone to see.

Jagger, with his dark brown hair and thick eyebrows, wide eyes slightly tilted down at the outer corners, the broad planes of his cheeks and the heavy five o'clock shadow—he looked more like a lumberjack than a businessman. Kevin would bet he'd be something to see in faded jeans and a red plaid flannel shirt. *Oh, lumbersexual! Now I get the appeal!*

Even though he'd be a damned stud in plaid flannel, the suit was good, too. High quality, Kevin would bet. He glanced at Jagger's lips. *Those were just made to be wrapped around—*

No, no, no! Kevin leaned forward and rested his elbows on the desk. There was only one file on the surface, and he was careful enough not to touch it. He dipped his head down and howls and cheers came from the people watching behind him.

He reminded himself that this wasn't a strip-o-gram and he was in an office setting. Well, that hadn't meant anything before, but he wasn't supposed to be emulating giving head. Kevin rolled over and scooted up onto the desk. He sat with one leg cocked and the other straight, toes pointed, arms flung wide, and he bellowed the rest of the lyrics with his head tipped up toward the ceiling.

He couldn't look at Jagger. The man's scent was such a turn-on, whatever cologne it was. Kevin wanted to bury his nose against Jagger's neck and sniff out the source of it, discover the true core of the man buried under the fragrance. He wanted to lick that skin and—

Oh shit, now he'd done it. "Happy birthday," he warbled, the last two words to the song made much louder by everyone else shouting them along with Kevin.

Kevin rolled his eyes enough to kind of see Jagger. The man was blurry, but he was still watching Kevin. *Maybe. Maybe not.* Kevin was getting a crick in his neck.

And the damned bunny ears fell off. "Whoops." Kevin twisted around to see if they were on the desk behind him. His hand slid and he toppled backwards. In that split second, he braced himself for pain.

What he got was much better. Jagger moved so quickly that Kevin knew he wasn't purely human. The instant before Kevin would have gone head first off the desk, he was jerked into Jagger's lap.

"Woo-hoo! Jagger caught himself a bunny wabbit!" someone hollered. There were catcalls and whistles and Kevin was absolutely going to burn to ashes from his complete humiliation.

"Are you okay?" Jagger asked, that deep, low voice barely more than a breath beside Kevin's ear. "Calm down," he ordered to everyone else. "It'd be a shame if the boss came through and saw this."

"Too late," another voice said.

Kevin tried to scramble up but as close to the desk as Jagger had been sitting, he was kind of pinned. That, and Jagger had an arm around him, which felt really nice. Kevin wanted to snuggle right in, but he knew better.

"Who is responsible for this debacle?" a snooty-voiced man demanded to know.

Kevin felt Jagger take a deep breath and knew he was going to take the blame.

"I am," Kevin squeaked out instead. He pried himself up and off Jagger, easier done once Jagger had rolled the chair back and let go of him. Kevin dusted off his butt just to annoy the man who was standing in the doorway and looking down his stub nose at Kevin. "It's just a singing telegram, and I fell off the desk. I mean, I almost fell off and — "

"A singing telegram?" Snotty Man said with almost enough derision to annihilate Kevin. "Since when do people like you dress like strippers?"

Kevin wanted to vanish. Why the hell hadn't anyone developed personal teleportation devices already? *We can put a damned thingie on Mars, but nooooooo. No teleportation devices in existence. That. We. Know. Of.*

"And why would you be on the desk?" Snotty Man continued. "Wouldn't you be doing a singing and dancing routine instead of a — whatever that was?"

"He twisted his ankle," said the woman who'd been in the office. She glared at Snotty Man. "He was doing his singing and dancing routine, as you called it, and he twisted his ankle. He sat on the desk and finished the song. That's probably" — she leaned close and whispered loudly in Snotty Man's ear — "a potential lawsuit, so I'd be nice if I were you."

"A — " The man looked him over. "He isn't limping."

"I'm not walking," Kevin countered. "In fact, I may need to be carried out of here."

Oh hell. That's not a nice smile on Snotty Man at all.

"I'm quite certain that can be arranged. Security is right behind me."

Well, fuck. This year sucks.

Chapter Three

"Wait a minute, Mr. Renner, that's a bit excessive." Jagger would have argued more, but Mr. Renner glared at him and shook his finger as if Jagger were a child to be scolded.

"No, it's not. There's a hooker running around in this office. *That's* excessive." Mr. Renner turned to Debbie. "And don't tell me you didn't do this."

"I'm not a hooker!" Bunny Boy shouted. "You pompous—"

"Security!" Mr. Renner stepped aside as he hollered. "Get this piece of trash out of here!"

As big a dick as Renner could be, Jagger had to keep this job. It grated against his instincts to step back, but he didn't know what else he could do.

Well, besides slip Bunny Boy a tip. And maybe keep him from getting arrested.

"Sir, I'll make sure he leaves. I'll escort him out myself."

Mr. Renner sniffed and rolled his eyes. "I'm sure that's all just to help me out. I saw him on your lap."

"I fell!" Bunny Boy snapped. "Wow, are you a dick!"

Mr. Renner stopped the first security guy, Chuck. "Don't be gentle."

Chuck, who was bigger than any linebacker Jagger had ever seen, smiled and it was scary enough a sight to make many adults cry. "Yessir."

Bunny Boy whimpered and touched one of the badly covered bruises. "Not again. I'm gonna get fired for the second time this month."

"Second time?" Jagger repeated while trying to sneak his wallet out of his back pocket.

"Hey, you'd better not hurt this guy," Debbie told Chuck. She glared at Mr. Renner. "Law. Suit."

Mr. Renner glared back. "Un. Em. Ploy. Ment."

Debbie narrowed her eyes even more. "You are aware of what century we're living in, right?"

He planted a hand on his hip. "You are aware we live in Texas?"

Debbie growled and Jagger just managed to take a few bills out of his wallet and shove them in the back of Bunny Boy's shorts.

Bunny Boy squealed and spun around — and stumbled right into Jagger.

"See?" Debbie yelled. "I told you he was hurt!"

"Fine," Mr. Renner groused. "Chuck, throw him out, but don't completely break him."

"What?" Bunny Boy yelped as he was plucked up by Chuck. "No! Stop it! You big dumb ox!"

"I wouldn't be calling him names considering he's hauling you out of here," Mr. Renner said snottily. "Oh, whatever. Have at it. Chuck needs the exercise anyway."

Chuck hoisted Bunny Boy up over one shoulder in a fireman's carry. Jagger growled just like Debbie had but no one paid him any mind.

Mr. Renner turned his attention to Jagger. "I suggest you see what you can do to convince me not to fire you and your team." He turned and left right behind Chuck.

Jagger clenched his fists. If he didn't need the money so bad, he'd have told Renner to fuck himself with a two by four.

"Come on, have a seat. And put your wallet away, for Christ's sake," Debbie muttered as she took him by the arm. "How much money did you give that guy anyway?"

"I don't know. Not enough for putting up with being called a hooker and possibly hurt." Jagger looked in his wallet and gulped. "Er. Shit. About three hundred?" That was going to hurt him financially.

"Three hundred?" Debbie screeched. "Jesus, he wasn't even a decent singing telegrammer! I doubt he can strip for crap either! Three hundred!"

"I didn't realize," Jagger said in defense of his stupidity. "I was just trying to get money to…to… Aw hell." He sat and dropped his head in his hands. "That was Syn's grocery money. God damn it."

"I can pitch in on the tip," Debbie offered. "I mean, I was going to tip him anyway. Not anywhere near three hundred bucks, mind you, more like, I dunno, twenty if he was really good, but—"

"Just keep it." Jagger sighed and tossed his cashless wallet onto the desk. "I can stop at the ATM and get some more money." Jagger looked up at Debbie. "I don't want Chuck to break that bunny. He was already bruised up."

"I noticed." Debbie bit her cheek, then nodded. "I have to use the lady's room. Wouldn't you know? The one on our floor is packed." She darted out of the office.

Jagger owed her for that. Or maybe not. After all, she'd set the whole disastrous event into motion.

He picked up the file for the account from hell. Renner was really going to be on his case now. Jagger hoped he could find a way to keep the account and not lose money for the company he was employed by.

Otherwise, he might have to try to get a gig delivering singing telegrams himself.

* * * *

Overtime didn't mean shit money-wise unless Jagger snagged a new account during it. He didn't get paid by the hour. But they'd managed to come up with a new, cheaper ad campaign that he thought might work. If it didn't... Well, he would deal with that if it happened. For now, he was going to remain positive. *Ish.* Okay, not exactly positive, but at least not so pessimistic he wanted to kick his own ass.

He'd sent his team home hours ago. Jagger was surprised to see that it was after nine when he stood up and tried to stretch the pain out of his back. Didn't happen. He was worn out, hungry, thirsty, and damn it all, he had to be back at work as early as possible the next day.

He still needed to go to the ATM and stop by the grocery store before going to Syn's house. If he was lucky, he'd get away in under an hour, but Syn was a needy person sometimes, and she was clingy and demanding and... It was a good thing she was his sister and he loved her. She probably told everyone he was lucky she put up with him, and that was the truth, too. They were as dysfunctional as two loving siblings could be.

Of course, the fact that Syn couldn't leave her house was something else entirely. Ever since she'd been shot by a poacher four years ago, she'd become reclusive. More than that. And Jagger didn't know how to help her.

Taking her groceries or giving her money to pay the delivery boy probably was enabling her or something. He should stop doing it. Except he knew she'd seriously let herself starve to death before she left her home.

He'd tried to talk her into seeing someone to help her, but as Syn had pointed out, there weren't any shifter psychiatrists, and she couldn't really tell her truth to a human.

So Jagger worked, and took her money and whatever else she needed, and hoped for a miracle.

Tonight he was feeling less than hopeful. He was scared he'd lose his job, and it wasn't just Syn who was counting on him to keep working.

The near-constant worries and stress were pushing Jagger closer to a breaking point he couldn't fathom the depth of. He didn't know how to stop it, either.

But when he stepped outside the building into the cool winter air, all those worries and fears were blown away on the wind as a familiar scent tickled his nose.

Jagger turned and saw a shape huddled in the darkness at the edge of the building. "Bunny Boy?"

Well, that sounded really stupid. Apparently, he'd reached his intellectual zenith at thirty-two, and it'd been a downhill slide since then.

A warm laugh came from the man.

Jagger watched him approach, noted the slow roll of trim hips and— He frowned. It was cool out, in the low thirties, and the man was wearing that awful pink tank top and no jacket. At least he had sweats on. A new bruise darkened the right side of his face. Debbie had said Chuck had already been on his way back when she'd gone to spy. Chuck had obviously been a fuckhead.

"He hit you?" Jagger asked.

Bunny Boy stopped a dozen feet away and cocked his head as he stared at Jagger. "How can you see the bruise out here? The lights aren't all that."

Jagger pressed his lips together and refused to answer, but Bunny Boy came closer and closer until he was right in front of him. Jagger was caught in that pretty gaze, much like a deer being spotlighted.

"I thought you wanted to deck me earlier today, then you went and shoved three hundred bucks in my ass crack. I kinda want to know why you did that."

Jagger didn't have an answer that wouldn't sound stupid. Or make him sound stupid. He wasn't going to admit that he'd accidentally tipped the man that much. Besides, there was that new bruise, and three hundred bucks wasn't enough to make up for it.

Bunny Boy's nose twitched as he sniffed. He moved closer.

Jagger's insides jittered. He flushed hot. "What're you doing?"

"Smelling you. D'ya know, I could just…" He moved another half step closer. "Mmm, yeah, I'd just eat you up. Not literally, of course, that'd be disgusting, but I'd lick you right here" — he touched the side of Jagger's neck before dragging a fingertip from the base of it to right beneath Jagger's ear — "all the way up. I'd lick until I knew your taste like I know good chocolate. That's how you smell, how it affects me."

Jagger's cock couldn't possibly get any harder. He could barely breathe, he was so turned on.

"So how'd you see the bruise, hmm?" Bunny Boy asked.

Then he startled the crap out of Jagger by doing just what he'd said he wanted to. He stood on his toes and cupped Jagger's nape. In a flash, he was licking and Jagger was reaching for the man's hips.

"Are you...special?" the man asked. "A little different from other men?"

Jagger couldn't very well think to answer the odd questions, not when he was being licked like an ice cream cone.

It wasn't until a moment later, when he drew in a deep breath, trying to get some control before he slammed Bunny Boy against the nearest flat surface and fucked him until they both melted, that he detected the barest hint of the *other* in Bunny Boy.

And it was just *barely* detectable. Jagger pulled back and frowned at Bunny Boy. Something was very weird with the guy. Jagger had better than human senses, and he had always drawn an easy bead on other shifters.

So why could he barely pick up the *other* in Bunny Boy? "What are you?" Jagger demanded to know.

Chapter Four

Apparently, Jagger was long on good looks and short on brains. Kevin cocked one hip and tried not to shiver his balls off. "You first. I asked questions and you evaded. If I freeze to death out here waiting for answers, you'll have to live with the guilt."

Jagger snorted and it made white puffs appear in the cold air. Kevin snickered, thinking Jagger looked like a bull. It wasn't very cool that he didn't get to make the white puffs when he exhaled. *Lame. That's what happens when you start losing body heat, I guess.*

He reached for the pink feather boa around his neck, then groaned when he remembered he'd had to hand it over after being fired.

"Here." Jagger set down the briefcase he'd been holding and began to remove his coat.

Kevin waved him off, panicking just a little. "What? No, no way. That thing probably cost more than I've earned in months and if I touch it, it'll get ruined."

Jagger scowled and held the coat out. "Don't be ridiculous. You just guilted me into taking it off."

Kevin took another step back and caught his heel on an uneven spot on the cement. *Of course I did.* He was more amused and resigned than anything else as he fell onto his butt. "Oomph!"

Jagger crouched down and studied him. He tossed his coat onto Kevin, too. "How in the hell did you get a job doing singing telegrams? The dancing part of it…" He shook his head.

Kevin pouted at him for a few seconds, then shivered and gave up the coat fight. He slid his arms into the long sleeves, settling the coat on him backwards. It wasn't like he'd be keeping it on for long. He just wanted to defrost for a minute or two.

"You're saying my dancing sucked," he accused, stung because, as they said, the truth hurt.

"I'm saying you're as graceful as an elephant trying to walk a tightrope," Jagger said in an unmistakably droll tone.

Kevin didn't appreciate the insult at all. He raised his foot and pushed against Jagger's knee. Jagger's eyes went wide before he toppled over backwards. "You should talk," Kevin huffed. "Klutz."

"You pushed me!" Jagger said indignantly. "That's not the same thing!"

"I should have pushed you harder." Kevin got up slowly, aching from his tailbone all the way up to the top of his head. He was suddenly too exhausted for any more sparring, verbally or otherwise. "Look, I don't know why you gave me such a big tip, but I can't take it unless I know you meant it. That's a lot of money." He dug the bills out of his front pocket. "And the more I think about it, the more certain I am that you didn't mean to do it. I can see now that you were freaking out over that dickhead busting you for getting a lap dance you didn't want."

"You weren't—"

"And you have too much pride to just tell me the truth, which makes it tempting for me to keep it, but you know what?" Kevin tossed the bills down onto Jagger's chest. "Fuck it. I may not have a job, or anything else to brag about, but I do have some self-respect left. You might not believe that, what with the bunny outfit, but it's the truth. At least I wasn't panhandling on the streets. I was trying to earn a living."

He took the coat off and dropped it onto Jagger, too. He was done with this entire day. "I'm not Bunny Boy anymore, either." Now he was Unemployed Boy, and didn't that suck monkey balls?

"You were fired?"

Kevin turned to leave. He had a long walk home. Expending the energy for more sarcasm was stupid. "Yeah."

"God, what a shit day," he heard Jagger mutter.

Kevin paused. He could roll around in self-pity sometimes and miss other people's misery. Was that what he was doing now? He turned partially around and eyed Jagger. "Did you get fired, too?"

Jagger was getting to his feet. "No, but—"

"Eh." Kevin turned back around and resumed walking.

"Wait! You still have a tip coming."

Kevin was torn. He actually took another few steps before common sense kicked his pride's ass. "Is this going to be one of those shitty tips, like, *don't get caught on a customer's lap,* or *look both ways before crossing the street?*"

"Those are both good tips, but not the kind I had in mind." Jagger approached him from behind. Kevin was strangely reluctant to turn around. He was getting a weird, kinky enjoyment out of feeling stalked.

Then he sensed the heat from Jagger's body behind him. The man had stopped really close. Inappropriately so, possibly. Kevin craned his neck and Jagger cupped his chin. It was an awkward angle, but Kevin found himself held in place more by Jagger's expression than his hand.

"Did Chuck hit you?"

Kevin's mouth watered inexplicably as he stared at Jagger. "No. I tripped." If he wasn't careful, he was going to drool. Kevin tried to swallow and choked on his spit, which led to an embarrassingly wet cough right in Jagger's face.

Jagger quickly let go of him. Kevin wanted to just die then and there and be done with it. He was mortified. "I'm sorry," he squeaked out, and with the weight of the horrible day threatening to break him, Kevin took off, running as if his heels were on fire.

At least that warmed him up. Kevin had been waiting outside the building for hours. He'd been about ready to give up when Jagger had finally come outside.

Maybe he should have just kept the three hundred and not had any qualms about it, but if being cursed had taught him anything, it was to be as good a person as he could.

Not that it's helped break the curse.

That three hundred had been a shocker to tug out of his ass crack, and while Kevin had been thrilled at first, he'd started doubting that Jagger had meant to give him that much. Then he'd pictured Jagger having to do without food or other probably ridiculous scenarios. Someone wearing a suit and coat like the ones Jagger had wouldn't be hurt by losing three hundred bucks.

Maybe. It wasn't Kevin's place to decide that, in the end. He'd done what was right.

The guys he shared the motel-apartment with wouldn't be happy. At least Kevin hadn't told them about the money. He owed fifty for that week's rent. He was twenty short on it, and he didn't have any money to pitch in toward food.

If he got kicked out, he'd be screwed six ways to Sunday, but he'd deal with it. There was a homeless shelter three miles or so from where he lived. Tomorrow he'd go stand around Home Depot with all the other day laborers hoping to be picked up and put to work.

Kevin wasn't going to lie down and let life stomp him out. He was going to fight and keep trying to get past the stupidity of his youthfulness. Smarting off to a curandera—one he'd known was the real deal—had been the dumbest thing he'd ever done. Jesus, he could be a moron sometimes. He was lucky she hadn't made him impotent, too, though as seldom as he got laid, she might as well have.

Kevin glanced behind him. He had the distinct feeling he was being pursued, but he didn't see anyone. He scolded himself for being a dork. Of course he'd want the handsome, probably financially well-off stud to hunt him down, though what exactly he'd want Jagger to do if he caught him was a mystery.

Besides the obvious things Kevin would like him to do. Jagger was very appealing on a sexual level. However, the verdict was still out on his intellect.

Kevin chuckled and told himself to get over the *Pretty Woman* fantasies. He wasn't going to be rescued by a wealthy businessman who'd free him from a life of hardship.

No, screw it. He'd find a way to do that himself.

Chapter Five

It took Jagger almost a week to hunt down Sonny, but he'd finally found the little shit at his country club. Jagger liked to think it was his verbal skills and not his badly hidden urge to turn Sonny over his knee that had made the man finally agree to the new ad campaign. He was a little more gruff than he should have been, and Sonny had looked a tad nervous.

With that crisis averted, Jagger wanted to crawl into bed and sleep for twenty-four hours, but he couldn't.

Sleep, that was. He'd been haunted by Bunny Boy's bruised visage, by the way he'd turned and run, by... Jagger wasn't sure what all the reasons were. Somehow, Bunny Boy had gotten under his skin, which was crazy. They didn't even know each other.

But you'd like to know him. Jagger snorted at the thought. Wanting to fuck someone and wanting to know them were two different things. "Kind of." He shook his head. "No, they are. They *are.* I'm just feeling guilty because he..." *Looked like a scared rabbit. Lost his job. Got the shit whapped out of him. Had to wear those tiny, tight pink shorts that showed off every ridge and curve of —*

Jagger groaned. He was pathetic. And he was never going to fall asleep if he didn't get his brain to shut up. He rolled onto his stomach and shoved his pillow under his cheek. His eyes were gritty and his body ached like he'd spent hours at the gym.

Stress was going to kill him. That was all there was to it. He had to get a handle on that before it was too late.

Jagger exhaled and forced himself to relax, one body part at a time.

Eventually, he fell into a restless sleep, haunted with images of a man whose name he didn't even know.

* * * *

The ringing of his cell phone dragged Jagger's eyes open. It was Syn calling, and he groaned as he sat up, reaching for the cell at the same time.

"'Morning." Well okay, it sounded more like *mrnghng* than anything else, like all his vowels were still asleep, but whatever. It was unfair to expect him to be coherent without coffee.

"Good morning, sunshine!" Syn all but sang.

Jagger flopped onto his back and flung one arm over his eyes. She giggled and went on singing some obnoxiously cheery wake-up song. As soon as she stopped, Jagger found his tongue and got it unstuck from the roof of his mouth. He'd swear little fairies stuffed invisible cotton balls in his mouth while he slept. "Ugh, Syn. You freak. It's unnatural to be happy in the morning."

"You are *such* a grump. I thought it'd be best to start off trying to cheer you up before dumping the bad news on you."

Jagger buried a sigh. Of course there'd be bad news. "What happened? Is everyone okay?" He wasn't overly worried that they weren't since Syn didn't sound upset.

"They're fine. Jelly and Max are good."

Jelly and Max were her cats, aka her babies. Calling them pets would get a guy whacked upside the head. He would know.

"Uncle Sal is fine, too," Syn continued. "But he almost wasn't. He stepped through the porch."

"What?" Jagger sat up and scowled. "We just had the porch rebuilt last year!"

"I know, and if you see that contractor, I hope you smack him with the two by four that gave out on Sal. Do you have any idea how loud a sixty-three-year-old man can scream, and how much he sounds like a three-year-old girl when he does?"

"He's not hurt?" Jagger got out of bed and started for the bathroom. "Are you sure?" he asked when Syn said Sal was fine.

"Positive. He got scraped up but he shifted and is snoozing in his room. He'll be fine when he wakes up. It was just scratches."

That was good, at least. "I'm surprised he didn't head back out."

"Uncle Sal said he needed to do some things in the city. I think he has a lady friend he visits for a nooky call."

"No," Jagger groaned again. "No, I don't want to think about Sal and sex. That's disturbing, Syn."

Syn snorted. "Please. People have sex. Well, most people have sex. Apparently you and I are the weirdos."

Jagger felt sad more than anything else at that. Syn should be out and having fun, maybe not out screwing around, but not imprisoned by her own fears.

"Anyway, the porch needs fixing, and I was hoping you could replace the broken board?"

"I'm going to call the contractor I paid to do the job in the first place," Jagger told her. "He'll fix it, or else I'll—"

"Ohhh, spam his Facebook page with complaints?"

"No, I'll—"

"Hunt him down and kick his ass? Break his porch? Oh! The flaming bag of poop! I've heard stories about that!"

"How much coffee have you had this morning?" Jagger asked.

"Three cups," Syn answered. "And a whole bag of chocolate donuts. I am *happy*."

"Hyper," he muttered. "I'll be over in half an hour."

"Okay. Take longer if you need extra time to shake the grumpies."

Jagger grunted and hung up. He took care of his morning necessities and found some comfortable clothes to wear. He might be forced into suits and ties for work, but he hated the damned things.

His softest jeans fit him like they'd been tailored to accentuate every good thing about his lower half. Jagger liked them because of the feel, though. He was a tactile person and loved soft things against his skin.

Unless it was a man. He liked certain parts of his men to be harder than Wolvie's claws.

A flannel shirt and his hiking boots, and Jagger was dressed for the day. He made and drank half a pot of coffee, spent ten minutes arguing with the contractor he'd paid three grand less than a year ago to fix the porch, then got the asshole to agree to send someone over to Syn's.

Jagger made sure he understood that Jagger wasn't paying another dime for the porch to be fixed. It took the threat of a lawyer, but the contractor finally saw things his way. Sort of.

After that, he was ready to leave, taking the last cup of coffee with him on his drive over to Syn's. She didn't live very far away, but Jagger had other errands to run later so he didn't walk like he often did.

He wished, for more than the first time, that he'd followed Bunny Boy all the way home that night. Jagger had started to, but it'd been late, and he'd clearly not been wanted. Plus, there'd been Syn to take care of.

Maybe tonight, he'd go out and get laid. Clubbing wasn't his favorite thing, but he did it on occasion, long enough to find a willing man and get off together. It might help him get over his fixation on Bunny Boy.

If he didn't really feel that enthusiastic over the idea of sex with a stranger, it was just because he was still tired.

He needed to shift and spend some time in his bear form, too. That would help.

Jagger parked in the drive at Syn's house and shut the car off. He got out and went over to look at the porch. Since it was a covered one, it hadn't been rained on and exposed to the elements.

Jagger chuckled. Nothing in their part of Texas had been rained on in a long time.

Syn had been less than forthcoming about the damage. It wasn't just one board that had given way, and now that Jagger looked closely, he could see several were bowed. He glanced up as Syn opened the front door and peered at him through the screen one.

"Hey, you made it, and look, just in time. There's the contractor!"

Jagger heard the engine and turned, trying to keep himself from striding to the beater truck with the *Cole's Contracting We Do It Right* sign on the side of it.

He narrowed his sights on the driver, hoping it'd be the owner, who was the same guy who had done the original work.

And his jaw dropped open.

His wasn't the only one. Bunny Boy stood gawking at him from the other side of the truck.

Chapter Six

No way. Kevin's heart thudded and about a foot and a half lower, another part of him had a rather enthusiastic reaction to seeing Jagger standing there scowling like his ass was on fire.

I'm gonna get fired again. And I just freakin' started today! He'd had to beg Jody, one of his roomates, to get Jody's uncle, Cole, to hire him.

Kevin couldn't think about that just then. All he could do was gawp back at Jagger. The man was dressed as Kevin had imagined him back in the office — faded jeans, boots and a flannel shirt. Well, it wasn't red flannel, but the blue looked really good on him, and yeah, he just needed an ax in hand to pull off the lumberjack stud fantasy Kevin would be whacking off to later tonight.

Then he thought about that scowl. Okay, maybe no ax.

The silence stretched on way past the awkward stage. Finally, a woman poked her head out the screen door. "Jagger, you ass! Don't scare him off unless you can fix the porch after all!"

Jagger jolted and Kevin did too. Kevin whacked his knee on the truck door and black dots speckled his vision as he yelped.

"The fuck," he heard Jagger snarl.

"You killed him," the woman called out in a disturbingly chirpy voice. "You frightened him to death."

"Don't sound so freakin' happy about it," Kevin mumbled as he hopped on one foot, trying to hold his knee in his hands. About the time he wondered why he was bouncing around like a complete fool, he went down on his ass.

"See? Dead!" the woman crowed.

Kevin stuck his tongue out at her. Not that she could see him, but still. Jagger appeared at the front of the truck. "You should probably keep that tongue in your mouth so you don't bite it off the next time you take a dive."

Kevin closed one eye and glared with the other. "If I tell you to F-off, would you narc and get me fired my first day on the job?"

Jagger strolled over and squatted. He looked at Kevin, at every inch of him it seemed.

Kevin's insides did a weird little jittery dance.

"You just started this job?" And before Kevin could answer, Jagger added, "Do you even know how to do construction?"

"I'm fine, thanks," Kevin said as he gave up the one-eyed glare. Obviously, Jagger hadn't been intimidated. "Nothing broken except maybe my knee cap. But that's okay, 'cause I have another one and— Hey!"

Jagger grabbed him by the arms and Kevin barely had time to screech before he was tossed onto the man's broad shoulder. "What the— Put me down!"

"Ah hahahaha! This is priceless! Let me get my camera!"

Kevin quit squirming long enough to pop Jagger on one very nice butt cheek. "Who *is* that cackling harpy?"

"My sister, Syn," Jagger snapped, and the swat he gave Kevin in return was heavy enough to sting. "Whom I adore."

"Got it. Now put me—" Kevin's breath rushed from his lungs when Jagger stepped up onto the curb. His backside burned, but not because of the swat. No, it was because Jagger still had his hand there, and... Kevin's insides did their frenetic dancing again. He was *kneading* Kevin's butt!

"Say cheese," Syn called out. "Oh, turn around and let me get his face. Not that his ass is bad, not at all."

"This is sexual harassment!" Kevin yelped.

Jagger sat him down on the porch's edge with a thump.

"Ow." He glared at the big man. "So much for you being a gentle giant."

Jagger snorted. His sister burst out with a bawdy laugh.

Kevin twisted around to check her out. She was standing in the house with her phone in one hand, holding the screen door open with the other. She was tall and well-built, maybe a little on the muscular side, but what did Kevin know about women, really?

She had the same dark hair and pretty eyes as her brother, but whereas Jagger had a serious, almost stony look on his face most of the time, she was grinning like she'd never had a bad moment in her life.

"Who names a kid Sin?" Kevin asked her. "Did you, like, try to hang on to your mom's uterus during childbirth?"

Syn wrinkled her nose at him. "Gross. That's a disturbing thought. Jagger should keep you." She smiled broadly. "It's rare to find someone as warped as me."

"Syn…" Jagger rumbled. He turned his attention on Kevin. "It's a family name. Syn, with a *y*, not an *i*. Comes from a Norse goddess."

"And it fits," Kevin said. "You'd make an awesome goddess." He didn't even have to lie about that.

Syn beamed. "Oh, you are so keeping him."

Kevin pointed at her. "You stay out of this. I'm not anyone's kept boy."

"You look like a man to me," she told him.

"Bunny Boy." Kevin turned his finger on Jagger. "According to him."

Interest gleamed in her eyes. "Oh *reallllly*?"

"Later, Syn. I need to make sure he didn't fracture anything." Jagger's cheeks were a dusky pink that made Kevin think of the flush a man got before he came. Jagger's nostrils flared as he inhaled, and Kevin had to fight the urge to spread his legs and beg Jagger to sniff all he wanted.

"I want to know all about this Bunny Boy stuff," she warned. "Obviously you two know each other. Have y'all had sex?"

"Syn," Jagger warned.

Kevin choked on his denial, because he had been jerking off to fantasies about having sex with Jagger, and that was kind of guilt by association, wasn't it?

Jagger sat and patted his thigh. "Put your foot here."

Kevin had a burgeoning erection that would be obvious as hell if he moved his leg. "It's fine. God, I'm not fragile, just cursed to be clumsy."

"Clumsiness is usually carelessness disguised as bad luck," Jagger said.

Kevin stared at him. "What?"

"Never mind." Jagger reached for Kevin's ankle.

"No! I'm fine!" Kevin scooted away but Jagger caught his foot.

"Wow, this is like the mating dance of the socially inept," Syn murmured. "I should film it for a documentary—"

"Syn, why don't you—?" Jagger snapped his mouth shut as he tugged on Kevin's ankle. The second Jagger had grabbed him there, Kevin's cock had done the rest of the 'hey there, come shake my hand and give me a kiss' thing and perked up fully.

And Jagger was staring at it. Him. His dick. *Whatever.*

Kevin heard the screen door pop shut, but he couldn't look away from Jagger, who was still staring at his groin. Staring, and licking his lips like he wanted to devour Kevin.

Jagger's hand tightened around his ankle. Kevin felt the imprint of every finger.

Then those fingers began to move, first in soft caresses, then slowly, slowly, up to massage Kevin's calf.

His dick reacted predictably—and there was a bad joke he'd save for later—pushing up even harder at his zipper.

Jagger leaned in and inhaled.

The movement was primitive, and it called to a part of Kevin he hadn't been able to pull out in over a year.

Like calls to like. He'd heard it before.

"What are you?" he whispered as Jagger slid his hand up farther to the inside of Kevin's thigh.

Kevin's lungs seized when Jagger turned a hungry gaze up to him. "I'm going to be your lover."

Every smartass comment Kevin might have made shriveled up and blew away under that heated stare.

Jagger ran his hand back down to Kevin's ankle, then up again, this time brushing the side of his hand along Kevin's balls. "Nothing to say?"

Kevin had plenty to say, but since it would all be embarrassingly needy stuff, like *please get naked and fuck me*, he figured silence was the wisest course.

"No pain?" Jagger asked as he went back over Kevin's knee.

Kevin managed to shake his head. Jagger's expression darkened as need rolled off him. Even with Kevin's dimmed shifter senses, he could still smell Jagger's arousal. It was unfortunate that with the way the man was sitting and bent, Kevin couldn't see his crotch. He'd have liked to have gotten a glimpse at just how aroused Jagger was.

Which didn't matter, because Jagger grabbed his other ankle, and with a tug, Kevin slid forward, his legs going on either side of Jagger's. Kevin knew his eyes had to be the size of saucers — *okay, maybe more like anime character size* — but damn, he was really turned on by this bossy man. Surprising, since he'd always had a problem with authority figures. *Hence the curse.*

Jagger ran his hands up Kevin's legs and rested his thumbs against Kevin's nuts while framing his package with the rest of his hands. "If you don't want me touching you, taking you home and fucking you until you can't think of anything but me and how I feel in you, you'd better speak up soon."

"Not before you fix this porch," Syn said, saving Kevin from babbling about just how much he wanted Jagger to do all kinds of dirty things to him.

Jagger jerked his hands away and twisted around to glare at his sister. "Syn..."

"Porch," she said firmly. "Then go get laid. Try not to run this one off. He's funny."

Jagger sighed.

Kevin's dick would have told Syn to butt out if it could have. Kevin was glad it couldn't speak, because he was pretty sure Syn would have kicked the shit out of him for it.

God, the things that went through his mind. *A talking dick, really?* He giggled and slapped a hand over his mouth when Jagger snapped his head around to look at him.

"Talking dicks," Kevin said through his fingers. Syn started laughing, but Jagger only looked confused at first, then like he thought Kevin was a bit on the unstable side.

Well, he was probably right there. Kevin uncovered his mouth and started to get to his feet. Jagger was up in an instant, helping him.

"I'm not going to fall again," Kevin assured him.

Jagger bent and put his lips right to Kevin's ear. "Maybe I just wanted to touch you."

"Oh." *Oh shit.* He was going to end up so distracted he'd hammer his thumb and God only knew what else.

Chapter Seven

Jagger felt Bunny Boy's heart racing just like a skittery…well, rabbit. It excited Jagger unbearably, a call of prey to his inner hunter, and he pressed his hand more firmly to his intended lover's chest.

"Kevin," the man whispered.

No man liked hearing another's name on his guy's lips. Jagger scowled. "No, I'm Jagger—"

"Duh, donut, I'm Kevin," Bunny Boy got out between giggles. "And before you ask, yeah, I know you're not a donut. It's a saying from when I was a kid."

Jagger's cheeks heated with embarrassment. "Oh. Kevin's good, but… I think I like Bunny Boy better, at least sometimes. You remind me of a rabbit, all skittish and wide-eyed, smelling like—" Jagger closed his eyes as he sniffed right below Kevin's ear. "Mmm."

"If you say I smell like a rabbit, I'm so going to thump your nuts." Kevin sounded a little miffed. "Rabbits can't smell sexy."

The threat to his balls was what got Jagger's eyes back open as he jerked his head up. "You'll what?"

Kevin rolled his lips in and something very much like delight sparkled in his pretty eyes.

"I think he said he'd thump your balls," Syn called out from the doorway. "Seriously messed up mating ritual. Stop before you both completely kill each other's libido. Come inside, introduce yourself, er, Bun Boy—"

"Bunny," Kevin snapped along with Jagger.

Syn waggled her eyebrows. "I saw his butt. I'd go with Bun Boy. He's got quite the peach-shaped ass, isn't that what those bubble butts are supposed to be called? Or is it an apple-bottom? Heart-shaped?"

Kevin made a strangled sound and Jagger gave his sister a look promising retribution. She flipped him off.

"Anyway, I have homemade cinnamon and pecan rolls I just pulled out of the oven—"

Jagger began moving and dragging Kevin behind him before Syn ever finished speaking. "Inside. Oh my God, Syn made breakfast of the gods."

"How'd we go from you wanting to jump my bones to cinnamon rolls being the biggest turn-on ever?" Kevin complained. "I'm insulted, I think."

Jagger pushed Kevin in front of him, over the threshold and into Syn's home. "You won't be once you try one. Although—" Jagger's cock perked up even more as a filthy idea came to him. "She makes this frosting for them that I'd love to lick off of you—"

"Jagger, if you'll control yourself long enough to let Bun Boy fix the porch, I'll make you some of my frosting to play kinky sex games with," Syn offered. "But I want details."

Kevin stopped walking, his jaw dropping open. "Details? That's— Dude, your sister wants to know about your sex life?"

Jagger took advantage and palmed Kevin's butt while Syn cackled.

"Why not?" Syn asked. "I don't want pictures, and I only want to hear about you naked. Basically, just your part of it. I already know what my brother looks like naked."

"Syn!" Jagger barked out, letting go of Kevin's ass to instead cover his own face with his hands. "Ugh!"

Kevin scooted to the left. "Uh, maybe you two are closer than siblings ever should be."

Syn thwapped Kevin on the forehead. Kevin yelped and jumped back, elbowing Jagger.

"Ooomph!" Jagger stumbled and tripped over one of the hall table's legs. He flailed his arms, knocked off the mirror hanging above the table and managed to send the lamp flying, too. He grabbed for anything, trying to prevent breakage, and got Kevin. They went down in a tangle of limbs and glass.

"You deserved that for being a pervert," Syn said as she squatted beside them and glared at Kevin. "Gross. I've seen my brother naked because I walked in on him with a boyfriend when he was about sixteen. I was traumatized until I got an eyeful of Don Mackey's ass. Man. Maybe that's when I developed my fascination with male asses." She sighed and smiled. "He could give you a run for the money in the sexy buns department."

Jagger finally got his breath, only to lose it again when Kevin squirmed on top of him. That very fine butt Syn had been talking about rubbed right over Jagger's cock. Jagger gave up on trying to talk and let his head thump lightly against the floor as need boiled in his veins.

"Sorry," Kevin muttered. Jagger didn't know who he was yakking at. "I— Er, oh wow," he whispered, wiggling his butt eagerly. "Wow."

Jagger gritted his teeth and tried not to shoot off in his pants.

Syn snickered. "Hey, Bun Boy, I'm right here, remember? No sex in front of me unless you want the pics posted online."

Kevin apparently had forgotten about her, because he let out a loud curse and tried to get up. Jagger opened his eyes just in time to see a pained look streak over Kevin's face. "Shit. Glass."

Kevin nodded and paled. "Ow?"

"First aid kit." Syn leaped up and darted to the bathroom.

Jagger locked his arms around Kevin. "Up we go."

"What am I? An idiot?" Kevin grumbled.

"That remains to be seen." Jagger was only joking, mostly, and didn't think he deserved the pointy elbow to his diaphragm that he received. He loosened his hold on Kevin as pain spread out over his torso.

Kevin scrambled to his feet, grimacing and cursing.

Jagger sat up and realized Kevin wasn't the only one with some damage done to him. There were little nicks and cuts on his hands, and his back stung in a dozen or so places.

"Jesus," Kevin whispered. "You're bleeding."

"So are you," Jagger pointed out. He looked at his wounds. All shallow, they'd heal easily. The ones on his back were hopefully no worse.

"You two are never going to make it to having sex," Syn said as she returned with the kit. "Look at you both. Come on, into the kitchen." Syn held a hand out to Jagger. "Ew. Blood. Don't you dare drip on the rolls."

"Wouldn't dream of it," he grunted as he got up. The rolls were not going to be ruined by him. "These are just minor scrapes anyway."

"Mmmhm," she murmured. "How's your back?"

Jagger tried to peer over his shoulder and she laughed at him.

Kevin stopped him with a hand to Jagger's chest. "Be still." He walked behind Jagger. "Um. There's some blood?"

Syn sighed as if she were being tested to her wit's end. "Ugh. Fine, come on." Then she brightened. "Oh, hey, Bun Boy gets to see you shirtless. I bet he drools."

Jagger hoped so, but he merely rolled his eyes at his sister. Kevin snorted but there was definitely an eagerness in his expression.

"What's all the damned fuss?" Uncle Sal bellowed. "I'm trying to take a damned nap! Do I smell cinnamon rolls?"

Jagger groaned. "Please, let him go back to sleep—"

"Not happening," Kevin said close to his ear. "There's an old shirtless guy in his boxers coming down the hallway. I think maybe my curse has rubbed off on you."

Chapter Eight

Between the blood and the cuts, the repairs to the porch took much longer than Kevin had hoped. Plus, there was Uncle Sal, who said he knew more about carpentry than Jagger or Kevin. He certainly talked a lot about what they needed to do, and that should have been handy, yet wasn't. Maybe if Sal had just offered tips instead of getting in the way and trying to help, things might have gone smoother. There were too many people in with hammers in too small of a space for them.

"You hammered your thumb again," Sal pointed out quite unhelpfully.

Kevin had just yelped and stuck his thumb in his mouth to suck on it while he glared at the geezer.

Jagger sighed and took the hammer from him. "Pretty sure he's aware of that, Uncle Sal." Jagger thumped the nail in with two solid smacks. "Don't you have a girlfriend to go see?"

Uncle Sal waved him off. "Already saw her before I came over here. That's why I was too worn out to notice the porch was verging on collapse. Martha can ride a man like—"

"We don't want to know," Jagger said sharply. "Seriously, Uncle Sal. I don't tell you about my sex life."

"Well, why would you?" Uncle Sal asked, face scrunched up in confusion. "I mean, I don't wanna know about two guys putting their sausages in each other."

"Sal!" Jagger yelled, dropping the hammer. "God, stop talking, please, I'm begging you. Between you and Syn going on about sex, Kevin's going to think we are the weirdest family ever."

Sal cackled, sounding very much like Syn.

"Not the weirdest *ever*," Kevin assured Jagger. "But right up there, sure."

Jagger huffed. The man was adorable, all big and muscly and miffed. Kevin liked him, a lot.

Syn pushed the front door open and watched them while she sipped something from a cup.

Kevin noticed that she never actually came outside, not any of the times she opened that door. He frowned and wondered if he had any business asking about that. Probably not, he decided.

Which wasn't going to stop him from being nosy as soon as he got Jagger alone.

Although, looking at the man's muscular body, and the big bulge right *there* out of reach, Kevin wasn't sure he'd be doing any talking at all once he got Jagger to himself.

And naked. Can't forget naked. As if he ever would. Was he really going to do that, to let Jagger take him home and fuck him?

Jagger turned back to look at him and Kevin's stomach dipped and quivered. Yeah, yeah he figured he was. He hadn't been with anyone in far too long, and

Jagger, for all that he was a scowly bastard, was also sexy as fuck. He probably wouldn't be nearly as appealing if he was smiling all the time. There was just something very hot about a brooding man.

Mysterious man, too. Kevin had noticed the way the cuts and scratches were healing rapidly. The man was some kind of shifter, and a powerful one at that.

Kevin leaned forward, unable not to, and inhaled deeply. His eyelids fluttered shut as he filled himself with the musky scent of the man under his cologne. Strong, earthy, like damp forest and fresh grass, Jagger's scent was potent.

"Don't even think about leaving until this porch is done," Syn told them. "I won't make Uncle Sal come inside if you two are going to run off the second y'all are left alone."

"Hey!" Uncle Sal exclaimed. "What am I, a kid?"

"Not hardly," Syn replied. "Unless you're an old, wrinkly one."

"Brat," he muttered.

"You raised me," she pointed out. "Mostly. Come on, leave the two horn dogs alone."

Sal grumbled the whole way in, but he finally did go with Syn, and Kevin still didn't move back. He was content to just breathe Jagger in until he came in his pants, apparently, which was a real possibility.

Of course, the way things had been going, he'd probably shoot the zipper pull off and blind one or both of them...

The likelihood of that happening had Kevin sitting back on his heels and opening his eyes. He stared into Jagger's darker ones. There was power there, and something else, something...big. "What are you? Stop bullshitting me. I know you're a shifter. You're healing. You don't smell human."

Jagger's nostrils flared and he had a hand around Kevin's nape in a heartbeat. He pulled Kevin forward, which made him have to knee-walk over the uneven planks. He didn't care, because as soon as he was close enough, Jagger was slanting that hard mouth over his and pushing his tongue into Kevin's mouth.

Kevin's pleasure center was not just one spot, but his entire body. He tingled and burned — in the good way, not in the need antibiotics kind of way — all over. His toes and fingertips felt hot, too, and his groin — well, God, he was close to spurting like a virgin getting touched for the first time.

It *had* been a while, after all.

Jagger pulled him even closer and that slick tongue found every one of Kevin's favorite places to be licked. In his mouth, anyway. Kevin had no doubts it'd be equally as thorough on the rest of his body.

Oh geez! Thinking like that wasn't going to keep him from humiliating himself, either.

Jagger's hands were huge, big like the man himself. That bulge was damned impressive too, even when it'd been soft. Now with it growing rapidly between them, Kevin wanted to both quake with fear and build an altar to that large cock.

Jagger made a hungry, growly noise that vibrated right into Kevin. He clenched everything, trying to keep from giving way to his orgasm.

Unfortunately, that included his teeth, even though it was only briefly.

Jagger shoved him back just as Kevin unclenched. "Sorry, oh God, I'm sorry, I—"

Jagger wiped his mouth and laughed as he shook his head. "You are something else, aren't you? I think I'd better tie you up and gag you when we fuck. For both of our safety."

Kevin's apology died as his brain shorted out. The idea of being tied up was…well, it was so far beyond erotic Kevin could hardly wait for it to happen.

The gag part, he wasn't so sure about.

"Bear."

Kevin blinked away the filthy image building in his mind of him, naked, helpless, spread open and—"What?"

Jagger smirked and licked his swollen bottom lip. "You asked what I am, and I figured I wouldn't answer your question with a question this time. I'm a bear."

"Duh," Kevin said, staring at the bulky, hairy chest. He knew it was hairy because there was a thatch of dark curls peeking past the solitary unfastened button. "Of course you're a bear, but I'm not really a twink—Ohhhhhhh," he dragged out while slapping himself on the forehead. "God, I'm dense."

Jagger snickered and Kevin blushed so hard he felt his skin heat up.

"Now, what are you?" Jagger asked in return.

Kevin shrugged. "Nothing now, I guess. I can't shift. Used to be a pronghorn, once upon a time."

Jagger's smirk stretched into a wide leer. "Oh, good. Prey."

Chapter Nine

Prey. Jagger's body thrummed with anticipation. There was a distinct sort of fear-lust-eagerness coming off Bunny Boy. "Kevin," he growled, more at himself than not, but Kevin jumped like he'd been walloped on the ass with a fire poker.

"What?" Kevin squeaked, skittering back a few feet. Jagger forced himself to look away from Kevin long enough to check the porch over. They'd worked on it all day, with intermittent breaks. He decided it'd do for now.

And with that decision made, he reached for Kevin.

"Hey!"

Jagger had Kevin on his shoulder before the word was all the way out. He cupped Kevin's ass with one hand, feeling a primitive sort of ownership he'd never experienced with another man before.

"Put me —" Kevin swatted him on the ass. "Where're you taking me?"

Jagger didn't miss that Kevin hadn't finished the demand to be put down.

"Jagger— Oh, never mind," he heard Syn holler before she burst out laughing.

"Do you have to return the truck?" Jagger asked Kevin.

Kevin swatted him again. "Well, *duh*, that's not my name on the signs on it!"

Jagger was tempted to smack Kevin's ass back for that, but he didn't. Instead he curled his fingers over the taut mound of flesh and squeezed.

"Jesus," Kevin whimpered. Jagger could feel the rigid press of Kevin's cock through his jeans. "Uhn—"

"When do you have to return the truck?" Jagger ground out. Even the blood in his veins seemed to heat with the need throbbing up from his dick.

"T-tonight," Kevin stuttered. Jagger squeezed again, pushing his fingers hard against Kevin's hole. "Later. Sometime. Job came with it sort of—uh, I. T-tonight."

The near-incoherent babbling was nice. Jagger approved. "Not much time then," he murmured more to himself. The sun was quickly setting. "I have such plans for you…"

Jagger heard Kevin's gulp and grinned. He did have very filthy plans for the man. Some that would involve hours of exploring Kevin's nude body, but he wasn't going to make either of them wait long enough to get to his place. *Yet.*

"Jagger," Kevin began. Jagger tripped over the curb and jostled them both, but kept them from falling.

"Sorry," he muttered.

"It's the damn curse." Kevin wiggled and Jagger gave his ass another firm caress. "Oh… Do that—"

"There's no such thing as curses, unless you mean the bad words kind." Jagger had never been so glad for his sister living out in the boonies as he was then. While there wasn't anything like a forest to run in, there were trees scattered about, and shrubbery that provided cover for miles before leading to even more private places.

But Jagger was aiming for close, and just private enough to get off. Having run and played in the area since he'd been a small child, he knew just where he wanted to go.

"Where—?" Kevin started to ask again.

"Somewhere I can strip you down and blow your mind, among other things," Jagger told him.

Kevin moaned and shoved one hand down the back of Jagger's jeans. "Yes, please. Especially the blowing part."

Jagger strode through the first wave of bushes just as he heard Syn's cackling.

"Your sister's a nut," Kevin said.

It was hard not to take offense. Jagger knew Kevin didn't mean anything bad by it, that he was just referring to Syn being fun and unique. But, the fact that she did have problems made the comment rankle.

Still, he refrained from snapping. Saying anything defensive would just point out that Syn wasn't like everyone else. That she needed help he hadn't yet gotten for her.

Fortunately, Kevin seemed oblivious to Jagger's internal debate. He was too busy curling his fingers against Jagger's butt cheek.

Jagger wanted Kevin naked, wanted to touch bare skin, too. He walked faster, catching a thin branch or two in the face in his hurry to get them farther away.

The sun had finally set, perfect timing, Jagger figured, because he loved the cover of night and the freedom it afforded from prying eyes. Not that he believed anyone other than him and Kevin were out there. Still, even if there was, Jagger was done waiting. He stopped and lowered Kevin's feet to the ground, only to immediately push him against the nearest tree.

From there, it was a frenzy of hands and lips, teeth and tongues. Jagger wanted to devour Kevin, to burn the taste of him into his own DNA, to memorize the feel of him under his hands.

Kevin's lips parted eagerly and he pushed his tongue into Jagger's mouth. Jagger wasn't ceding control, couldn't, or he'd lose it completely and frot away against Kevin.

He fisted one hand in Kevin's hair and pulled his head back. Kevin shuddered and ripped at his clothes, sending buttons from Jagger's shirt flying.

Jagger nipped Kevin's lips and sucked on them, then his tongue. He used his other hand to cup Kevin's throat. Every time Kevin swallowed, the bob of his Adam's apple against Jagger's palm added to the need inside Jagger.

He swept his tongue over Kevin's swollen bottom lip. Kevin shoved at Jagger's shirt. When he rubbed his hands down Jagger's chest, fingers grazing his nipples, little bolts of electric pleasure shot out from Jagger's chest, right down to his balls.

It drove him wild with want. He pushed Kevin's head aside, not rough enough to cause him harm, but enough that Kevin moaned for him and clutched at him.

Jagger zeroed in on a spot lower down on the side of Kevin's neck. He bit at it, turning the skin pink.

"Gawd," Kevin rasped. He dug his nails into the skin at Jagger's waist.

The pain caused Jagger's cock to harden even more as lust enveloped him. He sealed his lips around that succulent skin and marked Kevin with several deep, sucking draws.

Kevin cried out and shook against him. Jagger shoved a hand down between them and squeezed Kevin's cock through his pants. The spreading moisture there told the tale just as surely as did the heady, musky scent of spunk that reached Jagger.

More! More, more, more! He needed so much more that he shook with it. He couldn't get enough of Kevin's taste, of the sounds he was making, the scent of his cum—

Jagger tugged on the skin with his teeth, then released it to drop quickly to his knees.

"I already came," Kevin said, his voice gruff and shaky.

Jagger merely opened his pants and mouthed the still-erect cock covered by thin cotton.

"Fuck. That's so…good." Kevin ran his hands over Jagger's head. "Oh man, better than— Oh, sensitive! Don't stop!"

Jagger had started to pause, afraid Kevin wasn't enjoying it once he'd said he was sensitive. Instead, with Kevin pulling at his head, Jagger lapped at the tip until he knew every nuance of Kevin's spunk.

He rolled Kevin's underwear down and freed his balls. Jagger hefted them in hand, enjoying the warmer temperature of them, the frizzy hairs rasping against his palm.

But Kevin's dick was the true prize. Thick, veiny, wider in the middle and topped with an enticingly broad crown. Jagger didn't make himself wait any longer. He parted his lips and took the tip in, rolling Kevin's balls at the same time.

"Jagger!"

Kevin's shriek made Jagger's ears ring. He didn't know if it was shock—or why it would have been, if it was—or what that forced the sound from Kevin.

Maybe it was just because Jagger sucked dick like a pro. He did, and he knew it, and reveled in every quiver and whimper Kevin let loose with.

Jagger closed his eyes and sank into the blow job. Every lick and suck became his focus—Kevin's pleasure became his focus. He kept playing with Kevin's balls while taking his cock in to the base. Jagger barely managed it. Kevin was better built than the prior lovers he'd had.

When he swallowed, Kevin yelped and bucked. That pushed his shaft in even deeper. Jagger held his position for a second, then came up and loved on the crown while he got his breath. He tongued the slit, seeking out the salty moisture there.

"Please, please, suck me again," Kevin begged. He didn't pull or push Jagger this time, merely rested his hands on Jagger's head.

Jagger wasn't a merciless man. He gave the tip one last lick, then sucked, hard, all the way down Kevin's length.

The sounds Kevin made... Jagger had never heard such eagerness, such need. He soaked it all in while taking Kevin's cock in again and again. Kevin's responses were addictive, and Jagger would have loved sucking him off all night, but Kevin eventually began to push at his shoulders.

Jagger felt those heavy balls draw up. He opened his eyes and sought out Kevin's gaze in the dark. Moonlight cast silvery strands around them, and the gleam of it in Kevin's eyes was fascinating.

"Coming," Kevin whispered in a raw voice. Jagger unzipped his own jeans and shoved his hand in to press against his dick. Stroking wasn't even going to be necessary. A few rubs would be all it took.

"Do it," he pulled off sucking long enough to say. Jagger licked Kevin from tip to base, then came back up for the whole length again.

At the same time, he pushed up on Kevin's balls and rubbed his palm against his own dick. The second he swallowed around Kevin's shaft, Kevin shouted, a torn, ragged yell that sounded like it came from his core.

Along with the pulsing of Kevin's dick and the first hot shot of his cum into Jagger's throat, it set off Jagger's climax as well. Jagger jerked as heated bliss filled him, growing brighter with every jet of spunk he shot out.

He gasped, leaning back a few inches. Kevin's cock emptied the rest of his cum onto Jagger's tongue. Jagger came harder then than he possibly ever had before. Kevin's release turned him on to a greater degree than he could process at that moment.

When Kevin's shaft was soft, Jagger let it slip from his mouth. He was too shaken to stand yet, so he rested his head against Kevin's hip.

Sucking Kevin had been the most intense sexual experience of Jagger's life.

He figured it must have shaken Kevin up pretty good, too.

But when Jagger finally found the strength to look up at him, Kevin had nothing but what appeared to be trepidation in his gaze.

Chapter Ten

Kevin's heart was going to beat right out of his chest. He still couldn't believe Jagger had knelt and sucked him off. If asked before that moment, he'd have sworn Jagger would be the bossy kind of lover who insisted on being the one who got sucked off, not the other way around.

Kevin's world-view was shifting…or, at least, his Jagger-view was. But that hardly mattered, because —

"I gotta go!" Kevin pushed at Jagger's shoulders and squirmed, but the man didn't let him go. Kevin whimpered.

"Why're you panicking on me now?" Jagger demanded while caressing him gently. "Are you trying to say you didn't want — ?"

"No!" Kevin snapped, quickly adding, "That's not what I'm saying. Yes, I wanted it, but you have *no* idea…" Kevin did, though. He pushed harder.

"Kevin," Jagger growled. "Stop."

Kevin couldn't. "No, you gotta let me go, now!"

Jagger let go of him, sort of, rising to his full height and pinning Kevin to the tree with his body instead of his hands, which landed on either side of Kevin's head. "Not like this. Tell me what I did wrong."

"Wrong?" Kevin was confused. "That was the best blow job I've had in my entire life. You've ruined me for others—"

"Good," Jagger said with a smug grin.

"No!" Kevin wailed, frustration pouring out of him. "You don't understand! The curse—"

Jagger snorted.

Kevin whacked him on the arm. "Stop being a dick!"

"There's no such thing as a curse!" Jagger retorted.

Just then, an ear-splitting crack of thunder rent the air, followed quickly by a brilliant flash of lightning. Kevin was positive he felt both of those all the way through his body.

"What the—" Jagger began, glaring up at the sky, or trying to, around the overhang of leaves from the tree they were under. "There wasn't a cloud in the sky, and it never rains in this part of Texas."

"I tried to tell you—"

A second heart-stopping slam of thunder and Kevin couldn't hold back the squeak of terror. Lightning followed again. He hated storms, hated being out in them—

"If you mention a curse, I'm going to have to remind you, this is Texas. Crazy shit happens with our weather. Last week it was freezing, and now it— Fuck it all!" Jagger sputtered as rain poured down on them both, the tree doing little to shelter them.

"You said yourself there wasn't even a cloud in sight!" Kevin argued. "Now it's raining and thundering and lightning!"

"Hell!" Jagger shouted.

"I know! I'm mad too!" Then he yelped again. "Ouch!" Were they under a pecan tree?

"*Hail!*" Jagger yelled. "Hail, hail, *hail!*"

"Ouch! Ouch! Ouch!" Kevin flung his arms over his head and hunched. "Run!"

For once, Kevin didn't end up on the ground when he tried to move. The same couldn't be said for Jagger, who spun on his heel and ran three steps before sliding into a face-plant. Kevin saw it all in his peripheral vision but wasn't able to do anything to help.

And the hail came down harder.

"Fuck!" Kevin shouted. He waved one hand up to the hateful sky. "Enough already!"

Lightning hit a tree not twenty feet away.

Kevin quivered inside and out, but he dove for Jagger and grabbed at his arms. "Come *on!*"

Jagger slipped and slid his way up to his feet. Kevin pulled his shirt up over his head, trying to form some sort of protective cocoon for his noggin while Jagger did the same.

And they ran, feet sloppy in the mud that seemed entirely too deep and wet for the circumstances. The hail pelted them, and it stung like fiery hell when it hit just right. Kevin was going to be covered in black and blue bruises.

They cleared the wild land hell, and Kevin bolted right for his truck despite Jagger telling him to head for the house.

Fuck that, he'd brought his curse down on Jagger today. First in the house, then outside with all the fury of Mother Nature aimed at them.

He was going home, alone.

Kevin ran for the truck. He'd worry about the tools on the porch later, maybe beg one of his roomies to come by and get them. He'd almost made it when strong arms locked around his waist and a loud growl made his eardrums vibrate.

"No," Jagger snapped at him. "You are not running away from me again!"

They crashed into the side of the truck, Jagger spinning just before impact to take the brunt of the fall.

"You can't make me stay with you," Kevin rasped, heart aching more than his body. "You can't. I don't want to be here. Don't want to be with you! Let me go!"

Jagger opened the truck door and shoved him inside the cab. Kevin immediately hated that he'd done what needed doing and pushed Jagger away.

But then he realized he hadn't, because Jagger crawled in right on top of him. He gripped Kevin's jaws in both hands and glared down at him. For several seconds, Kevin lay perfectly still, frozen under that look, Jagger's earlier description of him as prey holding suddenly, fiercely true. He was caught, and unable to free himself. Not wanting to free himself.

Jagger finally rubbed one thumb over Kevin's lips. "Liar," he said. Nothing more, just that one apt description before he dipped his head down and nibbled at Kevin's bottom lip.

Kevin gasped, heat blooming all throughout his body.

And Jagger kissed him, decimating any more protests Kevin could have built.

Chapter Eleven

Jagger didn't know why Kevin kept mentioning a curse. Bad shit happened to people, and Texas weather was crazy.

He supposed there was a chance Kevin might really want to ditch him, except that wasn't what he saw in Kevin's eyes, or what he felt when he tumbled on top of Kevin in the truck and kissed him.

Kevin opened right up for him, and clung to him as if Jagger were the shelter from the storm. Hail pelted the truck, rain doused it, wind buffeted it, but Kevin curled his fingers around Jagger's biceps and held on, moaning as Jagger feasted on him.

As tempting as it was to lose himself in Kevin again, Jagger forced himself to raise his head and end the kiss. Almost. He had to dip down for another quick taste of those swollen lips, then he put a few inches distance between his mouth and Kevin's.

Kevin muttered a protest and opened his eyes. He blinked, as if confused, then he shook his head slightly and asked, "Why'd you stop?"

It was the opening—well, one of them—that Jagger needed. "You didn't mean what you said, so why did you say it?"

Kevin blinked a few more times. "Huh?"

Jagger was delighted that his kisses had scattered Kevin's thoughts but he needed the man to answer him now. Jagger raised up onto his knees, which forced him to hunch over Kevin. "You told me you didn't want to be with me. You lied."

Kevin's eyes rounded and he gulped.

Jagger waited, noting every flinch and move Kevin made.

Finally Kevin got a stubborn look on his face right after the pinging of the hail increased. "I did mean it," he shouted, most likely to be heard over the ruckus.

Jagger decided space between them wasn't his friend. He lowered himself down onto Kevin, covering as much of Kevin's wet form as he could.

He felt Kevin shudder beneath him, smelled the sultry tinge of arousal roll off him at the same time he felt the thickening of Kevin's cock against his.

"Liar," Jagger whispered, almost brushing his lips over Kevin's. "Are you lying to me, or to yourself? To us both?"

Kevin loosed a whimpering sound and wrapped his arms around Jagger's nape. "I—" He closed his eyes. "It's—"

Jagger sucked on Kevin's bottom lip until Kevin mewled and rubbed against him. Then he asked, "It's what?"

Kevin shook his head, kept his eyes shut and mouth open. He licked his lips and Jagger ran his tongue over Kevin's. "Tell me," he demanded.

Kevin's eyes popped open. "I already *did*!" he wailed. "And you don't believe me!"

Jagger heard the misery in Kevin's voice loud and clear. It was what kept him from scoffing about the curse again. Even though Jagger didn't believe in such nonsense, Kevin clearly did, and scorning Kevin's beliefs would just make Jagger an asshole.

"The curse," Jagger said quietly.

Kevin's frantic nodding almost caused them to smack their heads together. "Yes! I told you, I'm cursed! It's true."

Jagger arched an eyebrow at him. "And that's the whole reason you want me to leave you alone?"

Kevin snorted. "Please, what sane person would reject you otherwise?"

Jagger had a list of exes who thought he was a jerk, or a loser, or too involved with his job and family. Okay, he had three, and a handful of one-offs, but whatever.

"I mean, look at you," Kevin continued. He squirmed and Jagger sat up again. Kevin scooted into an upright position on the bench, with his back to the door. The hail lightened up to a fainter pinging on the truck. "You're fuckin' hot, man. You're my lumberjack fantasy come true — except for the whole actually being a lumberjack part, but that's okay, because you'd reek after a day's work and I really like the way you smell now. It's way better than eight hours of intense man sweat. I know some people like sweaty men, and I'm okay with a minimal amount of sweat, or any amount that comes up due to fucking, but having a sopping wet guy who smells like funk and —" Kevin slapped a hand over his mouth. "Mmmph." He parted two fingers. "Sorry."

Jagger was amused and wanted to cradle Kevin in his arms, a novel desire for Jagger. He weighed whether or not to say what was on his mind, then decided to go for it. "You're adorable, Kevin. I want to keep you."

Kevin's entire expression registered shock.

Okay, maybe that was too much. Quick recovery — umm distraction! Jagger hoped it worked. "Tell me about the curse. How did that happen? Or do you just mean in a general way? Was there an actual witch with a wart on her nose or what?"

Kevin's shock turned to irritation. "Don't make fun, and don't be a douche about witches. I know some and they're awesome, and the only warty thing about them is their exes. You just don't fuck around with a witch."

Jagger held up his hands. "No offense intended, Kevin. I was trying to make a joke but obviously I was just being a jerk."

Kevin sniffed. "I'll forgive you this time because you're so sexy. Next time, you have to strip naked and swing your dingy for forgiveness."

"Swing my —" Jagger snapped his mouth shut. Holy rollers, the things Kevin said.

Kevin nodded. "You heard me. I'll expect a song of sorts when you do it, too. Maybe something like, *I can swing to the left, I can swing to the right, I can swing a ding dingy all day and night.*" He frowned. "No, that's a sucky song. Do you think you can make it go in a circle?"

"Kevin." Jagger laughed nervously. He wasn't sure if he should say more, lest he risk a repeat offense and have to strip and…swing.

Kevin shook himself. "Right, whatever. The thing is, I have a smart mouth. Not as bad as I used to, because once a curandera curses you, and everything goes to shit, you learn a lot of humility. And humiliation. That happens a lot, too."

"A curandera," Jagger repeated. He was pretty sure he knew what that was. "How did you —?" Jagger stopped himself from saying, *how did you piss off a curandera*. He was fairly certain that would just be the wrong thing to ask. "What happened?"

Kevin gave him a shrewd look. "Nice save."

"I try."

"Uh huh." Kevin pushed at a chunk of wet hair that flopped onto his forehead. "So I used to think I was hot shit. I mean, I was worse than most twenty-year olds. I was vain, and thought I had to have the last word on everything." He huffed and rolled his eyes. "Gods, I was such a fuckhead. I thought being a smartass was the same thing as being smart."

Jagger shrugged. "Sounds like most kids I know. I think we all go through that obnoxious 'I'm an adult now and I know everything' stage."

Kevin pursed his lips then shook his head again. "No, you have no idea. I was spoiled, rich, and totally believed I was better than almost everyone else."

Jagger sat back and studied Kevin. He couldn't picture the man being like that. His skepticism must have shown on his face.

"It's true. I'm surprised someone didn't just kill me to rid the world of one more obnoxious asshole," Kevin admitted. "I was in college, pretty much floating through life on a haze of sex, money, pot and booze. The things a shifter can handle ingesting…" He chuckled sardonically. "Well, anyway. Mommy and Daddy would buy my way out of any trouble. I knew it. They wouldn't have the family name besmirched. Dad actually used that word, besmirched."

"Where are your parents now?" Jagger asked. Kevin was living— Well, he didn't know exactly where or how he was living, except that he obviously didn't have a lot of money now.

Kevin looked away. "They disowned me after I got arrested for possession with the intent to distribute.

Right after that, they lost everything, too and both of them are in prison. Embezzlement, fraud, insider trading… I can't even name it all off. It's like the curse got them too."

Jagger's mind was boggled.

"Well, I mean, they *did* bring that prison stuff down on themselves, but the timing was… Whoa." Kevin leaned toward him. "I wasn't selling or dealing or buying drugs. It was a simple mix-up at the gym. I had a black bag, so did half a dozen of my friends. We were all there together working out. In fact, they were there watching when I laughed at the little old…er, elderly lady working out on the elliptical. I kind of said something about the loose skin of her arms being wind-flaps—"

Jagger gasped.

Kevin bobbed his head. "I *told* you I was an asshole. That lady stopped working out and got off the thing like she was sixty years younger. She was in my face and waving her finger, muttering things about gods and goddesses and like punishment—I don't even know. I heard 'curse' and laughed again. Then I felt like someone kicked me in the balls. And less than ten minutes after that, I was tackled to the sidewalk outside the gym, accused of being some drug lacky. Mule. Runner. Whatever. It's been all downhill from there."

"You have a record?" Jagger asked. "I don't believe you were a hardcore druggy—"

"I wasn't," Kevin said emphatically. "Most I ever did was smoke a joint or two. Meth? No way. I really did pick up the wrong bag, which was how the lawyer was able to get the charges dropped and all."

Chapter Twelve

"That didn't all happen because of a curse," Jagger argued. "Your parents had to have been committing crimes for a long time if they're still in prison."

"Oh yeah, they are, and not likely to be out anytime soon," Kevin muttered. "And yes it *was* because of the curse! Using your own argument, if it wasn't the curse, then I shouldn't have gotten busted toting a duffel full of meth, because I hadn't ever done meth, much less been doing it for years. So my folks may have had prison coming, but I didn't."

"And you didn't go to prison, either." Jagger could see Kevin was going to be stubborn about this. Maybe if he prodded, Kevin would give him more examples, and he'd be able to point out to Kevin how illogical—

"The cops let me go, Mom and Dad got arrested two days later. Everything was frozen. They'd already paid for that semester at my college, but I didn't have any money to live off of, and anyway, I couldn't hang around that place anymore once they'd been busted. I had friends that were as loyal to me as I'd have been to them," Kevin scoffed. "And since my parents fucked over most of their parents, financially, I was a pariah overnight. I even got beat up a couple of times before I got it through my head that my friends weren't my friends anymore."

Jagger had a vision of Kevin back then—young, cocky, pretty and scared. Only one of those things would be unfamiliar to him—scared, fear, Jagger would bet Kevin hadn't dealt with that particular emotion much until then. The other three things would have been a source of comfort up until that point, until they likely contributed to his former friends hating him.

Well, and money. You just didn't mess with other people's money. "You must have been so scared," Jagger said before he could consider the wisdom of it.

"Terrified," Kevin admitted.

"Come here," Jagger told him, opening his arms in a gesture meant to tell Kevin how much Jagger wanted to hold him. He expected hesitation, but Kevin bolted into his arms. Jagger felt him trembling and his heart broke a little for Kevin.

"I know I was an ass, I do, but I don't think anyone deserves the harsh things my friends said to me, and did to me," Kevin whispered. "They beat me like they'd hated me all along, and they probably did. Maybe I did deserve—"

"No," Jagger snapped. "Unless you had kicked the shit out of every one of them when they were down, you didn't deserve it. But I bet you were free with your cash."

"Buying friends, yeah," Kevin admitted. "That's what I did. Should have gotten better quality for the dough I tossed out." He laughed and hugged Jagger. "I'm wet and cold and worn out. You don't believe me about the curse, do you?"

Jagger wouldn't lie. "No, but I know you believe it. Does that count at all?"

"Honestly, I don't know. Maybe."

Jagger held Kevin tighter. "Come home with me."

Kevin grunted and burrowed against him. "Can't. Gotta have the truck back."

Jagger snorted. "And that means you can't come home with me? When I can follow you to the office or wherever to drop the truck off, then pick you up from there?"

Kevin stiffened. "Oh." He squirmed until Jagger loosened his hold enough that Kevin could peek up at him. "Oops? I'm going to blame the hail. It hit my head. Otherwise I'd have thought of that." Then Kevin frowned. "But you have to understand. Something bad will happen if I come home with you. It always has when I've tried to have sex with anyone since —"

"Whoa, whoa, whoa," Jagger cut in. "Can we not bring up the exes yet? Whatever happened with them, it has nothing to do with us."

Kevin frowned harder. "Well, that sounds like *someone* has some exes he doesn't want to talk about. You have a string of broken hearts you've left behind?"

Jagger almost laughed himself unconscious over that question. When he finally wiped at his eyes and caught his breath, Kevin was still frowning.

And he was sitting out of easy reach, with his arms crossed over his chest. "Figures. It's that damned curse. It's spreading to you and making you lose your marbles."

Jagger's amusement vanished. "No it isn't. You just have no idea how laughable that idea of yours is. Every boyfriend I ever had dumped me and never looked back. I've been the string of broken hearts, not the person leaving them behind."

Kevin's eyes went wide then he flung himself at Jagger. "That's awful! What kind of idiots have you dated?"

Jagger knew none of his past boyfriends had ever been right for him. None of them had fit so perfectly in his arms, like Kevin did. Jagger thought maybe they could have something special and rare together.

Then again, he'd always put all his eggs in one basket rather quickly, as his last ex had pointed out to him. That had been the reason more than one man had dumped Jagger.

Too clingy, too needy, too monogamous — Jagger had been called all those things and more.

"Come home with me?" he asked again, just in case his laughing fit had changed Kevin's mind.

"Okay, but I warned you. If your house burns down or all your pipes burst, remember, I tried to spare you."

Jagger huffed a soft laugh. "None of those things will happen."

Kevin hummed and wiggled closer. "What *will* happen?"

Lust spiked down to Jagger's dick. Someone wanted to play. "I'm going to take you home, strip you down, and fuck you —"

"Whoa, whoa, whoa, whoa!" Kevin said. He was back to pushing away from Jagger. "I think you forgot something there. Actually, I think you forgot several things!"

Jagger cocked his head.

Kevin held up one finger. "Kissing. There has to be lots of kissing." Then a second finger, and one more for each point he ticked off. "And foreplay. What is it about men thinking foreplay doesn't exist? I want some groping and rubbing and more sucking! Then — No, before the foreplay starts, but it can be during foreplay, too—a shower. Gods, a nice, hot shower." Kevin's eyes gleamed. "The two of us, naked, soapy, rubbing all over each other. But no soap for lube, that burns." Another finger went up. "Food. I might even need that before all else, except maybe the kissing. If it's garlicky food, then—"

"Might as well start on some of that now." Kissing Kevin was as necessary in that moment as it was for Jagger's heart to beat.

Kevin, with his quirks and conviction that he was cursed, drew Jagger in like no one else ever had. Jagger wanted to hold him, to protect him, to make Kevin's life better. Easier.

He wanted to wipe away the memory of betrayal, of friends who'd turned and delighted in Kevin's downfall.

Jagger wanted Kevin, wanted all of him, and the intensity of it was unsettling.

And irresistible, just like Kevin was.

When Jagger was finally able to make himself stop kissing Kevin, he was shaken inside. His bear wanted out, or wanted to mate, something. Jagger wasn't sure, but his gut cramped as he forced himself to release Kevin.

Kevin's eyes were glazed over as he flopped backward. "Ohmygodsssss," he hissed. "So perfect."

After the digs about foreplay, or the lack thereof, Jagger had just a tiny need to prove that he wasn't like every other guy Kevin might have known.

And Jagger did want to take his time and really love on Kevin.

"When you're ready to drive, I'll follow you," Jagger said.

Kevin blinked, then did it again. "Huh? Oh. Oh!" He sat up and looked out of the window. "The storm passed!"

"Yeah, it did."

Kevin took a deep breath then expelled it slowly. He looked up at Jagger through thick lashes. "You really want me."

Jagger almost snorted at that. "Wasn't me blowing you a clue?"

Kevin rolled his eyes. "I meant, maybe for more?" But he didn't sound so certain.

Jagger thought of how Kevin had been used and ditched. Whatever he said, he needed to be honest for both their sakes. He didn't want to be one more person in a long line of people who'd hurt Kevin.

"I think there's something more than sex between us," Jagger said. "I'd like to get to know you."

"But not before we have sex, right?" Kevin asked in a rushed way. "I mean, we don't have to run through twenty questions first, or have six dates, or —"

"No. Nothing like that, unless we get back to my place, and you decide you don't want more than a shower, food, kissing and foreplay. Not necessarily in that order."

Kevin's smile started slowly, but then he was beaming at Jagger. "Okay. I think I'm ready to drive now."

Jagger had to force himself out of the truck. The urge to take Kevin in the front seat was strong, yet he resisted. He was glad he had when Syn hollered at him and waved from the doorway.

Jagger waved back. "See you tomorrow, maybe." He ran for his vehicle, and fifteen minutes later, was putting it in park while Kevin handed off the keys to the truck to someone else.

Then he had Kevin in his car, and Jagger's mouth went dry at the look Kevin gave him.

"What I said about the foreplay…" Kevin began.

Jagger grunted, his dick hardening at just the thought of touching Kevin's bare skin.

"Maybe we can skip it after all."

Jagger gave a long, slow shake of his head. "No, I don't think so." He was going to drive Kevin crazy with need before he pushed into that tight ass.

Kevin whimpered and cupped his own dick. "Oh, gawwwd," he drawled. "You're gonna tease me until I beg."

Jagger grinned.

Chapter Thirteen

Jagger wasn't sure he'd be able to restrain himself, but he did keep it to just resting a hand on Kevin's thigh while Jagger drove them to his place.

Kevin was quivering with nerves, and he kept looking around, head on a swivel, as if he expected a boogie monster to jump out and tumble the car over.

The curse. Kevin believed something bad was going to happen to them. Well, Jagger was going to make sure that some very, very amazing fucking happened instead.

He liked the nervous little looks Kevin kept shooting his way. It wasn't the bad kind of nerves, either, but the kind that came from anticipation.

Jagger did his best to keep that anticipation high. He moved his hand up another inch or so, until his pinky almost brushed over Kevin's dick.

Kevin whined and slumped in the seat. Jagger moved his hand down almost to Kevin's knee.

"Jag," Kevin said. "Just a touch!"

Jagger turned into his drive and parked the car rather than answer. He shut it off, then unbuckled. Kevin beat him out of the vehicle.

"Which way? Which— Oh."

Jagger chuckled. There was only his house, set on a good seven acres. Kevin had been too distracted to notice until then.

But it was private.

And perfect.

Jagger tipped his chin down as he began to stalk toward Kevin.

"Um," Kevin began, eyes widening as he took a step back. "Wait, why would I *do* that?"

The question brought Jagger up short. "Why would you do what?"

Kevin snorted. "Back up."

Jagger started to take a step back, then he got it. "Instinct." He took another step forward and Kevin shivered before crossing his arms over his chest. Jagger moved even closer. "Your animal knows it's being hunted." And another.

Kevin gulped, but his dick was erect and pressing against the denim of his jeans. Jagger licked his lips as he thought about the way Kevin tasted, the sounds he made as he came.

"Oh fuck," Kevin panted, "me."

Jagger leered at him. He intended to do just that, to fuck Kevin until the man couldn't remember that anyone else had ever had him before Jagger.

That possessive surge might scare Jagger later, but for now he went with it.

Growling, he held his arms loosely at his sides as he approached Kevin. Kevin, who was cupping his own dick and whimpering.

Jagger had promised him slow, torturously erotic love-making. He'd give Kevin that if it killed him to do so. Jagger would bet no one had taken the time to really love on Kevin like he deserved to be loved.

Kevin went for his pants, working the button free then pulling the zipper down. Jagger's gaze zeroed in on the unveiling. The way the moonlight played on Kevin's fingers was entrancing, but not nearly as much as the thick cock that he revealed.

Jagger had seen it, touched it, tasted it, but he didn't care. It still took his breath away. Kevin's dick was perfect, big enough that a man could feel it, but not so big it'd be uncomfortable — for long. Probably.

The ground was wet, soaked, really, which was the only reason Jagger didn't tackle Kevin and start licking him all over right outside. He'd do that another time, in broad daylight. Even though his place was private, it'd still feel kinky and dirty to fuck outside in the sunlight.

Tonight, he had other plans.

Jagger stepped right up to Kevin and batted his hand away from his dick. Jagger fisted it instead, and at the same time, he used his other hand to grip Kevin's nape. Jagger slanted his mouth over Kevin's and slid his tongue right past those parted pink lips.

Kevin clung to his shoulders, giving himself over eagerly. Jagger swept his tongue over every inch of Kevin's mouth he could reach while tugging on his dick.

When Kevin started trying to hump his hand, Jagger stepped back — but he held on to Kevin's dick. "This way," he said wickedly. Kevin gasped and began shuffling forward as Jagger led him by his dick.

Jagger knew his property like he knew his own body. He didn't miss a step as he kept his grip on Kevin and walked backwards. Once he reached the steps, he carefully went up them. Kevin followed along perfectly, still breathing heavily, eyes gleaming with excitement.

Jagger unlocked the door and gave Kevin's dick a harder tug. "Inside." He let go of Kevin only long enough to let him get in, then Jagger followed and closed the door. He had his hands down low immediately after, one on Kevin's dick, the other palming his balls. Jagger snuck those fingers back and pressed on the smooth skin of Kevin's taint.

Kevin's sharply inhaled breath pleased Jagger to no end. He wanted so much more than a quick fuck in the entryway, though. Jagger kissed his way down Kevin's neck.

He also left off fondling Kevin to instead push his pants and underwear down.

Then he realized he'd forgotten to take off Kevin's boots and socks.

Kevin snickered and Jagger dragged his blunt nails down Kevin's hips, not hard enough to leave a permanent mark, just enough to warm Kevin's skin.

"Please," Kevin whimpered, and Jagger wondered how much Kevin liked, how far he could push. Not tonight, he told himself. Tonight was for making Kevin his in more ways than one.

Jagger knelt and rubbed his cheek over Kevin's bobbing erection. There was pre-cum on the tip, and Jagger rubbed that on his skin, too. Then he kissed the slit, letting his tongue delve in after the salty liquid there.

Kevin moaned and began petting Jagger's head.

Jagger enjoyed that, but he wanted Kevin naked. He went to work on the left boot, unfastening the laces. He saw how worn those shoes were, how thin the soles were. Jagger even found a hole in the left one. "Pick up your foot," he said, and Kevin obeyed immediately. "Other one," Jagger told him after removing the first boot and sock.

Then he tugged Kevin's pants all the way off, along with his briefs. Jagger ran his hands over Kevin's body, from his freakishly long toes to his hips. He nuzzled Kevin's balls, tugged at his pubes with his teeth, then rose slowly to his feet as he peeled Kevin's shirt off.

He saw the little tits, hard and pointy, and had to play for a bit. Jagger nipped and pinched until the flesh was hot and Kevin was begging him for more.

Jagger kissed him again, sucking on Kevin's tongue then palming one firm ass cheek. Kevin's butt was a work of art, round and firm with a smattering of fuzzy coating. Jagger gave it a squeeze, then he popped it and Kevin moaned again.

A second swat, then Jagger forced himself to step back. "Shower," he said in a voice so gruff he almost startled himself. "Down the hall to the left. You get in there and I'll be right behind you."

Kevin turned and sprinted. Jagger was stunned by the view—not just Kevin's ass, but his whole body. Jagger shook himself then scooped up Kevin's clothes. He darted into the kitchen and pulled two steaks from the freezer, then went into the bathroom.

Kevin was in the shower, and steam was rolling out over the glass partition. The bathroom was muggy but that was okay. Jagger didn't mind. He stripped and was delighted to see Kevin push the door open enough to watch him.

"Oh, man," Kevin said with more than a little wonder. "I want that in me!"

Jagger hefted his shaft in one hand. "You'll get it. Eventually."

"Jagger." Kevin poked out his bottom lip in a pout.

Jagger strode to the shower and cupped Kevin's chin. "I'm going to wash every inch of your body, then I'm going to lick you and rim you until you come. Then I'll fuck you, once you're ready for round two."

"Round three," Kevin whispered. "Oh fuck, I'm ready now!"

Jagger nibbled on his lips then Kevin stepped back and Jagger joined him in the shower.

And Jagger took great pleasure in running his hands all over Kevin's body, in making him squirm and hump and moan. Kevin was so responsive, soaking up every kiss, every caress as if he were starved for them.

He probably was, Jagger realized, and that made him go even slower, making certain he didn't miss any spot. Kevin squealed and giggled when Jagger sucked on his toes — honestly, that second one on each foot was damn near the length of Jagger's pinky fingers — and licked the soles of his feet.

But the backs of his ankles, the bends of his knees and the underside of his ass were all places that made Kevin shake and beg.

Jagger licked over his spine, up to his ears. He left purple marks when he could, when he wasn't moving to taste the next place and the next.

Kevin's little nipples were swollen and dark red by the time Jagger was done sucking and pulling on them. He avoided Kevin's cock, but sucked on his balls until Jagger had every wrinkle and hair imprinted in his brain. He wanted to know everything about Kevin, everything that drove him wild or caused him to pull away. Those things, Jagger made sure not to repeat.

Kevin didn't like his belly button tongued, and licking over his hip bones made him squirm away. He was good with the left arm put being lapped at, but the right was a no-go.

"I don't know why, it just bugs me," Kevin offered as he shrugged. "I'm not manly, I guess."

Jagger snorted and pushed the showerhead away from them. He didn't want to drown. "That has nothing to do with manliness. Now this right here"—finally, he touched Kevin's dick, trailing a finger around the glans—"this is manly. It's perfect, you know."

Kevin frowned. "Uh, please. It's not as big as yours—"

"Perfect," Jagger said firmly before taking the cap between his teeth.

"Ungh," Kevin got out.

Jagger slid his hands around to cup Kevin's ass. He kneaded those taut cheeks and pulled them apart repeatedly. He didn't take any more of Kevin's dick in, though, and Kevin tried to thrust. Jagger had been waiting for that show of impatience. He pulled off and spun Kevin around.

"What—?" Kevin wailed, then he really let loose with a shout as Jagger shoved his face in Kevin's ass crack.

Jagger went right for his asshole, licking and rubbing his chin over that tender skin.

"Aw, gawwwwd," Kevin drawled, spreading his legs apart. He got one foot up on the tub ledge and arched his back. "Pleasedon'tstop," he garbled.

Jagger pushed his cheeks apart as far as he could and ran his lips over that tiny pucker. He pressed his teeth over it, just letting Kevin feel them, not biting. Then he squeezed those round globes hard and pushed his tongue into Kevin's ass.

Kevin cursed and arched some more. "Never—" he got out, then he was gasping, pushing back against Jagger's face. Jagger slid one finger in alongside his tongue. He worked that digit in as deep as he could while he filled himself with everything Kevin—taste, scent, sounds, touch—everything.

When Kevin began moving back and forth with more force, Jagger had to move his head back or risk some damage. He pushed a second finger into Kevin's hole, then a third in rapid succession.

Kevin howled and rocked back even harder. Jagger curled his fingers with each penetration, and when he stroked over Kevin's gland, Kevin went stiff, those inner muscles clenching and gripping. Jagger's eyes crossed as he tried to imagine those silky walls milking his dick.

Kevin reached for his own shaft and barely touched it before the scent of his spunk filled the shower stall.

Kevin shook and shook, then his legs gave out. Jagger just managed to slip his fingers free before that happened, and he eased Kevin down to sit on the shower floor.

Jagger quickly washed his hands under the water, and his face. He rinsed out his mouth and started to spit before he realized Kevin was sitting right by the drain. Jagger leaned out of the door and spat in the toilet, then he was back in the shower and turning off the water.

"Come on," Jagger said, holding his hands out to Kevin. "We aren't anywhere near done."

Kevin blinked up at him then a slow, sexy smile stretched his lips. "Well I should hope not. There was the part about fucking, and food…"

Jagger hadn't forgotten. He helped Kevin out then toweled them both off.

And once that was done, he began making love to Kevin all over again, with slow, thorough kisses and sweeping caresses.

Kevin melted right up against him. Jagger's cock had been hard for so long, but he was waiting, waiting, until he felt Kevin's cock stir, felt the shaft lengthen and stretch, harden while Jagger was kissing Kevin's collarbones.

Jagger gently nudged Kevin's chin up and kissed him again. Kevin's lips were just as swollen and red as his nipples were.

"Bed," Jagger got out between kisses. "I want you in my bed."

Kevin nodded and Jagger had him there in short order. "Please," Kevin asked, his eyes heavy-lidded and chest heaving, "please. You've licked and kissed all of me. Please, I want—" Kevin reached for Jagger's dick and groaned when he touched it. "Oh, yesss!"

Jagger wanted, too. He stretched an arm out and got the lube and condoms from the drawer. "On your belly," he urged. He needed hard and deep, at least at first. It'd be torture holding his orgasm back, but he wanted to work Kevin up again, then roll him over and watch his face as he fell apart for Jagger.

Kevin rolled and came up on his hands and knees. "Hurry," he urged.

Jagger opened the lube and pulled one of Kevin's cheeks aside. He squirted the liquid down Kevin's crack, the lewd sound the goop made turning him on even more. He was, he decided, more than a little bent. Jagger tossed the lube down.

He worked the slick over Kevin's hole, then into it with two fingers. Kevin made incoherent, needy sounds and Jagger enjoyed them until he was on the verge of ramming his cock into the tight heat clamping around his fingers.

Then he withdrew those digits and opened a condom package. His hands shook as he slid the rubber on. Kevin lowered his shoulders to the mattress and watched him with eager eyes.

Jagger quit torturing them both. He lined up his cock and rubbed it over Kevin's pucker.

"Jagger," Kevin wailed, and Jagger thrust.

The tight, gripping heat almost did him in immediately. Jagger had to close his eyes and concentrate on finding some self-control. He'd just managed it when Kevin cursed and pushed back, impaling himself on Jagger's cock.

"Jag!" Kevin yelped, and Jagger started to panic. He was afraid Kevin had hurt himself but no, Kevin said his name again and started curling his butt, moving his hips and fucking himself on Jagger's shaft.

Jagger grunted and pressed his chest to Kevin's back. He took over, rutting and fucking deep and hard, letting himself feel and revel in the clenching inner walls that held his cock so perfectly.

Jagger pounded away at Kevin's ass, nearly mindless. His plans for slow and thorough were being trounced by a need he couldn't contain.

Until he had a flash of an image — Kevin's face in the truck as he'd talked about everyone abandoning him.

And it tore at Jagger's heart. He lost his rhythm but only for a moment, because then he pulled out. "Roll over. Let me see you," Jagger said when Kevin started to protest. "Let me see *you*."

Kevin's stunned expression told Jagger he'd been right — no one had cared about Kevin when they'd fucked him. No one had really seen him.

Jagger helped Kevin get onto his back. Kevin was silent, watching, waiting. He seemed scared and hopeful — Jagger didn't want to ever let him down. Somehow, this one man had gotten under his skin like no one else ever had.

Jagger fitted himself between Kevin's legs, got his cock right where they both wanted it to be. He dipped his head down and kissed Kevin, taking his mouth at the same time he took his ass.

And slowly, thoroughly, he filled Kevin up. Kevin wrapped his arms and legs around Jagger. Jagger thought he felt Kevin's lips quiver, thought he tasted a salty tang of tears.

But Kevin wouldn't loosen his hold. The man was strong, wiry and strong and determined that Jagger wasn't getting off him.

Jagger understood. Kevin's pride was involved, but more than that, Kevin felt so right beneath him, and he suspected Kevin thought he felt just right, too.

So Jagger began to move his hips, little thrusts, not pulling out much at all before pushing back into Kevin's body. He twined his tongue with Kevin's, let Kevin explore his mouth in return as he made slow, sensuous love to the man.

Jagger could have stayed inside Kevin forever. Would have, if such a thing had been possible. But his orgasm creeped over him, into him, as surely as Kevin had slipped under his skin. Kevin bucked beneath him, an urgent press of hips, and Jagger felt the first wet shot of cum between them.

Knowing Kevin was coming was the final push. Jagger shook from head to toe as he undulated, as his balls released and sent spunk jetting from his cock.

It was the most exquisite orgasm, and it flowed through Jagger, bled into Kevin, bound them together.

Maybe he was being a romantic fool, but Jagger would swear it was the truth.

And as his climax drained the strength out of him, Jagger let himself be eased down to lie beside Kevin. He opened his eyes enough to see that Kevin was practically glowing with pleasure, and that was good. It was enough for the moment.

Chapter Fourteen

Oh wow. That was all Kevin could think as he lay there beside Jagger, trying to get his breath back. Jagger had made love to him, something Kevin didn't think anyone had done before.

And there was a difference between that and fucking. He might not have known it before, but he sure as hell knew it now.

"Gotta toss this," Jagger said a moment later. "Might have to crawl to the trash can."

Kevin snorted. "You don't have a handy can by the bed?"

Jagger snorted right back. "I don't get laid often enough for that."

Kevin turned his head and eyed Jagger. "Get one. Put it right here." He patted the side of the bed. "You're gonna need one."

Jagger smirked and puffed his chest out. "Well, if you insist."

Kevin nodded as enthusiastically as he could manage when he'd been plowed into the mattress and reduced to a puddle of sated man. "Uh-huh."

"No more worrying about a curse?" Jagger asked as he got up.

Kevin groaned. "Aw, why'd you have to go ruin my afterglow, dude?"

Jagger chuckled. "Glow away, sweet stuff, nothing bad is going to happen."

A chill washed over Kevin. "You know that's tempting fate, or God, or Mother Nature, someone. You just don't say stuff like that."

"Why not?" Jagger asked with a shrug. "It's true. We're going to rest for a while, then I'll grill us some steaks and you can make the potatoes—"

"I don't cook," Kevin admitted with no small amount of embarrassment. "Not since I started a fire the last three times."

Jagger paused mid-condom removal and looked at him. "Three…times?"

Kevin nodded. "Well, the first time wasn't my fault. Someone had left a dishtowel on the microwave and it fell off while I was boiling water for spaghetti. I heard the popping and smelled this nasty odor. Luckily, the countertop only had about a six-inch portion burned. Then there was the grease fire." He rolled onto his stomach and kicked his legs up. "Did you know, you don't put water on a grease fire?"

Jagger grimaced. "Er, yeah, I did know that. The whole water and oil thing."

"Okay, smartass," Kevin huffed. "I thought that only worked with oil spills. Cooking oil should be different! I don't even like fried foods anymore after that."

"The third time?" Jagger asked.

Kevin glanced at him and snickered. Jagger frowned then looked at the condom he was holding up. Jagger arched an eyebrow and swung the rubber threateningly.

"You wouldn't dare," Kevin muttered, going still. "You'd get spunk all over your bed."

"Not if I hit where I was aiming," Jagger said with a leer.

Kevin flipped him off. "I'll roll all over your pillows, dude."

"That's gross." Jagger trotted off to the bathroom. Kevin ogled his ass and his balls, then his muscular thighs and—well, he was horny again by the time Jagger returned. He just needed his dick to catch up to the rest of him.

Jagger scratched his balls and yawned, then looked at him. "Third time?"

Kevin licked his lips. Jagger had fat balls that hung down nice and low. He'd like to get a mouthful of those—

"Bunny Boy, the third fire?" Jagger prodded.

"Bunny Boy," Kevin mumbled. "I'm gonna burn those pink ears. The third time was totally my fault. I was trying to warm up a tortilla and was too lazy to use a pan. It stuck to the burner, and yeah. I melted the spatula, too, trying to scrape it off. Guess it helps in times like that to turn the burner off, too."

"I'll make the potatoes," Jagger said. His stomach rumbled right before Kevin's did. "And I reckon I'll start dinner now, since we're both starving."

"I can come watch," Kevin offered. "And I can set the table."

"That'll work." Jagger went to his dresser and Kevin sighed unhappily when he slid on a pair of shorts. "Not putting my dick and balls at risk, sweet stuff."

"Sweet stuff," Kevin repeated. "You've called me that twice."

"Yup, I have." Jagger tossed him a pair of sweats. "I've tasted every inch of you. I think I get to decide what you taste like, and sweet works."

Kevin wrinkled his nose at Jagger. "I'm not sure that's any better than Bunny Boy."

"They're both endearments," Jagger said.

Kevin thought about that then nodded. "Okay then, either one works."

Jagger grinned, until Kevin added, "But I get to call you Pooky Bear."

Oh, the sound Jagger made! Not quite a growl, but close.

"No? Snuggle Sausage? Cutie Patootey Cakes?" Kevin was going to keep going, but Jagger sprang for the bed and Kevin squealed as he was pinned down under Jagger's hard, hot body. "Tweety Buns?" he gasped out just as Jagger began tickling him.

Kevin howled, laughing and squirming. He didn't miss the fact that Jagger was rubbing a semi-hard-on against his ass after a minute or two, or that the tickling turned to caresses shortly thereafter.

"Maybe dinner can wait a little longer," Jagger whispered roughly in his ear. "We can—"

Whatever else he was going to suggest was lost in the crack and thud that followed. Kevin's lungs were just about squished out of him when the bed collapsed and Jagger landed on him. Before either of them could move, the headboard groaned, and Kevin heard Jagger yelp a split second after a sickening *thunk* sounded.

Chapter Fifteen

"Mother—" Jagger bit off the rest of the curse word as he swatted at the headboard.

Kevin pushed up from beneath him, lifting the piece of wood. "At least it was padded?" Kevin said tentatively.

Jagger snorted and maneuvered around to the side of the bed. He got his feet on the floor and his body out from beneath the headboard. Then he shoved the whole damned thing up against the wall. "Piece of shit!" He struggled for calm. Usually he did not lose his temper like this.

"I dunno, seems like good quality materials to me." Kevin got up and Jagger's fit died as he ogled the naked man.

"Yeah, really good quality," Jagger mumbled, gaze gliding down to Kevin's dick. "Good, good—"

"Er, hey, my face is up here," Kevin said. "Gawd, now I know how women feel with their boobies always getting stared at."

Jagger guiltily snapped his eyes up to Kevin's. What he saw was delight there and he realized Kevin was teasing. "I can ogle your tits, too, if you want. I'm an equal opportunity leerer." *When it comes to you, at least.*

Kevin batted his lashes. "How about this?" He turned around and wiggled his ass.

"I can definitely —"

The headboard fell down again. Jagger ignored it, and so did Kevin.

Well, Kevin almost ignored it. "I told you, I'm cursed."

Jagger gave a slow shake of his head. "That was an old bed, and old frame. I'm two-hundred twenty pounds, and I ran. And leaped. I broke the bed, sweet stuff, the curse didn't do it."

Kevin opened his mouth and Jagger just knew he was going to argue. He had better plans for that mouth. It must have shown on his face, because Kevin blushed and sputtered, "T-the bed, it's broken."

Jagger stalked around it, gaze trained on Kevin. He could see the pulse fluttering at the base of Kevin's neck. "Are you seriously going to tell me you've never had sex anywhere else besides a bed? Because that will just mean I'll have to break in every room and piece of furniture…"

"I have," Kevin said, but he averted his gaze. "Uhn. Like where?"

"Like for now —" Jagger lunged and dipped. He had Kevin hoisted over one shoulder without missing a beat. "I need to feed you, but first, I'm going to make you come again."

"I can't," Kevin wailed.

But Jagger went right for his ass, pushing a finger into his warm hole, still slicked with lube. "You can," he countered as he began to walk. He had the perfect spot for Kevin, on the kitchen island. Later he'd fuck him in there, but for now, he just wanted to watch Kevin burn for him.

Which reminded Jagger, he needed to keep Kevin away from the stove.

"Jagger," Kevin gasped while Jagger wiggled his finger. "Oh hell. Fuck!"

Jagger grinned. He knew what the cussing was about. Kevin's cock was firming up against Jagger's shoulder.

"I'm gonna be dehydrated," Kevin whined.

Jagger stopped walking and frowned at him. He didn't, however, withdraw his finger. "From coming?"

Kevin grunted in agreement.

"That's not possible," Jagger assured him, then resumed making his way to the kitchen. Once there, he slid his finger out and lowered Kevin to the floor, helping him stand—just long enough to turn him and bend him over the island. "Stay just like that."

"What're you gonna do?" Kevin asked nervously. "I don't want food stuck up my ass!"

Jagger chortled in surprise. "I wasn't planning on that. I only laid out steaks, but I might have a cucumber."

"Which I would beat you with," Kevin grumbled.

Jagger grabbed his butt cheeks and squeezed. "Well then, I'll just have to use what I was born with." He pushed two fingers in deep.

"Ungh!"

An incoherent Kevin was fun. Jagger used one hand to pull back an ass cheek so he could watch as he sunk his fingers in then slid them out of Kevin's pink hole. "Like that, honey?"

Another syllable-less answer that had Jagger's cock stirring again. He wasn't worried about coming, not for himself. He wanted to see Kevin fly.

"How about another?" Jagger twisted his wrist and pulled back, then slowly worked three fingers into Kevin's ass.

Kevin panted and clawed at the countertop. He also tipped his butt up and wiggled it around.

"Yeah, you like it," Jagger crooned. "So do I. I could play with your ass for hours. Just put things in it."

"Things?" Kevin yelped, finally getting an actual word out.

"Yeah, things. Fingers, toys — and before you ask, I mean adult toys, like fat dildos and anal beads, not a teddy bear or monster truck."

Kevin laughed but Jagger turned it into a long moan by caressing his gland. "So yeah, and my dick, too, of course. My tongue. Maybe after I had you open and gaping, my fist." Probably not though, because he had hellishly big hands. He was a big guy, period. But it was fun to talk dirty and work them both up.

"You'd like that, wouldn't you?" Jagger asked as he began thrusting his fingers in harder. "You'd like to be so full of anything I gave you that you couldn't feel anything else but that. Every breath you'd take, you'd cry out, because you'd be falling apart for me. You wouldn't be able to do anything except lay here and take it because you want it so bad."

"I do," Kevin stuttered out. "So much."

Jagger hoped that meant he wanted it so much. He thought that was what Kevin meant, but regardless, he would never do most of those things without a lot of prep.

"Think about it. Imagine me pushing my hand into you," he murmured, leaning over Kevin's back. He pressed harder with his fingers. "You'd have to stretch so wide."

"It'd burn." Then Kevin wailed and shoved a hand under his belly. His arm jerked as he began beating off.

"This little thing would open for me." Jagger pressed against the outside of Kevin's pucker with his thumb. "Let me right in, then it'd grip and clench around my fingers as they slid past it. When my knuckles hit it, you'd tremble and beg." Shit, Jagger was close to getting off on this just like Kevin was. He could see the images in his mind, and he also saw the reality. The combination, along with the silky hot grip around his fingers and Kevin's whimpers, were all driving Jagger close to the edge.

He wasn't going to fall. He had plans for Kevin later.

"You'd want my hand." Jagger turned his wrist, stroking those inner walls.

Kevin mewled and shook.

"When you finally opened for me, my hand would slip in. You'd milk it, squeezing and rippling around it. I'd be inside of you, slowly spreading my fingers. Then—"

"Aargh!" Kevin shouted loud enough to wake the dead as his ass clamped down around Jagger's fingers. Kevin grunted and moved his hips while his orgasm ravaged him.

When he calmed, going limp and nearly sliding onto the floor, Jagger gently pulled his fingers out. He caught Kevin under the arms. "Come on, I think you need a nap on the couch before dinner."

Kevin stumbled more than walked, and Jagger kept an arm around him. He got Kevin settled on the couch, then swelled with pride when Kevin gestured for him to lean down.

It wasn't the expected kiss that he got though.

Kevin whispered in his ear, "Promise me you'll wash your hands really good."

Chapter Sixteen

Everything was going good.

Kevin was scared. Nothing *ever* went good, not for long. He hadn't even hit his thumb with the hammer in the past two days.

Good. Scary.

And he was supposed to have a date with Jagger tonight. They'd been together once since their first time. Kevin had returned to finish Syn's porch, and Jagger had gone with him since they'd spent the night together. After the porch was done, they'd spent their second night learning each other's body, and Kevin had been longing for a third night ever since.

Five days later and he was getting it in the form of a date. A real date, with dinner and a *Grease* sing-along at the movies. Kevin wouldn't admit it to anyone else, but he'd had a hell of a crush on John Travolta when he'd been a kid. Him, not John. With those blue eyes and dented-in chin, not to mention a very fine ass, John T had been the recipient of many, many of Kevin's dirty fantasies.

Well, as dirty as an innocent boy with no clue about what went where could be.

God, he'd probably have a boner the whole time they were in the theater. Kevin snorted. Who was he kidding? He was going to be hard before Jagger even got halfway in the door.

No, no wait. He wasn't going to let Jagger see the inside the crappy apartment. Kevin would make sure to be ready fifteen minutes early and be waiting outside.

Or maybe half an hour early, because he could envision Jagger showing up about that early just so he *could* come inside and see where Kevin lived.

He'd be ready an hour before then.

"You finished with that cabinet, or are you trying to memorize the wood grain of the inside of it?"

Kevin closed the kitchen cabinet and patted the door. "I'm just making sure it's hung right, Terry. I'm kinda proud of myself."

Terry gave him a thumbs up. "You did good, kid. Everything's level and nothing got broke. Now let's pack up and go home."

Kevin nodded. He liked Terry. Maybe some people would look at him and be scared, because Terry was like *whoa* big and tattooed and pierced on his face. The beard hid most of the tattoos. The face ones. And some of the neck ones.

But he was friendly and smiled a lot, and laughed often too. He was a great lesson on why it was bad to judge someone on their appearance.

Kevin made sure he had all his tools packed up. He swept the debris out of the cabinets, little shavings of wood from the screws going through.

"Oh, those look so nice," Mrs. Williams said when Kevin showed them to her. "You boys did a wonderful

job. My Joe would have been right in here helping you."
Though she sounded wistful, Mrs. Williams' smile
conveyed a love that Kevin envied. "He was always
wanting to build things and fix things, but oh my, he
was awful at it."

Kevin chuckled along with Terry. Mrs. Williams
shook her head. "That man. I can't wait to be with him
again."

Kevin didn't know what to say to that. Nothing
sounded right in his head. Mrs. Williams went on about
more things she wanted them to do to the house. She
had a list for them, and Kevin wondered if it all needed
doing or if she just wanted the company. Maybe he'd
drop by to see how she was doing in a couple of days,
because he knew what it was like to be lonely.

With his luck, she'd think he was a psycho stalker.
He'd try anyway.

He didn't give any thought to whether or not he'd get
anything out of doing so. All he had in his heart was to
help ease another person's loneliness. It wasn't
something he'd have ever considered back when he'd
been a dickhead.

Traffic sucked on the drive home, and Kevin fought
against panicking that something bad was going to
happen. The scenarios he came up with ran the gamut
from possible to utterly ridiculous. A wreck was
possible, but giant earthworms swallowing all the
vehicles on the highway was something that only
happening in awesomely bad movies.

When he got home, he had to wait for one of his
roommates to get out of the bathroom. That wasn't
bad—usually there was a line and Kevin was at the end
of it. One person was actually a great thing. There was
even some warm water left, and Timmy, the guy who'd

showered first, was in a cheery mood instead of bristling with his usual emo 'tude.

It wasn't until Kevin was sliding on his nicest jeans that he realized how well everything was *still* going.

And fear seized him as sweat broke out all over his body.

The sweat, in turn, shook him out of his fear. "Aw, man! Ugh!" Kevin pushed the jeans off, set them on the towel bar, and stepped back into the shower. Another quick rinse and he forced himself to keep his mind blank, or as blank as he could make it, which meant reciting equations in his head. Blank didn't work for him, but busy brain work did.

Kevin got dressed and checked himself in the bathroom mirror. He looked as good as he was going to get. The gray button-up set off his eyes and fit his shoulders really well. Kevin tried a sexy look then grimaced. If *that* was the face he made during sex, he needed to make sure he was always on his knees or belly.

"People make stupid sex faces." Kevin could point to any number of ex-hookups or porn videos. "Maybe I should practice—" He pursed his lips and lowered his eyelids until he could barely see. "Mmm, mmm."

Okay, no. That was *not* a good look for him. He just couldn't do duck lips for shit. Kevin parted his lips and tried a breathy moan. He had to open his eyes a little more or he'd look like he was dying.

"Mm, ya big stud," he purred. Kevin cleared his throat. That had sounded kind of phlegmy. "Give it to me, stud. Oh! Oh!" He did a little shimmy. "I've got it!" A quick check in the cabinet and he wrinkled his nose. "Well, it'll work. I guess." He picked up one of Jane's tampons. For a second, he considered opening the little package, because yeah, how that fit—

Kevin shook his head then rolled his shoulders back. He cocked one hip and held the tampon between his right thumb and index finger. He tried for sultry as he looked at himself in the mirror. "Tell me about it, stud." He dropped the tampon and stepped on it.

"Very good."

Kevin yelped and spun around to find, much to his horror, Timmy and Jagger both watching him with amused expressions.

"Except Jane is going to shove that tampon up your ass if she finds out what you did with it," Timmy said. "But other than that, *braaavo!*" He started a slow clap.

Jagger blushed, of all things, and he shot Kevin a sympathetic look. "I, uh, got here a few minutes early."

"And aren't you glad you did?" Timmy snarked. "You got to see your date—"

"Being adorable," Jagger cut in with such challenge in his voice that Timmy couldn't miss it.

Not that Timmy seemed to care. He rolled his eyes. "Sure, whatever. You don't have to flatter him. Pretty sure Kev would hand his ass to you on a tray." He leered at Jagger. "I would."

"I know just how to dispose of the tampon," Kevin muttered, picking it up while glaring at Timmy. "Up your—"

Jagger didn't even glance at Timmy. "I'll pass. And FYI, maybe I'll be the one handing him *my* ass if he'll have it."

A rush of lust went right to Kevin's dick.

Timmy rolled his eyes again. "Ugh. That's like false advertising. If you look like a top, you ought to have to be one!"

Jagger took Timmy by the shoulder and pulled him back. In a perfect world, Jagger would have broken into John T's lines and started singing about having chills, but what he did next was even better. He strode right up to Kevin, hooked a hand around his nape, and kissed Kevin like there was no tomorrow.

And Kevin knew, without a doubt, that he was falling in love for the first time in his life. It scared him to his core, and filled him with hope at the same time.

Chapter Seventeen

When Jagger had seen Kevin doing his best Sandy imitation, his heart had tumbled right out of him and into Kevin's hands. Not that Kevin was aware of that, but it was true. The man was simply adorable and had a good soul, something Jagger knew for a fact was priceless, and beyond Kev's weight in rubies and all of that. Jagger's exes were all pretty much selfish guys if you dug very deep. He'd been kinda slow on the uptake, though.

But Kevin was the real deal. Maybe that had something to do with having lived the life of a spoiled brat up until a few years ago. Something about lessons learned, though Jagger still didn't believe in the curse.

Kevin did. He railed about it as Jagger led him from the apartment.

And that apartment… Jagger didn't want to send Kevin back to it, but he didn't really have a choice. He was certain that Kevin wouldn't appreciate being tossed over Jagger's shoulder and moved into his place immediately.

But it was a goal for Jagger to work toward. Planning was something he was good at—he'd spend some time coming up with the best way to get Kevin to agree to move in with him.

At the theater, he slipped an arm over Kevin's shoulders once the lights went down. They were one of only four other couples in the place, and they had the back row all to themselves.

"Normally I'm more restrained," he said, after singing *Greased Lightnin'*.

Kevin cocked his head, and Jagger grinned wickedly before kissing him. Public displays in Texas could be risky, but the theater was dark and no one else was looking. Plus, half the other couples were men.

So Jagger got to kiss Kevin, and kiss him he did, pushing his tongue into the welcoming heat of Kevin's mouth. Kevin's inhalation was immediately followed by him twisting and trying to get closer to Jagger. There was a scuffle between them, a silent battle with teeth and tongues for dominance.

Jagger couldn't escape the belief that Kevin didn't truly want control, but rather that he wanted to test Jagger in some way, maybe his strength, to see if he could handle Kevin.

And he could, though he wouldn't hurt the man. Jagger canted his head and gripped Kevin's nape. He squeezed just enough to make sure Kevin knew he was holding him, then he urged Kevin to tip his head. Kevin resisted for all of a second, then he moaned and leaned even further into Jagger.

Jagger swallowed the sound down and his bear exulted in the dominance he had. It wasn't a constant need for Jagger—he liked to switch, to hand over the stresses and worries and let someone else lead.

But Kevin needed him, needed *this*, and Jagger was happy to give it to him. Kevin melted so sweetly, so eagerly, when Jagger touched him.

Jagger's cock was hard enough to split the seam of his pants. He had to pull back and nuzzle along Kevin's cheek while he tried to keep from dragging him out to the car to ravish him.

Ravish. Jagger almost snickered. He was becoming one of the characters out of his mom's romance books. He nipped Kevin's earlobe, needing to break the sexual tension between them before they got tossed from the theater.

"What's so funny?" Kevin whispered, tipping his head back to look at Jagger.

Jagger waggled his eyebrows and brought his lips to brush against Kevin's ear. "I want to ravish you, like a hero in one of those romance novels."

Kevin's breath stuttered out of him. He licked his lips.

Jagger adjusted his cock before he did himself permanent damage.

Kevin glanced down and Jagger could feel his stare like a heated touch over his shaft.

"Take me home," Kevin whispered, laying a hand on Jagger's thigh.

Jagger twined his fingers with Kevin's. "Soon." It almost killed him to say that instead of *hell yes*, but anticipation was good and he wasn't going to cut their date short. He wanted Kevin to have this night out, and wanted it for himself, too.

"Jag," Kevin whined softly, yet there was a light in his eyes that said he got off on being told, even gently, that he was going to have to wait to, well, get off.

Jagger slid Kevin's hand up over his cock and pushed into the hold. "I'll take you home after this, and then I'll take you, hard and fast, until you scream my name."

Kevin panted and closed his eyes. After a moment, he cracked one open and glared. When he spoke, his voice was a bare wisp of sound. "I'm close to screaming it now from sheer frustration." Then he grinned and gave a subtle shake to his head. "The things you do to me."

Teasing him in the theater was nothing compared to what would happen when they made it to Jagger's place. He was going to do many, many things to the man. Not all of them tonight. Jagger was hoping they'd have a lifetime together to play and make love.

The rest of the movie went by quickly, for which Jagger was grateful. They waited until the other couples had left before standing and leaving the theater themselves. Jagger's cock was almost soft again by then, but watching the sway of Kevin's ass had it perking back up.

Jagger had been careful to keep a little space between them when they walked outside. As much as he wanted to hold Kevin's hand, it wasn't a good idea where they were at.

But if he had been, he might have been able to prevent Kevin from falling when he tripped over God only knew what.

Kevin went down as if he'd been rammed by a bull.

"Shit!" Jagger hissed as he reached Kevin and squatted beside him on the sidewalk. "Honey, are you okay?" Jagger reached with shaking hands to touch Kevin, who'd landed with a thud that had made Jagger's stomach churn.

Kevin moaned and Jagger touched his head, his shoulders, looking for what, he didn't know. Kevin looked at him and Jagger was the one who felt like he'd been rammed by a bull when he saw Kevin's split lip and bloody nose. "Shit. Let me help you up."

Kevin looked stunned and didn't answer.

"He all right, man?" someone said from Jagger's left. "He fell hard."

"We aren't responsible," a second voice chimed in with.

Jagger turned around just enough to glare at the theater employee.

"Dude, not cool," said the first guy. "And sure you are. I saw him trip on that rug you got out front. It was curled up at the corner. So yeah, y'all are at fault."

The theater employee sputtered and the other guy seemed to get a kick out of causing duress.

Jagger focused on Kevin. "Kev, honey, can you get up?"

Kevin blinked then drew in a shaky breath. "Ow."

Well, that was some kind of acknowledgment. "Kev?"

"Hurts," Kevin gasped out. "Ow."

Jagger's heartbeat raced as he tried to figure out if he could touch Kevin. "Where? Where does it hurt?"

Kevin started to sit up. When he put his hands down to push up, Jagger reached for him. At the same time, Kevin yelped and would have collapsed had Jagger not caught him first. "My wrist!" Kevin muttered. "My face."

Jagger gently pulled Kevin into a sitting position. Beside them, the two guys argued about liability. Jagger heard one say something about a lawyer, but he didn't care enough to parse it out.

"Your wrist?" he murmured, running one hand down the length of Kevin's right arm. When he reached the wrist, even as lightly as he touched it, Kevin hissed and tried to pull it back. *Not good.* "Damn it, if I'd taken you home—"

"I'd still have tripped," Kevin cut in, his voice slightly slurred. Jagger saw that his lips were swelling, the top not as much as the bottom, but still, the split was bleeding and here he was wasting time on self-recrimination. "S'the curse," Kevin got out.

Jagger wasn't going to argue. "I'll pick you up and carry you to the truck, okay? Unless you'd rather I call an ambulance."

"No!" the theater guy hollered.

"Definitely!" countered the other man.

Jagger ignored them both as Kevin's eyes glistened. "I'm going to lose my job again," he mumbled. "Wrist—"

Jagger brushed a chunk of hair back away from Kevin's brow. Blood was smeared there too and he decided he'd already waited longer than he should have. "Come on. Up we go. Don't worry about your job. If you do get fired…" Jagger spared the theater employee a glance then before looking at Kevin. "Tell me if it hurts anywhere else. I don't want to hurt you when I pick you up."

"Just m' wrist and face," Kevin rasped. "Oh geez."

Jagger slid an arm beneath Kevin's knees and another around his back. "All right. Here we go."

* * * *

Six hours later, Jagger settled a doped-up Kevin into his bed. The hospital had been packed, and he guessed they were lucky it had only taken six hours to get Kevin treated. A broken wrist, stitches on his bottom lip, and a few other contusions and scrapes, but Kevin would be all right. He didn't have a concussion, at least, for which Jagger was grateful.

It wasn't how either of them had intended their night to go. Jagger wished with everything in him that Kevin hadn't been hurt, not so they could have had sex, but because, damn it all, he hated to see Kevin in pain.

And that curse. Kevin had gone on and on about it. To Jagger, to the nurses and doctors, to everyone.

Jagger had thought about it all night. Whether the curse was real or not, Kevin believed it. It caused him more pain and suffering, too, and for all Jagger knew, Kevin's subconscious might work to prove that curse true.

By making him trip, or whatever.

So Jagger made up his mind. He was going to find a way to break the curse.

Chapter Eighteen

At some point, Kevin remembered being woken up and handed a pain pill to swallow. That preceded him waking up later, horny as hell.

Kevin knew where he was — Jagger's place, in Jagger's bed. And he knew how he'd ended up there — not the way he'd planned, that was for sure. Nope, rather than seduce his sexy lover, Kevin had tripped and broken his wrist and bashed his face in, too.

He sure wasn't going to be a pretty sight for Jagger to wake up to.

That realization almost had Kevin trying to sneak out of the bed.

But.

He was *so* horny. Maybe abnormally so, if such a thing was possible for a guy. He wondered if pain meds made dicks go wonky.

Or hormones. Or something. Sheesh. There was also the possibility that his shifter nature combined with human meds was sending his libido into overdrive.

Because he was ready to tear the blankets off Jagger and rub all over the man.

Kevin very carefully turned his head, just in case the pain wasn't really dulled.

Nope, he felt pretty high, like everything in him was swimmy, except, obviously, the erection that seemed to weigh five pounds where it rested against his belly.

He cracked an eye open, and his heart did a series of somersaults when he found Jagger watching him.

"I look like shit," he tried to say, but okay, he was definitely stoned. He wasn't even sure what he'd gotten out sounded like English. "Ungh." Well, that sounded right.

Jagger brushed at some hair on Kevin's brow. "You're soaring, aren't you?"

Kevin's grin probably looked as loopy as it felt. "Yeah. Fuck me."

Jagger frowned. "Huh? You didn't— Nah, of course not. You're hurting and—"

Thick-headed, stubborn… Kevin's wrist was broken, not his legs or ass and definitely not his dick. Maybe his face was a little broken too, but not for real broken, just 'look I'm beat up' broken.

Kevin sat up and flung himself onto Jagger, which jarred his head a little, but—*bonus!*—Kevin's dick got some good friction, so the spinny-head thing was totally worth it.

"Kevin," Jagger gasped, eyes wide and startled.

Oh, that was intoxicating, rattling the bigger man. Kevin went to caress his face.

Which would have worked *way* better had he not had the cast on.

"Shit!" Jagger yelped, cupping the side of his face.

"I'm so sorry." Apparently, guilt could make clear speech possible. Kevin straddled Jagger's waist and hunched over to kiss the spot he'd whacked. "Sorry, sorry."

If he was kind of humping on Jagger a little, that was okay, wasn't it?

Because Jagger was naked, and there was a lump of sheets in just the right spot when Kevin bent over, giving him something to thrust his dick into. Plus Jagger, naked, all hard and hairy and—

"Ungh."

Okay, the speech thing had only been temporary.

Kevin shivered and hunched over more. He rubbed his balls over Jagger's groin. Was Jagger even hard?

If he was hard, and Kevin had just hit him, did that make Jagger a kinky dude?

"Kev, honey," Jagger said, and maybe he didn't sound nearly as horny as Kevin felt. Kevin sat up and looked down. There was his own hard-on. Where was—

"Oh." He twisted around. Of course Jagger's dick would be *behind* him. "Duh." *Oh wait. He's not hard. What's wrong?*

Kevin turned back around to glare at Jagger. "You don't want me 'cuz I'm ugly now?"

Jagger scowled. "What? I know you're having trouble talking because of the, er, the swelling, so you couldn't have said— Okay I don't know what you said. You could write it—"

Kevin held up his right hand. Could he write with a broken wrist? Maybe. He wasn't eager to try.

"Um." Jagger nibbled his bottom lip.

Kevin's bottom lip was probably the size of a small planet.

And Jagger was *not* getting the point. Kevin glanced down at his own pecker. Then back at Jagger. Then down again. *Come on, man, you aren't stupid!*

Jagger twitched beneath him. "You want—you want to get off?" he asked in a tentative voice.

"Woohoo!" Kevin tried to whoop. If it sounded like he was gargling pebbles, oh well.

Jagger scowled some more. "You're stoned."

Kevin bent down. He concentrated really hard on being kind of articulate. "M'horny. Fuck me."

Jagger opened his mouth up and Kevin tried to lick his way into it.

The pain pills weren't *that* awesome. He hissed and pulled back an inch. "Fuck me," he demanded, and added a wiggle of his butt along with it. In case it still wasn't obvious, he tried fisting his dick with his left hand. Too bad he wasn't ambidextrous.

Jagger touched his cheek. "You're sure?" he asked so seriously it almost killed Kevin's boner.

Yes, Kevin was sure that he wanted to be fucked by this magnificent man when he was floating on cloud nine thanks to the best medications *ever*.

Whether he said anything like that or not, he didn't remember. His brain kind of fizzled and popped when Jagger reached behind him and pulled Kevin's cheeks apart.

Oh yeah…

Jagger pushed against his asshole.

Kevin whimpered and wiggled backwards. Jagger's cock was still softish, but it was beginning to get interested.

Kevin arched his back. He left off jacking himself to return to humping the sheets.

And Jagger pushed the tip of one dry finger into his hole.

It wasn't enough. Kevin was going to burst from being horny, just blow right up and leave behind a pile of spunk that needed to escape.

Oh wow, drama king.

Jagger sat up and that brought Kevin's dick up against the firm wall of his muscles as the sheet slid down. Kevin moaned and closed his eyes as he — carefully — looped his arms around Jagger's neck. He went from zero to sixty, rutting fast against Jagger's abs.

"Slow down, honey," Jagger said in a rough voice. "Let me catch up."

Jagger was just going to have to skip ahead to do that. Kevin dropped his forehead to rest it on Jagger's shoulder and kept right on thrusting.

Jagger growled, and that finger went deeper before a second was added.

The burn might have been greater had Kevin not been on the pain meds. As it was, he wanted more.

"Lube," Jag muttered. "Condoms. Let me get them, then I'll take care of us both. You gotta let me get them, though. Let go of me long enough for me to grab them. Can you do that so I can fuck you? Is that what you want?"

What Kevin *wanted* was for Jagger to shut up and just do him, but that wouldn't happen if Jagger didn't get the lube and —

Kevin let go of him, trying to pout but, *Ow.* He settled for jacking himself sloppily with his left hand while Jagger reached for the nightstand. In short order — but not quickly enough — he had a condom on and was pushing slicked fingers into Kevin's ass.

"You want to ride me?" Jagger asked. "Or is that too hard on you? How are your knees?"

Well, now that Jagger had brought them up… Kevin tried to shuffle onto his back. There was the matter of the fingers in his butt, and changing positions turned into a more complicated act than Kevin had expected.

Jagger's erection had dimmed some, probably due to the couple of contacts with Kevin's knees and elbows. Kevin was still ready to go. He reached down, left-handed—yay, he was remembering!—and fondled Jagger's balls.

Jagger's breath left him in a gust and he pulled one of Kevin's legs up. Kevin didn't know if it was right or left because Jagger's cock was nudging at his pucker and Kevin couldn't think worth a damn at that point.

Then Jagger was filling him, using that thick cock to spread Kevin open and touch him in ways beyond the physical.

Whether it was the drugs or the fact that Kevin was just unwilling to fight it, he felt Jagger all the way to his heart.

Scary stuff, probably, though Kevin didn't feel spooked. What was the point? Jagger meant more to him than anyone ever had, honestly. Kevin wasn't counting family. That was too squicky when you were having sex.

So he let Jagger melt him, let himself open to Jagger on every plane possible—which might have only been physical but it felt like a spiritual experience.

Jagger pushed in so deep Kevin expected them to merge into one being.

Then Jagger pulled out and did it again.

And again.

And again!

Kevin mewled and he tried to say things that it was probably too early to say, to make promises that Jagger wouldn't be ready to hear. Whatever came out probably wasn't coherent and that was okay.

Kevin still meant it, all of it.

Jagger began to pant, and all he said over and over was Kevin's name. When he palmed Kevin's dick, Kevin's entire world turned inside out.

Then Jagger kissed him, and it was such a gentle, bare brush of lips, it made Kevin's eyes burn.

His orgasm hit him totally unexpectedly. He'd thought there'd be a maelstrom of *more, more, more,* but that tender kiss, it did something to him, loosed something in him that he hadn't known was there.

And that overpowering thing, that ball that suddenly expanded, it filled him with an emotion stronger than any he'd felt before. It sent Kevin spiraling into a climax that wasn't about the physical release.

It was the emotional one, the feeling, for the first time in his life, that he had someone to love completely and without inhibitions.

Jagger wouldn't reject him, or mock him. Kevin knew it with a certainty that set him free.

Chapter Nineteen

Jagger watched Kevin sleeping. It was a wonder that he wasn't passed out, too, after the way Kevin had woken him up. Granted, Jagger maybe had opened his eyes before Kevin, but he sure hadn't been awake-awake until Kev had asked to be fucked. Demanded it, was more like it.

And Kevin had completely let go with him. Jagger hoped it wasn't the pain meds that had made that possible. He wanted Kevin to feel safe with him, to know there was nothing he couldn't do or ask for that Jagger wouldn't accept or give.

Jagger rubbed his forehead and sat up a little straighter in the chair. His back ached down toward his butt from slumping. Kevin snuffled and licked his lips. Jagger's heart shouldn't have raced but it did. Kevin was sprawled out on the big bed, taking up entirely too much space for the size of his body.

The pale yellow sheets were twined around his left calf and draped over most of his groin. Jag could see a bit of dick, which made him feel tantalizingly voyeuristic. Kevin's tight stomach was highlighted by a stream of sunlight slipping past the blinds and curtains. His chest rose and fell steadily, and Jagger's gaze was drawn for a moment to the taut nipples plumped up and all but begging for a touch.

But Kevin's face—he looked so young and peaceful. Jagger wouldn't disturb him for his own pleasure. He watched Kevin a little longer then got up and left the bedroom. In the living room, he took his laptop from the case and set it up.

Once he had made a pot of coffee and drank a cup, Jagger took a second helping of it with him and made himself comfortable on the couch.

Then he started looking, Googling, searching. The things he found boggled his mind.

"Apparently a lot of people believe in curses," he muttered as he clicked the link on the tenth website promising freedom from such things.

Jagger couldn't help it. Every time he opened up such a site, he got the definite feeling the place was a scam. Honestly, there was so much information that he couldn't begin to sift through it and weed out the tiniest bit of truth. He needed more than the advertising businesses that made their money scamming people who wanted a miracle. He needed something that Kevin would believe would work.

Because Jagger *was* going to help him through this. He was going to do whatever it took to make Kevin happy, and that meant getting rid of the curse—

Jagger snorted. Now *he* was beginning to think that was real? "I'll give it a fair maybe," he decided. After all, he was a shifter, and so was Kevin. Obviously there was mystical shit in the world, right?

By the time he heard Kevin shuffling around in the bed, sounds of a man waking up, Jagger was no closer to finding anything useful. He shut the laptop down.

"I'm bringing you coffee," he sang out, sort of. His voice wasn't all that, but to him, anyone announcing the delivery of coffee would sound like a damned vocal god.

"Good," Kevin rasped. "Sugar."

Jagger thought he was being called sugar for a second, then he remembered that Kevin had taken sugar in his coffee before. "Ruins a perfectly good drink," Jagger said.

He grabbed his sugar dispenser along with the cup of coffee for Kevin. It was probably time for another pain pill too. Kevin sure looked like he hurt. He had bruises in places Jagger couldn't account for the bruising being, and his poor face... Kev was going to be hard on himself for it, probably. Jagger still thought he was adorable, swollen lips, bruised cheek, scraped nose and forehead, and all.

Sure enough, when he walked into the bedroom, Kevin had his face turned away. "Hard to drink coffee like that."

"Don't look at me," Kevin mumbled. "I'm scary, and I was a total slut earlier, unless I was dreaming—but my ass hurts, so..."

Jagger sat on the edge of the bed and put the coffee cup on the nightstand as he frowned. "Sore? I was too rough—"

Kevin huffed and gave him a sideways glance. "Please. I can take it rougher, I just meant that I had the just-been-fucked-good feeling back there."

"Good?" Jagger mused. "Honey, I fucked you better than good."

Kevin's lips twitched. "Ow. Don't make me smile. Or laugh. For that matter, can someone Botox my face until it heals?"

"Botox? What does that have to do with anything?" Jagger picked up the coffee cup. "You need to drink this so you wake up and make sense."

That got him a glare, with Kevin rolling over and no longer trying to hide from him. "I'm making sense. You have issues if you've never heard of Botox."

Jagger had, but he'd be damned if he admitted it. "We'll just have to agree to disagree."

Kevin sat up all the way and held out his hand—his right one, then cursed. "Oh God damn it, ugh!" He swapped it for his left.

Jagger handed him the cup. "Sugar?"

"I really just wanted it in here for decorative purposes," Kevin snarked. "That was a joke, but I can't waggle my eyebrows without my whole face hurting. And again, I'm hideous. Don't look at me."

"Enough of that," Jagger said firmly. "I'll hold the sugar and the coffee hostage until you get off the self-loathing bent."

Kevin growled, and it was the cutest sound Jagger had ever heard. If he hadn't been head over heels for Kevin already, that little growl would have pushed him over. "Here." Jagger opened the sugar and tipped it to the cup. "Say when."

Kevin stuck his tongue out and poked at the stiches as Jagger poured. "That's good," he said after Jagger had added enough sugar to kill off every sweet tooth he'd ever had.

"No spoon," Kevin said.

Jagger held up a finger and arched an eyebrow.

Kevin probably was trying to give him a stern look, but Jagger couldn't tell.

"Is it clean?" Kevin asked. "Because I know where that finger was earlier."

Jagger nodded. "Washed when I brushed my teeth."

Kevin gave a slight nod and Jagger only winced a little. The coffee was hot, but had cooled a bit during their banter.

"Look at you being all manly for me," Kevin teased.

Jagger lifted his finger out and sucked the too-sweet coffee off it. "Mmm. Instant cavity. And I'm always manly."

Kevin took a long sip then moaned. "Oh my gods. So good," he mumbled before slurping down half the cup.

"There's more. Why don't you take a pain pill while I go get the pot?" Jagger offered.

Kevin took another swallow before answering. "Nothing stronger than ibuprofen. I don't like drugs in the first place." Then he turned and looked Jagger in the eyes. "Did I…? Was it okay that I mauled you this morning?"

Jagger almost laughed, but he knew this was a very serious question for Kevin. It wasn't that Jagger thought it was funny, either, but only that Kevin had rocked his world so hard and didn't seem to be aware of it. Maybe Jagger *had* only fucked him good earlier.

Jagger took the empty cup from Kevin and used his other hand to gently caress Kevin's unbruised cheek. He could so easily lose himself in Kevin's eyes. "I was worried you might regret it. Please don't. You were free and happy, and you…" Gods, he sounded like such a corny idiot, yet he couldn't shut up. "You bloomed for me like you've never done before. Like you didn't hold back." *Like you know I love you, and you love me, too.*

Those words wouldn't come. Jagger wouldn't let them, not yet. He didn't want to spook Kevin.

"Oh," Kevin breathed softly. "Okay then. So stoned slut is a good look for me."

Jagger chuckled then gently kissed Kevin's brow. "Any look is good for you, and I wouldn't say you were a slut at all. Or if you were, so was I. I wasn't on the meds and I'm pretty sure I was flying right there with you."

Kevin tilted his head to one side, giving Jagger a considering look. "We can be sluts for each other. That's okay."

Jagger's heart did a slow flip in his chest. "Just each other," he pressed, wanting the commitment from Kevin.

Kevin dipped his chin down in a nod. "Well yeah. Like anyone else could ever live up to you, stud."

Though Kevin made it a joke, there was a seriousness there too, and the look in his eyes was a promise that Jagger recognized.

"Only you," Jagger said quietly, sliding his hand down to rest it over Kevin's heart.

Kevin sighed, and placed his hand on Jagger's chest. "Only you."

Chapter Twenty

Kevin kept thinking about that moment when he and Jagger had held their hands over each other's heart and vowed to be monogamous. That was what they'd done, he was pretty sure.

"Better have been what he meant." Kevin sighed and touched his bottom lip. The stitches felt gross, like a hairy bug on his lip. He'd almost shrieked like a nitwit when he'd looked in the mirror. There was no way Jagger was being honest when he'd said Kevin didn't look like shit.

Kevin rubbed at his chest next. There was a dull throb there, but it wasn't a physical ache. Considering the rest of him felt like it was one big bruise, he supposed he was lucky to have a not-sore spot.

He was going to trust Jagger with his heart. That was a damned scary prospect, but it was happening. Honestly, he already did trust Jagger. It was himself he doubted. Jagger was good and strong and nice and he hadn't ever done shit bad enough to get a cursed tossed on him.

Sometimes, though Kevin was loath to admit it, he thought that curse might have been the best thing to happen to him. Sure he got hurt a lot and life was a struggle. Yet if he'd gone on the way he had been back when money hadn't been an issue, what kind of person would he be today?

One that needed his teeth kicked in, that's what kind. Wouldn't have happened. No one would have laid a hand on him when he'd been such an asshole. Now, however, that layer of protection was gone. It made him wonder about that, why bullies and such were more likely to go after the poor and powerless than the strong and moneyed. He guessed it was the only way they knew to find a sense of power themselves, though to him, it would only underline their own weakness.

Human nature was an ugly puzzle sometimes, and Kevin wasn't ever going to fit the pieces together. All he could figure was that it took a great deal more strength and skill to wrestle a bear than it did a puppy.

Which brought him right back to thinking about Jagger. Kevin reached down and pushed against his rising dick almost unthinkingly. Even sore all over, he wanted Jagger again.

What would Jagger look like in shifted form? And if Kevin was ever able to shift again... Should he? How much of Jagger was in control when he was a bear, and how much was animal? It would really suck to get killed and eaten by his lover, and Jagger would be destroyed if he did such a thing.

Maybe it was better that Kevin couldn't shift. When he was a pronghorn, sometimes he got lost in his animal side. Well, he used to. It'd been so long since he'd shifted.

He heard the rumble of Jagger's engine and his stupid cock went to full staff. Kevin groaned and piled on the sheets. It was embarrassing how easy he got hard around Jagger.

"Kev? You awake?" Jagger called out in a raspy whisper.

Kevin shuddered as need flowed through him. He closed his eyes. "Yeah."

"We now have chicken soup, vegetable soup, beef broth, tomato soup, cheese soup—"

Kevin snorted softly and peered at Jagger out of one eye. "So every watery soup they make?"

"Pretty much, yeah," Jagger said as he appeared in the bedroom doorway. He took a slow perusal of Kevin, likely not missing the way he'd bunched the sheets. Jagger's lips twitched. "Which would you like first? You need something on your stomach."

Kevin had never been a soup fan. "Whatever you want to open, man. I'm easy."

Jagger nodded. "All right."

Kevin thought he was going to ignore the erection. He should have known better.

"Is that from the ibuprofen?" Jagger asked, tipping his chin at Kevin. Well, at Kevin's groin.

Kevin groaned. "Just ignore it. Somehow my dick's developed a mind of its own. Or something. Maybe it's possessed. Don't ask me how. I don't have a clue." He opened his other eye. "I would consider myself an averagely horny twenty-something, but you seem to be skewing that reality and making me—"

"Exceptional?" Jagger asked, arching an eyebrow.

"Yeah, or sexually demented."

Jagger laughed at that. "Ah, no, I don't think demented is the right word. It's not like you would let me use the cucumber."

Kevin maneuvered himself into a sitting position, then scooted to the edge of the bed. "Cucumbers have those sharp bumps, and besides — pesticides. And what about GMOs? For all we know, there could be firefly DNA in the cucumbers then I'd go to the bathroom and—" Kevin just managed to stop himself from making a bigger idiot of himself.

Jagger snickered and shook his head. "I can imagine you hollering at me to bring a net. Okay, you win. No cucumbers, unless they're peeled and organic."

Kevin started to scowl but stopped when his entire face ached worse. "No food at all." He cocked his head and studied Jagger. "Unless that's your kink?"

Jagger shrugged then walked over to him. He held his hands out to Kevin in an offer of assistance. "I really wouldn't know. I think it's more of a way to tease you than anything. Haven't ever messed with it, to tell the truth. I buy food to eat."

Kevin put his hands in Jagger's and got to his feet. Jagger pulled him right into a hug.

"Besides," he breathed against Kevin's ear, "there are plenty of toys made we can try, if you want."

Kevin leaned his head back to look at Jagger. "Do *you* want? Because no way are you putting that choice all on me and making me into the horny, gotta-have-it guy."

This time Jagger's laughter was almost silent, but he shook against Kevin, and his breath left him in short, warm bursts that wafted over Kevin's cheek.

"Yes, I want to try lots of things with you," Jagger finally managed. Those pretty eyes of his were intense as he stared at Kevin. "I want to do lots of things *to* you, and with you."

Kevin's dick was going to just spurt all on its own if Jagger kept talking about sex. "Like what?"

Jagger cupped the back of his head. He kissed Kevin so gently it didn't even hurt. "Come eat and talk to me.

I want to hear more about the curandera who cursed you."

Kevin groaned. "Aw, and you were doing so well."

"Your stomach has been growling this whole time," Jagger pointed out.

Kevin blushed. He hadn't even paid attention. His focus had been on his dick and on Jagger. "Sorry."

Jagger snorted. "Why would you apologize? I've been a bad boyfriend. Should have fed you sooner."

Kevin was going to argue that but Jagger looped an arm around his waist and turned so that they were side by side. "Come on. Soup, talk, then maybe a shower and some bone-melting sex if you're still interested."

"Talking about the curse might kill that desire," Kevin muttered as they made their way to the kitchen. "Why do you even want to hear about it? I know you don't believe."

"Because you do, and that's important," Jagger said. He settled Kevin in a chair. "I want to see if we can find the curandera and get her to reverse the…the spell. Surely she could undo it."

Kevin hadn't realized he was hoping Jagger would have a magical cure for, well, black magic, but his mood plummeted. "I tried that."

"Couldn't find her?" Jagger asked as he took a can out of a bag. "I can—"

"I found her," Kevin interrupted. He would have smiled had he been able to, but it wouldn't have been a nice, happy one. "And trust me, you can't get her to help you. She died six months to the day that she laid that curse on me."

Chapter Twenty-One

There was a lot of information online about curanderos. Jagger was still trying to weed through it over a week later. One thing had caught his attention repeatedly, and he wanted to ask Kevin about it as soon as Kevin called him.

Jagger had a thick stack of notes, some written, most printed out. He'd tried doing his own curse reversals, but in the past week, Kevin had gotten fired due to his injury. His boss wouldn't pay him when Kevin couldn't get out there and work like an uninjured man, and he said he didn't have any other job Kev could fill even temporarily.

Kevin was panicking over doctor bills, his pride not letting him check into programs to help the destitute. Jagger couldn't blame him. He understood Kevin's vow to work two or three jobs to pay off those bills.

He didn't have to. Jagger would help him, if he could figure out a way to make the offer without dinging Kevin's ego. Jagger wasn't as smart as he'd thought he was, because he hadn't come up with a way to do that yet.

Jagger also knew that Kevin's cell phone was almost out of minutes. He'd seen the message on the screen when Kev had set it on the counter yesterday.

There'd been the laundry incident, which had happened at Kevin's place. They had a community laundry center and someone had snuck in and stole Kevin's clothes from the dryer when Kevin had been dozing in a chair there. Jagger knew Kevin had one pair of jeans and a pair of sweats, a couple of shirts that hadn't gotten stolen. Not that Kevin would tell him so, but he had eyes, damn it.

The bus Kevin had been waiting for yesterday hadn't stopped even though Kev had been at the right spot. Two days before that, he'd gotten on the bus and it'd broken down ten minutes later in the middle of afternoon traffic.

Jagger would have picked him up both times, but Kevin was determined to do things on his own. Jagger got that, he just wished things were easier for Kevin.

And Kevin was having more pain because he'd tripped — twice — and his wrist had had to be recast.

Which was where he was right then. Jagger had wanted to take him but Kevin was as stubborn as he was. One of his roommates was giving him a ride to the clinic, and Jagger would get to pick him up later in the day.

Jagger tapped the keyboard, not hitting any keys. There it was again — this time on an official-looking Texas history website.

A curandero is a healer. His or her main enemy and combatant is Satan and those who make pacts with him. Called brujos (or brujas), which means witches, these work evil against people. They place curses, generally one of three types, and frequently appear as other animals.

"Shit. That sounds like a shifter." Jagger tried not to let the chill creep down his spine. Was it possible a shifter had cursed Kevin? Wouldn't he have recognized another shifter? Jagger really needed to ask Kevin those questions.

Jagger kept reading about the brujos, and the more he read, the more convinced he was that the lady Kevin had insulted hadn't been a curandera. Or if she had, she'd sicced a brujo or bruja on Kevin.

"I'm just confusing myself more." Except he wasn't, not really, because if he was going to agree—even if only for Kevin's sake-- with the power of a curandera being a reality, then he kind of had to believe in the brujo part too, didn't he?

Jagger printed out another dozen pages of notes. He started a new search then, looking for, hopefully, real curanderos.

When someone knocked on his door, Jagger jolted like he'd been poked in the ribs. He'd been so lost in his research, which was surprisingly fascinating, that he hadn't heard anyone on the steps. "Just a sec," he called out.

He tidied up the papers and got up. When he reached the door, he caught a whiff of Kevin. Jagger opened the door, smiling like the Cheshire cat. His smile died at the miserable look Kevin gave him.

"What's wrong?" Jagger asked, heart pounding. He couldn't fathom what bad thing had happened since he'd seen Kevin last.

Kevin didn't meet his gaze.

Jagger saw it then, the duffel bag at Kevin's feet. "Kev? Honey, come in and tell me what happened. How's your wrist?" Jagger had to force himself to look away from the bag. He was torn between feeling awful and elated, if that bag meant what he thought it did.

"My wrist is fine, except for the whole being broken part," Kevin said, his voice heavy with defeat.

Jagger couldn't stand that. He tipped Kevin's head up and kissed him, gently brushing his lips over Kevin's. The swelling had gone down almost completely. That didn't mean Kev was ready for an oral plundering.

"Whatever's wrong, we'll make it right," Jagger promised him. "Let me get your bag."

Kevin sighed and didn't argue. Jagger knew he was in a bad frame of mind then. Or a sad one.

Kevin came inside. Jagger picked up the bag. If that was everything Kevin owned, it was very light, and it broke Jagger's heart to think Kevin didn't have anything more.

He has me. He has Syn, because she'll be on his side. And he can sure as shit have the crazy uncle.

Jagger brought the bag in, shutting and locking the door as he watched Kevin plop onto the couch. Kevin had bags under his eyes and strain lines around his mouth. "You need something for the pain. Let me get the ibuprofen."

"Okay." Kevin leaned his head back on the couch. "Jagger?"

Jagger stopped midway to the medicine cabinet. He spun on one heel and turned to Kevin. "Yeah?"

"They kicked me out. Didn't even give me notice, just packed my bag and tossed me on your doorstep like garbage."

Kevin delivered those two sentences in a flat tone that had Jagger back at his side in a flash.

"You aren't garbage," he said fiercely, cupping Kevin's jaw. "They're assholes, too, to do this when things are—"

"Fucked up?" Kevin cut in with. He opened one eye and zeroed in on Jagger. "You're the only good thing I have."

The silent plea in those words just about undid Jagger in ways he couldn't have guessed at. "I'm not going anywhere. You're stuck with me for a long, long time, honey." *Like, forever.*

Kevin opened his arms and Jagger moved in for a hug. Kevin always fit so perfectly to him, and he to Kevin. "It's going to be okay, Kev. Better than okay," he promised as he ran his fingers through Kevin's hair. "It will. I think I have a lead on a curandero who can help us. I need to ask you about brujos."

Kevin craned his neck and frowned at him.

Words spilled out of Jagger faster than he could even consider them. It was hard to censor his heart, though, and he didn't think he was capable of doing so. "And you can stay here, honey. You can live here, with me, or we can move somewhere else if you want. I wanted to ask you, was going to when the time was right." He smiled a little at Kevin. "Seems to be now, and please don't think I'm an ass for saying that. You need a place to stay." Jagger took a deep breath, let it out. "And I need you."

Kevin's eyes welled and for a moment Jagger thought he was going to cry. He blinked rapidly then nodded. "I'd love to. Thank you, Jagger. I won't be a leech. I'll find a couple of jobs."

Jagger wanted to stand up and whoop, but they weren't done talking. "You can take your time. I'm not saying you won't find jobs, but you ought to let your wrist heal completely first so you can get a job in the first place."

Kevin frowned and stood up, leaving Jagger's arms. He paced to the windows then back. "I know, but the medical bills will come before that, I think."

Jagger bit back the offer to pay them. Kevin was on edge as it was. They'd deal with the bills later. For now, Jagger thought a distraction that might prove helpful was in order. "Okay, let's worry about those tomorrow. Today, I want your help with this stuff I've been reading up on. Maybe you can call a few of these people, too, and ask about their services."

Kevin followed him over to the kitchen table, where Jagger had been working. "They're curanderos?"

"Yeah, they are, and they are supposed to be the best I've been able to find at taking on brujos," Jagger explained, handing Kevin a list.

"Brujos." Kevin had a look of concentration on his face. "Doesn't that mean witch? Isn't it the same thing as a curandero?"

"Nope." Jagger pointed to two papers. "Read those. They explain the difference. I'd heard of curanderos, but didn't know their primary foes were brujos. Well, and Satan, but he's no one's friend anyway."

Kevin snorted out a laugh. "Yeah, he tends to make the afterlife miserable for eternity and all that not fun stuff."

Jagger sat down across from Kevin and handed him a third paper, this one with the names and numbers on them. "I think it might be difficult to get seen quickly with any of these, and we'll have to travel to them. None are very close."

Kevin took the paper. "South Texas, Mexico, New Mexico, Colorado, California." He looked at Jagger. "These are all of them? I'd have thought there would be more."

"There probably are more legit curanderos, but these are the only ones I could find. I don't know how other people do it. Word of mouth, I suppose." Jagger tapped the paper. "Try the top one first. He doesn't have a website. I found his name in a forum. People were talking about how he'd helped them."

Jagger hoped the man was available. He'd raid his savings if he had to in order to get the curandero to help them. It was only money after all, and Jagger had something more precious than money anyway.

He had Kevin, and a love he knew wasn't going to fade.

"Tell him we'll do whatever it takes." He waited until Kevin nodded at him, a serious expression in place. Then Jagger smiled and went back to reading up on the spells and curses curanderos and brujos used.

After five or so minutes, he slid his phone over to Kevin. "Use mine, please. I have unlimited weekend minutes."

Kevin took the phone without any arguing. He dialed the number, holding himself tense. When voicemail kicked in, Kevin slumped in his seat but left a message.

Jagger knew how he felt. And he knew how Kevin felt when the next four calls resulted in him having to leave messages. "Maybe there's a big curandero convention going on this week," Kevin muttered. "In Siberia."

Jagger laughed despite being disappointed. It wasn't like they'd been told 'no' by any of the people on that list. "Not likely. They're probably all very busy. One, if not more, of them will call back."

"I hope so. I hope this is all right. I did talk to two other curanderos after I was cursed, and they didn't do jack to help. Said they couldn't." Kevin glanced at him. "I'm afraid to believe any of these people will say different."

"They will," Jagger said firmly. "Maybe the ones you talked to couldn't help because they weren't real curanderos, or maybe the curse had to be on you for so long."

"Or I had to learn my lesson, like the Beast," Kevin said as he scratched at his casted wrist. "Damn, this thing drives me crazy."

Jagger thought Kevin might have nailed it with that last idea. It seemed to fit. "I think—" He stopped when his phone rang.

Kevin looked at it then paled. "It's the guy, the first one. I recognize the number."

"Answer it," Jagger urged gently. "Go on."

Kevin picked the phone and pressed accept.

Chapter Twenty-Two

"Nothing good ever comes easy," Kevin reminded himself. The first curandero sounded legit, but he hadn't been available for weeks. The second, third and fourth... Kevin had just gotten a bad feeling about them. And maybe he shouldn't have trusted it. What if it was the curse working against him, trying to convince him that those three couldn't help when really they were the best choices? And why was it so hard to get a hold of these people anyway?

"This lady seemed to know what she was talking about," Jagger said as they waited at the airport.

"Yeah, and she won't take any money other than the cost of the flight, so I'm..." Kevin swallowed, his nerves jangling. "I'm really hopeful she isn't a scam artist."

Jagger touched his hand, a brush of fingers over Kevin's palm. He wished they could hold hands like so many other couples did, but those other couples were straight and didn't have to worry about getting the shit beat out of them. The world could suck sometimes— but there was plenty of good in it too, Kevin told himself. That's what he needed to remember.

"She won't be a scammer. We're going to have to believe she can do what she says she can."

Jagger sounded so sure, which was funny considering how much he'd doubted the curse in the first place.

"It's just that easy?" Kevin asked him. "Just...believe?"

Jagger blushed a little but nodded. "Yeah, I think it is. I'm not sure I believe in all the curse stuff, but I'm not sure I don't either. It doesn't matter what *I* believe, though. You believe it. You need to believe that someone can undo the curse, too."

Kevin sucked on his bottom lip, glad as hell the stitches were finally out. He'd hated the way they felt, looked — everything. And he'd been pretty insecure about himself when he'd been black and blue all over. Now he just had the cast left to remind him of his fall that night.

Jagger's gaze went right to Kevin's mouth. "And also, I don't know everything," he murmured. "I'm not so egotistical that I think I'm always right. Just mostly." Jagger grinned at him and winked, too.

Kevin's insides melted in that way they did when love and arousal swamped him at the same time.

Jagger went on talking like he was unaware of what he was doing to Kevin. "I have faith that this is all going to be fixed somehow, and I think that counts."

Kevin bobbed his head and let his lip slip free from between his teeth.

Jagger moaned softly and the sound went right to Kevin's cock.

After glancing around them, Jagger leaned and whispered in Kevin's ear. "After we're done with the curandera, I'm going to take you home and fuck you so hard you can't feel anything but me. I'll be so deep inside you, that's all you're gonna be aware of. Me, my dick, your ass. All of me on all of you."

Kevin shivered right there in the airport, his dick growing erect through Jagger's promise. And it was a vow—Kevin knew Jagger would strip him naked in more ways than one, then cover him, that big, broad hairy body over his, chest to Kevin's back, curled around him as he pounded away into Kevin's ass. It was almost worth leaving the airport right then for.

"Soon," Jagger added, barely licking the top of Kevin's ear.

Kevin whimpered and had to adjust himself, screw being out in public. His dick was about to break through his clothing, it was so hard.

Jagger looked quite pleased with himself as he stood back again. Kevin glanced down, though, and saw the bulge Jagger was sporting.

"What a pair we make," Kevin told him, almost floating on a giddiness he kept experiencing at the oddest times. Jagger just flat-out made him happy.

Jagger raked him with a look, lingering on Kevin's groin. "We—" The rest of his sentence was cut off by the announcement of Flight 672 disembarking. "I didn't even notice it'd landed," Jagger said sheepishly.

Kevin hadn't either. "We were busy making plans." He turned and started watching for a woman who fit the description the curandera had sent them. Petite, a little heavy-set, with graying black hair, she'd said she would be dressed in pink and gold.

That right there boggled Kevin's mind.

Jagger shoulder bumped him companionably and Kevin smiled, happy despite the fact he hadn't found a job. He would, somewhere. Honestly he hadn't been out applying since he'd only gotten the stitches out yesterday. It didn't seem like he'd make a good impression being beat to hell. The cast was probably going to keep him from getting any job, too, but he'd try.

"That's her," Jagger said at the same moment Kevin spied a woman wearing a bright pink pantsuit. The gold came in with her shoes and purse. She had on blingy flats that could have blinded someone if the sun hit them just right. "Oh my."

"She has a presence about her," Kevin agreed. "I think I like it."

Jagger chuckled. "Yeah, me too. She looks…warm."

And she did. Kevin realized with a pang that she was probably someone's grandma, someone's mom, and he'd bet she wouldn't have disowned anyone she professed to love.

Of course, he told himself, judging someone by appearances was always a stupid thing to do. He was projecting his own wishes onto the curandera.

She turned her head and looked right at him, and Kevin felt exposed in an instant. He didn't even breathe as she walked over. She stopped in front of him and kept staring. He finally had to inhale or pass out.

"Mrs. Pena, thank you for coming," Jagger had the decency to say.

Kevin pulled himself from his thrall, or panic — whatever it was — and held out a hand to the curandera. "Mrs. Pena, thank you — "

She took his hand and heat shot from his palm to his shoulder. Kevin started to pull away but Mrs. Pena had a strong grip. "*Mijo*, this is a strong curse on you. The bruja who placed it left the earthly realm and now has more power as a spirit."

"Shit," Jagger muttered. "That's not good."

Kevin didn't think so either, but he couldn't speak. His tongue was stuck to the roof of his desert-dry mouth.

"Have you encountered this before?" Jagger asked her.

Mrs. Pena released Kevin's hand and looked at Jagger. "You are his partner?"

"Yes," Jagger answered immediately. "I'll marry him, soon."

"I will expect an invitation to the wedding." Mrs. Pena sniffed. "This state is gave in to equality kicking and screaming. As long as apathy—" She waved at him. "No politics. I will lose my temper, which is never a good thing for any of us curanderos. Did you get the things I told you to get?"

She waved again, this time encompassing the area around them. "Ever since the security crackdown, I have trouble bringing my herbs and other necessities on flights. These TSA agents interfere with many people's happiness and safety."

Kevin wasn't going to argue. He did finally manage to speak. "Yes, ma'am, we did get them. Er, we had to have a couple of things shipped to us." Overnight, and it'd cost a bundle. He'd pay Jagger back, one way or another.

"Call me Gabriela," she told him, turning her light brown eyes back his way. She smiled and an odd longing hit him. Kevin wished his own family had cared enough about him to keep in touch, but he hadn't been any better about it. Two letters to each of his parents, neither of whom had written him back, and he'd given up.

"Gabriela," he said almost reverently. "Thank you."

She cocked her head as she studied him. "You are a lost boy, though not as lost as you were." She gave

Jagger a knowing grin. "Love can do that to a soul, give you an anchor when you've been adrift for so long."

Kevin loved Jagger something fierce, not that he'd said those three words yet. It was stupid, but he wanted to be clean when he gave Jagger that confession. He felt like the curse still tainted him. Jagger would tell him it didn't, but Kevin had to be free of it.

"We can get started as soon as we are at your home," Gabriela said. "It will take many hours to prepare, and I always do my best work after midnight. Contrary to what many people think, the stroke of midnight isn't magical or powerful. Not for me, or anyone I know."

"You have luggage?" Kevin asked her.

She gave him a disbelieving look. "*Mijo,* do I seem like the type of woman who wouldn't?"

Kevin checked her out then shook his head. "Uh uh. I am not going to answer that. You could be, you might not. I don't know and I am not going to make a judgment on that."

She beamed at him. "You have come a long way, haven't you?"

Chapter Twenty-Three

Jagger was eager to get started. He felt certain that Gabriela would be able to help Kevin—help them. There was something about her besides her chosen profession that caught one's attention, too. Gabriela was effusive, warm, and she seemed like she could be a universal mother.

She simply gave the impression that she *cared*, and that was such a rare thing in today's world. Jagger even began to entertain the hope that they'd be able to stay in touch with her.

He missed his own mother and grandmothers. Syn would love Gabriela too, and—

Jagger sat up a little straighter on the couch. Kevin was in the bathroom, Gabriela had gone into the guestroom to take a short nap. He was by himself when he dared to wonder if Gabriela could help Syn.

Would a curandera know anything about shifters? Could he tell her what he, Kevin and Syn were? It was something to think about, and he did, for the first time in months feeling that there was a chance someone could do something for Syn.

"You're looking thoughtful," Kevin said as he walked over to join Jagger on the couch. "Care to share?"

Jagger shrugged. "I was just wondering if Gabriela could help Syn, if she knew about shifters and — Well I guess that was the brunt of it."

Kevin nudged him gently, looking at him with amusement. "Not wondering if she can help me?"

"Not really, no. I think she can." Either by breaking the curse or making Kevin believe it was gone and therefore...breaking it. He still wasn't certain on where he fell when it came to believing in such things. Sometimes he did. Sometimes he didn't, and most of the time he wasn't able to decide. "She's — I like her."

"Me too. She reminds me of the grandma I always wanted."

Jagger frowned. They hadn't discussed their families much. "What was wrong with your grandmas?"

Kevin snorted. "Uh, they were both even snootier than my parents. I saw them each maybe five times total in my life. Neither of them wanted anyone to know they were old enough to have grandchildren. I'm sure they've both completely disowned my branch of the family by now."

"Your family sucked," Jagger couldn't help but say. "Sorry, that's harsh."

It was Kevin's turn to shrug. "It was true. Is true. Whatever. What about yours?"

Jagger rubbed at his chest. "Well, mine were close. I grew up with both sets of grandparents being friends. It was nice." Until they'd all been killed together. That part had been the most awful time in Jagger's life.

"That's not a happy look," Kevin observed quietly. "What happened?"

"Tornado." Always a risk in Texas. "I was at college." Jagger shook his head. "I don't care to talk about it. I prefer to remember the good times. There were plenty, and someday I'll share some of them with you. But for now…" He tilted his head toward the guest room, where the slightest sounds were coming from. "Gabriela is up."

Kevin glanced at the clock. "She said she'd be up in an hour. I didn't hear an alarm. Did I just miss it?"

"Nope." Jagger stood, Kevin rising as well when the bedroom door opened.

Gabriela came out and held up a cloth bag. "If you will put this with the items you have for tonight?"

Jagger stood and walked over to take it from her. Gabriela smiled at him and patted his hand.

"You," she said to Kevin. "Please show me where the tea is."

"Sweet or —" Kevin began.

"Sweet, cold tea," Gabriela informed him. "I *am* in Texas."

Fifteen minutes later, they were on the road, the moon rising in the sky. Jagger didn't think it was just luck that Gabriela had been able to come to them on the night of the full moon.

He listened to Kevin and Gabriela talk, their voices somber as they discussed what would happen. Jagger wasn't weirded out about getting naked in front of anyone. He'd bet Kevin was a bit more prudish seeing as how his folks sounded. Jagger doubted they were the sort to strip and run with a pack or clan.

It was during the drive to the forest that he figured out the answer to his earlier question. His eyes met Kevin's when Gabriela mentioned their spirits being more tied into the supernatural plane than humans'.

"What do you mean?" Jagger asked.

Gabriela leaned forward from the back seat where she'd insisted on sitting and thumped him on the ear.

Jagger yelped. Kevin snickered. He got thumped too.

Gabriela clicked her tongue. "Don't play stupid with me. I understand why you must be careful, but you need to have some faith in me or all of this will be for nothing." She made that sound again. "Of course I know about shifters. One can't serve as a curandero does and be ignorant of the very creatures we're here to help. It isn't just human beings that we serve, and in fact our lineage, although we aren't all related, can be traced back to a wolf shifter."

"Sorry," Jagger muttered. "I didn't know you were given to fits of violence," he teased.

Gabriela laughed. Kevin looked panicked.

"You were thinking of your grandmother, on your father's side earlier. I felt her spirit," Gabriela said, her voice soft and comforting. "She watches you. They all do, but she in particular more than the others. She's been worried, but now, with Kevin here, she has hope that you won't end up alone. Your sister, however, is another source of concern for all of them."

"All of them?" Jagger asked, head spinning as he tried to take in everything she was saying.

"Parents, yes, and grandparents. You want me to see if I can help your sister, and so do they. She doesn't leave the house, has nightmares about the guns and panic attacks if she sees one even on the TV."

Jagger went numb and tingly simultaneously. Any doubts he'd had about Gabriela dried up then and there. He'd told her nothing about Syn, hadn't discussed his sister except to say to Kevin that she needed help. There was no way Gabriela could know the how and why of that.

"It will take longer with her," Gabriela continued. "Hers is not a curse, but a trauma. Those require repair to the soul."

"But you can? You will?" Jagger asked, hands tightening on the wheel.

"Yes, if she is willing too." Gabriela patted his shoulder. "Isn't that your turn?"

"Crap!" Jagger hit the brakes a little too hard, but he made the left turn and they bumped down the dirt road. "Thanks. I was distracted."

Gabriela hummed. At first he thought she was just agreeing, then he realized she was actually speaking words in a dialect he had no knowledge of. Goosebumps prickled his skin. Kevin shivered beside him. He held Jagger's hand.

Gabriela kept the chanting up, a low, constant sound that was both eerie and soothing. Jagger parked the car by a copse of trees. He shut it off and unbuckled. Kevin and Gabriela unfastened their seatbelts as well, then they all got out. Jagger went to the trunk and opened it. He and Kevin stripped right there. It wasn't any different from a run, something Jagger hadn't done in far too long.

Kevin looking longingly at the trees. "I wish… Maybe after tonight, I can shift. It's been years."

Jagger couldn't imagine. He tugged Kevin in for a kiss then they resumed undressing. Gabriela stood with her head tipped toward the moon, arms out in supplication or something. He wasn't sure what.

Once nude, Jagger took the bag from the trunk. Kevin shut it, and Jagger led the way to the clearing. Gabriela had said they needed an open space under the moon. Jagger had known just the spot. He'd gone there often with his family.

It was a two-mile hike, but they made it easily enough. Gabriela never once stopped whatever it was she was saying or chanting. Toward the end of the hike, Jagger felt a tightening in his chest. He turned when

Kevin hissed. Kevin shook his head and touched his chest. Yeah, he felt it too.

The clearing was beautiful. There was some grass, though the heat would kill it come mid-summer. For now, though, it was there, making the ground softer. Small white flowers were blooming. Jagger remembered them. He'd always marveled at a flower blooming at night.

When he reached the center of the space, Jagger stopped and set the bag down. Then he squatted and unzipped it. Kevin crouched beside him, and they began to remove the items they'd need. An altar, candles, herbs…and there were things he didn't want to think about touching while he handled them. Jagger set it all out as he'd been instructed.

Gabriela came and crouched. She arranged things on and around the altar. Photographs of saints Jagger couldn't name were set up. When Gabriela bowed her head, he and Kevin did too.

Gabriela's voice grew louder. Beside him, Jagger felt Kevin tense. Jagger turned his head. Kevin's eyes were open but had a glazed look to them. As Jagger watched, they rolled back until only the whites showed.

It was terrifying, yet Jagger couldn't move. He remained as if frozen in place while Gabriela's words worked over Kevin. Jagger could see it happening, as if each word formed part of a chain that wrapped around Kevin, protecting him, or perhaps covering the curse and overpowering it.

There was no climactic thunder, no streaks of lightning when the chanting ceased. The wind blew a little harder, and Kevin moaned as he toppled over backwards.

Jagger's frozen muscles held. He couldn't even get a word out—then he thought his heart might literally stop as a dark, inky shadow rose up from Kevin, exiting from his mouth and nose. His body convulsed and his teeth snapped together. A high-pitched screech rent the air, making Jagger's head throb and his ears ache.

Then the black thing came toward him.

Gabriela was there in an instant, her words and hands battling the substance away. It went out, scattering into a million dots of black so dark it was indescribable. Each one shot away from them and burst into tiny pinpoints of light.

And it was over. Jagger knew it because he flopped forward and just managed to catch himself with one tingling hand as he reached for Kevin with the other.

Chapter Twenty-Four

For one moment in time, everything ceased. Kevin felt it—his body froze, every molecule of it held in suspense while a chilling, oily mass worked its way through him.

Then he was hollow, just for a second or less, even, before sensation came rushing back into him.

He gasped, eyes rolling as a weight was lifted from him. Whatever had been done to him with the curse was now undone. Kevin felt clean and whole, and full of hope that he'd suppressed for too long.

Jagger was there when he opened his eyes. Kevin reached for him, hands shaking, heart following suit.

"Kevin," Jagger whispered, cupping his face.

Kevin held on to him in return, parting his lips for the kiss he needed more than anything at that moment. Jagger murmured his name once more. He pressed his lips to Kevin's and Kevin knew then he'd give his soul to make Jagger happy.

But Jagger already was happy—with him. Kevin pressed up against Jagger until they were both sitting, kissing, holding each other.

"You've loved me even with the curse," Kevin said when he tipped his head back. "You loved me homeless, unemployed, clumsy."

"I love *you*," Jagger emphasized. "All of you."

Kevin got that, fully and finally. "I'd do anything for you," he vowed, clutching at Jagger. "Give anything just to see you smile. When you laugh, you make me light up inside, and your joy spreads to me. I mean—" Well, he was getting there. "I mean, I love you, Jagger. I'd like to stay with you until we're both ready to walk into the afterlife together. And even when that happens, I'll be with you."

Jagger blinked then kissed him hard enough to make Kevin's lips ache in a way he was very fond of. "That's the sweetest thing, well things, anyone's ever said to me, Kev. You're pretty damned poetic when you want to be."

Kevin snorted though he was really pleased at the praise. "I ain't either. You just inspire me to try to speak good English is all." He laid on a horrible accent and Jagger started snickering halfway through.

"You two are both cute, but I wish you'd shift and run so it won't be morning before I get to bed myself."

Kevin jolted and cracked his head against Jagger's chin when Jagger also went to look at Gabriela. "Ow!"

Gabriela pointed at him. "Don't blame me. That wasn't a curse, that was clumsiness and guilt because you both forgot about me." She sniffed and crossed her arms over her chest.

Kevin didn't believe she was truly miffed. The corners of her mouth were twitching. "Have you ever seen anyone shift?" he asked her.

"Yes," Gabriela said without hesitation. "More than once. My last boyfriend was a hawk shifter."

"Oh wow," Kevin murmured. "I haven't seen one of those in a long, long time."

Jagger nodded. "Me either. I thought they'd maybe gone extinct."

"Nope, there's a whole bunch of them alive and kicking. Or flying." Gabriela waved a hand at them. "Whatever. Time's a wasting, boys. The sooner y'all shift and run, the sooner we get back to your home and you can go—"

"Got it, thank you." Kevin didn't want to hear any more. He was nervous, though. "I haven't been able to shift since I was cursed."

"It's going to hurt so bad you might be ill," Gabriela informed him.

"Then he shouldn't do it," Jagger grumbled.

Gabriela walked over and thumped him. "You be quiet. Of course he needs to shift now. It's rising in him. It's going to happen and it's going to hurt. And you, as his lover, husband, whatever term you want to use? You will shift, too."

"My bear—" Jagger began.

"Will respect that your mate is Kevin in whatever form he has." Gabriela proceeded to tap the toes of her left foot against the ground. "I'm waiting, and so are your beasts."

Kevin felt it, just as she said. His beast needed out before Kevin's skin split from holding it in.

But it did hurt, like someone was ripping him open from the innards out. He'd never experienced physical pain like he went through to shift again.

Even the backs of his eyeballs throbbed, every joint and length of skin burned like acid had been poured on it.

He wasn't going to flip out, or give up.

Kevin shouted as his bones and tendons gave. The agony was whiter and hotter than any he'd ever known.

Then he was shifting, his body turning into the familiar shape he'd missed so badly. Then it was done.

He was whole again. Whole and free and in love. Kevin bleated and bounded around Jagger, who smelled a lot like a threat but wasn't. There was the odor of a human and that of an animal about him.

Predator and prey. Kevin knew what they were. No, he knew some of what they were. Most of that was love.

He loved Jagger, and Jagger returned the sentiment to him.

Gabriela chortled and Kevin huffed as Jagger shifted. When he was done, the large bear beside Kevin threatened to freak Kevin out.

He saw the intelligence in those eyes, and knew he was safe. With Jagger, he always would be.

Jagger growled — more like coughed, Kevin guessed. He made a sound back.

Jagger stood on his hind legs and bellowed. Kevin butted him for being a noisy show-off.

Then the chase was on.

HAREY
SITUATION

Dedication

Thank you to The Blogees. Y'all are made of amaze and stardust!

Chapter One

Oliver Biggerstaffer wiped the perspiration off his forehead. He'd just stepped out of the San Antonio Airport less than a minute ago, and he was already drenched in sweat. The heat and humidity combined were sheer hell. He only had himself to blame for being caught unprepared for the weather—had he bothered to check what it'd be like, he sure wouldn't have worn a suit on the flight in from Boston.

If he hadn't wanted to get *away* from Boston so badly, maybe he'd have paid attention to where he was *going*. Instead, excitement had taken over when he'd received a call from a well-known headhunter. Oliver had packed and bought a one-way ticket, trying to feel optimistic about the potential job. An advertising firm based in Abilene was branching out, and San Antonio would be their first big venture. His interview would be with Jagger Osterman, and from what Oliver had been able to dig up on the guy, he was rather intimidating.

Well, Oliver wasn't easily spooked. In fact, he tended to be sly and devious when needed. It was business, and the advertising business in particular, could be quite cutthroat. Added to that was the fact that Oliver never liked to fail—and there went his brain, right back to Boston, his biggest failure ever.

Oliver shook his head and wiped his forehead again. He had his luggage, and if a taxi didn't stop for him soon, he was afraid he was going to melt from the heat and end up a puddle on the pavement. Fortunately for Oliver, a driver did pull up in right under a minute. He quickly stowed his bags when the driver popped the trunk, not caring to wait for help, then Oliver got into the cab and sighed in relief.

"Not used to this Texas weather, huh?" the cabbie asked.

Talking was beyond Oliver just then. He managed a grunt as he closed his eyes and leaned his head back. Then he remembered he had to give the address for where he was going.

"Hotel Emma," Oliver muttered. He opened one eye up and checked the meter. "I Google Mapped it, in case you need to know the shortest route." He closed his eye again. There was no way would he let some cab driver rip him off. Not that all of them were crooked, but he'd had a few try to drive 'the long way' around.

"One of those," he heard the cabbie grouse under his breath. "Hotel Emma it is."

Oliver considered checking out the San Antonio scenery, but really, he just couldn't dredge up the interest. Yes, he wanted—no, *needed*—the job he was interviewing for, but he had never considered living in the South, and certainly not in Texas, with rednecks and cowboy hats and those awful ball sac things hanging from the undercarriage of huge, jacked-up trucks.

Maybe he was stereotyping, but he'd seen pictures online and read plenty of stories about the Lone Star State, and Oliver wasn't impressed.

And it's hotter than Hell. Satan himself probably couldn't stand the heat.

Oliver started to sneer and quickly suppressed the reaction. He wasn't better than anyone else, not in Texas, not in Boston, not anywhere, and he'd do damned well to remember that. It'd been his ego and arrogance that had caused the trouble in Boston. He was smart. Smart enough to know he must learn from his mistakes, and that he *did* make mistakes in the first place.

And when he made them, they were colossal mistakes. No one could ever accuse him of doing anything half-assed.

Oliver was just beginning to feel like he wasn't going to broil in his own skin when the taxi came to a stop and the driver said, "Here ya go, bud."

Oliver bit back the urge to ask whether he was a flower bud, a beer, or some other type of bud. He knew the answer but detested the false friendliness. After checking the meter to make sure it was accurate, Oliver paid the cabbie and tipped him twenty percent. The man had done his job well and honestly. That was what mattered, not whether or not he called Oliver 'bud'.

The Hotel Emma wasn't the fanciest or most expensive hotel Oliver had ever stayed in, but it wasn't a dump, not at all. In fact, he quite liked the look of it, and the history it held. Oliver had done his research on the hotel before choosing it to stay in. He would have preferred to book one of the suites, but those were reserved well in advance, and he understood why after having viewed them online. They were works of art as far as he was concerned. Very few hotels managed to pull *that* effect off, despite being very expensive.

His room would hopefully be delightful to stay in.

"May I help you with your luggage, sir?"

Oliver glanced away from the hotel—he'd been looking at the name of it, the design—and gave his attention to the valet. Pert was the first word that came to mind when he saw her. She smiled as if she truly enjoyed her job, and despite her uniform, she wasn't sweating at all.

"Please." Oliver internally winced at the thought of the tip he'd have to leave her. His funds were low, but he had a certain image to maintain—that of a confident, successful man rather than a desperate one fleeing a bad situation of his own making.

And that image included tipping well and seeming at ease when inside he was trying not to panic and fret over what would happen if he didn't get this job.

Oliver checked in and was pleased with the efficient clerk. She was neither too friendly nor snobbish, and he appreciated people who could find that balance.

The interior of the hotel was aesthetically appealing and very well laid-out. A little of the tension he'd been carrying for the past two weeks eased off his shoulders. *Everything will be okay. I'll get this job. I'll fix everything.*

This was his new start, his chance at redemption, and Oliver wasn't going to blow it.

* * * *

Peter had to admit it—he had a weakness for uptight jerks. Every time he found a guy attractive and made a move or vice versa, he ended up being used for nothing more than sex. Did he learn from it? *Nope. Not once.*

As he eyed the tall, thin man with the weird accent— well, weird for Texas—Peter guessed the stranger was from one of those North-Eastern states along the Atlantic Ocean. Just hearing that strong accent made Peter's dick perk up.

"Stop drooling," Lucy said, but she was smirking at him and even her eyes lit up with her amusement. "Mr. Biggerstaffer is a customer. You can't jump him and lick him like a lollipop!"

Peter's mouth watered and he gulped, suddenly envisioning just such a thing—Mr. Biggerstaffer, nude, all that uptightness gone as he moaned and thrashed while Peter sucked his long, thick cock.

"Peter Ruiz, get that look off your face right now, mister," Lucy teased as she waggled a finger at him. "Or at least go on break and take care of *that*." She pointed to his erection, which was tenting his trousers. "Seriously, dude."

Had it been anyone but Lucy, his BFFaEaE—Best Friend Forever and Ever and Ever, not to mention his cousin—Peter would have been embarrassed. However, Lucy had been born on the same day as him, and their moms were not just sisters but also best friends, so of course, Peter and Lucy were like twins. They even looked it, both with black hair, dark brown eyes and slight overbites. Both were an even five-feet tall, and a hundred and twenty-two pounds dripping wet. Peter would have loved to put on some weight, but his metabolism was set at warp speed.

"Go take a break," Lucy urged, making a shooing motion at him. "I can smell your arousal and *ick!*"

Peter wiggled his nose at her, a trick they both had, but he left Lucy at the counter. He wouldn't want to smell Lucy's arousal, either... Well, he had, as close as they were and as much time as they spent together. Sometimes one of them *did* get laid, and that person tried to warn the other to stay away if the sex took place at their shared residence. A couple of years back, Lucy had texted him that she had a date she was bringing back to fuck.

Peter's phone had been dead. When he'd entered their home, the scent of sex, and the sight of his cousin bouncing away on some random guy she'd never dated again, had seared Peter's eyeballs. He tried not to think about it. The sex, and seeing his cousin naked, because both of those things were just wrong. Lucy was his sister, as far as Peter was concerned. Sex was something neither of them wanted from each other. As much as they shared, they never went into detail about that part of their lives.

Peter wasn't a fuck-and-tell kind of guy, anyway. He scurried to the employee restroom and was relieved to find it empty. His conversation with Lucy was all but forgotten as he let himself picture Mr. Biggerstaffer again — and wonder if his last name was a declaration or just a name.

For his sake, Peter wanted it to be a declaration. He was, unabashedly, all about size. More girth than length, but either made him happy.

So long, and thick, but not too long. Thick, yeah. Real thick. Peter dashed into the nearest stall then locked the door. He didn't bother with his belt or anything more than unzipping his pants so he could pull his cock out. Underwear was not something Peter bothered with. He licked his hand a few times, then bit back a moan as he began masturbating.

As usual, he'd barely started before he came. No more than a picture of Mr. Biggerstaffer's face had him shooting on the third stroke.

Not that he was done, not at all. Peter's cock didn't grow soft after he came. It remained hard and the cum from his release slicked his shaft nicely, making the second orgasm even more intense, and his third almost caused him to pass out.

Peter had to wait a few minutes for the fourth one, but when it came, his knees gave out and he plopped down on the toilet, hard enough to jar him back to reality. He looked at his hand—at all the cum on it, on his pants, his shoes, the floor. "Well, crap."

He froze, then sniffed the air. He was still alone, and he didn't detect any fresh odors other than his own, so no one had come in while he'd been jerking off. There was the whole problem of him having made a mess, but Peter had a change of clothes stashed at work, because he did at times tend to get *overexcited* and have to masturbate. Never as much as he'd had to today, but Mr. Biggerstaffer just really did it for him, and anyway, Peter wasn't unusual in his horniness. Everyone made jokes about people fucking like bunnies, but the same held true for hares.

If they only knew about hare shifters... Peter chuckled, then stood and began cleaning up his mess.

Chapter Two

After tossing and turning for most of the night, Oliver was having to work hard to suppress his crankiness, as well as his nervousness. Then there was the fear of failure gnawing at him, so all in all, he was an internal mess, wound tighter than an eight-day clock. That thought actually brought a smile to his face. His granny Alice had been from the South, and that had been one of the sayings she'd brought to Boston with her. When he'd been younger, he'd all but worshiped his granny. Now he missed her, especially in moments when her words popped up in his head. He felt a pinch in his chest, that not so dull ache of losing someone loved, then took a deep breath, closed his eyes, and remembered how much love he and his granny had shared.

The pain of loss eased and so did some of Oliver's worries. He'd be okay. His granny's memory comforted him, and though, he didn't know squat about the afterlife or religion, he felt her presence. Whether he was imagining it or not, it helped him be more confident and less tense.

Oliver checked his reflection in the mirror once more. His light auburn hair was perfectly coifed, short but not too much so, slicked back but not slimy with product. He'd shaved and not nicked himself — a small miracle, considering his mood earlier. The suit he wore was his best, a medium-gray wool and cashmere Armani that he'd coveted for months before he'd purchased it.

Assured there wasn't a wrinkle anywhere nor a hair out of place, and his shoes were polished and gleaming, Oliver turned away, then walked over to the table where he had all his personal documents and résumé laid out.

Presentation was everything in the advertising business. Though Oliver was a bit of a cold-natured man, he did not lack in creativity. There was nothing boring about his résumé, or the PowerPoint presentation he'd prepared to show Mr. Jagger Osterman exactly *why* he should — *no,* had *to* – hire Oliver.

Now, if he could just not melt in the heat, he might get the job. Showing up for the interview dripping sweat would not make a good impression.

Fortunately, the hotel was less than two blocks from the building where the advertising agency was opening a new office.

Oliver still took a cab. He had his briefcase with all his preparations inside, and he strode into the building confidently, even if he felt like he'd swallowed a netfull of butterflies. *Or possibly hornets.*

Oliver ignored the pain and smiled at the man working the security desk. "Good morning," he said politely. "I have a nine o'clock appointment with Mr. Osterman."

The security guard — Martinez, according to his name tag — checked both his phone and the computer before replying. "Mr. Biggerstaffer?"

"Yes," Oliver answered.

"I'll need to see your ID." Martinez held out his hand.

Oliver had expected such security and had prepared accordingly. He took his ID from his trouser pocket and passed it over.

Martinez scrutinized it, then ran it through a machine of some sort — Oliver could only guess it scanned the license and checked to see if it was fraudulent or if Oliver was on some wanted or watch list. He didn't ask what Martinez was doing. It didn't matter, as long as he let Oliver in.

Martinez nodded, then pressed a button on another machine. "Sixth floor. The receptionist will tell you where to go from there." He gave Oliver his license back.

"Thank you." Oliver tucked it away again then headed for the door Martinez gestured to.

"Elevators are to the left," Martinez added.

Oliver thanked him again. Once at the elevators, Oliver quickly gave himself a mental pep-talk. The down lit up and the elevator was there in no time at all. The doors parted and he entered, then pressed the button for the sixth floor.

Elevators tended to make Oliver nervous, much like flying did, but this one was smooth, not jerky at all, and there were no clanging or banging sounds, just a smooth ride to his destination. The oak interior was oddly calming. Oliver thought it should have made him feel enclosed, claustrophobic, but he licked his lips and smelled the wood, the age of it, the strength of trees that had grown for hundreds of years before whatever fate had led them to be used for such a purpose as becoming part of an elevator.

His wandering thoughts came to a jolting stop when the elevator doors slid open. The scent of filtered air hit him, cool and slightly off since it wasn't the fresh outdoors odor he preferred. He stepped out onto wooden floors which had been polished until they reflected the lights overhead. The heels of his shoes clicked with every step.

He spotted the receptionist immediately. Her gray hair was piled up in a large bun on top of her head and she sported black cat eye glasses, complete with purple chains running from the earpieces around to her nape. She had on a little makeup, and her genuine smile reminded him of Granny Alice.

"You must be Mr. Biggerstaffer, and you're right on time, which is always a bonus," she chimed. Her voice definitely held a musical lilt to it. "He does appreciate punctuality. I'm Mrs. Garza, and if you'll have a seat, I'll let Mr. Osterman know you're here."

"Yes, ma'am. Thank you, Mrs. Garza." Oliver found the plush chairs not a dozen feet away from Mrs. Garza's desk. They were lined up against the wall, and two coffee tables had been set in front of them. The surfaces were covered with myriad magazines. Oliver picked up the first one that caught his eye, a tabloid-gossipy one with a shirtless Channing Tatum on the cover. Oliver certainly wasn't going to be reading it for the articles. A little eye-candy always helped ease the mind.

Oliver heard footsteps — solid, sure — on the wooden floor, and his heart did a little pitter-patter dance as he set the magazine back down. He stood, eyes already on Mr. Osterman's, and Oliver caught just a whiff of something that made his senses tingle. He wetted his lips with his tongue and knew then he was shaking hands with a shifter—a big bear one at that.

Osterman narrowed his eyes and sniffed, his nostrils flaring. He arched one dark eyebrow.

"Jagger Osterman, and you must be Oliver Biggerstaffer. Interesting," Osterman muttered as they released hands. His lips quirked up on one side. "Come on into my office where we can talk."

Oliver picked up his briefcase and ignored the unease crawling down his spine. He silently assured himself that the gossip wouldn't have zipped down the line to Texas from Boston, at least not to a bear shifter. Most species stuck to their own kind. *But not all of them. Look at my family lineage.* Oliver hoped his wince had only been an internal one. He was relieved to note that Osterman wasn't glancing back at him.

Holding his head up high, Oliver entered the office behind Osterman.

"Sit, please," Osterman said. He closed the door once Oliver was in the office then rounded the desk and pulled out a plush leather chair.

The office was decorated in a way that spoke of wealth—old wealth that didn't need to be proclaimed in new-age furniture and bright colors. The pale golden walls were works of art themselves. Oliver didn't know what had been done to get the texture or color, but both were soothing to look at. Paintings, not prints, hung on the walls in delicately gilded frames. The back wall of the office was solid glass, with some kind of tint that kept the sun from blasting through while still allowing a nice view of the area outside.

Oliver sat in a chair directly across from the desk, almost sighing as he settled into the comfortable leather seat.

"Yeah, they really went all-out on the new location." Osterman patted the armrest lightly. His smile wasn't quite right, lacking in sincerity.

Oliver prepared himself for something bad. He tried not to tense up.

Osterman leaned forward, placing his elbows on the desk and steepling his fingers under his chin. He narrowed his eyes and stared at Oliver.

It was difficult not to squirm, but somehow Oliver managed to keep himself still, his breathing steady. His inner nature, that of his creature, took over. *Finally!* Though he'd resented the shifter part of himself for weeks, Oliver felt a rush of relief now. He didn't shift, but inside he chilled as he thought of it. Everything calmed, his heart slowing, breathing almost ceasing.

"Ah." Osterman leaned back, surprise clear on his face. "I didn't even *know* there were snake shifters! Bird shifters, yeah. Guess I thought it was only warm-blooded species."

Well, that's a relief. He couldn't have heard about the Boston screw-up then. At least not through the shifter gossip vine, and Ellis signed a non-disclosure agreement. He can't violate that without voiding the sale. But Oliver knew well that other people talked, and word could still have gotten out.

Worrying wasn't going to help him. He smiled at Osterman and licked his lips—scenting the air, really, though, humans never caught on to that. "I'm surprised you didn't know. There are snake shifters all over Texas."

Osterman shrugged. "Huh. Guess I don't get out enough. I knew there were other species, like I said. There was a curandera I met that had been with a hawk shifter, and my husband's a pronghorn."

"Prey and predator?" Oliver asked, curious about the match. "Does that ever cause, er, problems? And what's a cu—coo—coorannera?"

"Last question first. A curandera or curandero—the ending in an 'a' means female, the 'o' male—is a healer or a witch doctor, a shaman or a sorcerer or sorceress, depending on who you ask. They've been around in some form or another for a long, long time. Some of them are real, true, powerful curanderos, and some are quacks. Whatever you do, don't piss a real one off. As to your question about my husband, surprisingly, no." Osterman's grin was all teeth. "I'm never tempted to eat Kevin when we're in shifted form. Can't say there aren't other urges, though." He blushed darkly. "Sorry. That's not appropriate work conversation."

"Is any of this?" Oliver asked, shrugging. "We are what we are. It's in our best interests to learn about other shifter species. It will certainly make you think twice if you ever run over a squirrel."

"Squirrel shifters, man, I know." Osterman's blush vanished as he paled. "I don't know whether a shifter would run out in front a car like squirrels do, or what. I mean, is it instinct? Run out, run back to the curb, then at the last second, run back in front of the car? What if that's just suicidal shifters?"

"Hell, I hope not. I do everything I can to avoid hitting a squirrel, including stopping in traffic and refusing to move. It's caused problems a few times." As far as Oliver knew, there were shifters in every breed of animal. Insects and smaller birds—like hummingbirds—he wasn't certain about. Or fish. "All mammals, that I know of, and reptiles. I am unaware of other sorts of creatures' shifter potential."

"Wow. I wonder if Kevin has any idea…" Osterman shook his head. "Okay, well, thank you for teaching me something new today. Can I ask what kind of snake you are?"

Now Oliver had to fight a blush of embarrassment. "Copperhead," he managed, which wasn't a lie.

Osterman glanced at his hair. "Ah, the hair."

Though Oliver called his hair auburn, it was truly as bright as a copper penny. He just hated to admit it. Auburn sounded much less…coppery.

"Yesss," Oliver agreed, a little hiss escaping before he could censor it. He had heard plenty of ginger jokes and was very sensitive about the topic, though, he wished he wasn't.

Osterman looked surprised for a moment, then he cleared his throat. "So, let's get down to business. What made you decide to sell your advertising firm in Boston and look elsewhere for work in the field?"

It was the question Oliver had dreaded, but knew he'd face. "I'd built up a successful company and grew bored. I need to be challenged."

After a long moment of silence, Osterman said, "I'd press you on the veracity of that claim, but I don't think you'd change it."

"I would not," Oliver agreed, his heart beginning to flutter. Osterman clearly didn't believe his answer. It *did* sound suspicious, but the truth wasn't an option, especially not to another shifter. "I have never committed a crime or violated any ethical standards."

"Ah, so it was personal," Osterman guessed. "An affair?"

Oliver was taken aback. "*Never* in the workplace! And not as the owner of the company, either. I said I hadn't violated any ethical standards."

"I believe you. I supposed that's what matters, and your reason for selling the company you built is personal." Osterman nodded. "I can accept that. I've not heard a bad word about you. Let's discuss the position you're being offered. The sooner I get this place staffed, the sooner I can go home to Abilene."

"You won't be staying on here in San Antonio?" Oliver asked, relieved and idly disappointed at the same time. He'd have liked to possibly befriend Jagger Osterman and his husband Kevin. Friends were one thing Oliver was short on.

"No, I'm just here doing the interviews and hiring." Osterman tapped the desktop with one finger. "I'm going to tell you, this is all just for the sake of following the proper hiring procedures. If your résumé is as excellent as I suspect it will be, you'll have the job."

Relief rushed through Oliver. Granted, he'd be going from business owner to Executive of Account Planning for someone else, but it was still a job, a prestigious one to some in the business.

He wasn't a failure, not totally. Oliver's smile was the most genuine one he'd had in weeks.

Chapter Three

Peter knew the moment Mr. Biggerstaffer entered the hotel. Peter's cock began to harden and Lucy turned to him and rolled her eyes.

"Really?" she asked.

Peter shrugged. "Like you have room to talk? You were drooling when that blond guy checked in earlier."

Lucy nodded. "Well yeah. He is *fine*."

The implication there being that Mr. Biggerstaffer wasn't. Peter wholeheartedly disagreed. He and Lucy had dissimilar tastes in men.

And Peter was going to make himself known to the sexy, uptight man striding into the lobby.

"Good afternoon, Mr. Biggerstaffer," he called out, pitching his voice low so as not to draw the notice of everyone around.

Lucy snickered, but Peter ignored her. He focused his attention solely on Mr. Biggerstaffer. All he wanted was for the man to notice him. Peter wouldn't do anything on company time that he shouldn't, and though he'd jack off on break, he'd never once done more than that. He might be a horny hare, but he did have standards.

Mr. Biggerstaffer looked at him, a quick glance, then he slowed his stride and paused to *really* look at him.

The connection was instant when their eyes met. Heat zapped through Peter, lust and something else, something raw and primal. He very nearly shifted forms, and the urges to run and fuck battled with each other.

His nose twitched. His senses shrieked. *Predator! Run!*

Yet knowing in that instant that Mr. Biggerstaffer was more than human, and was, in fact, a snake shifter, a powerful one at that—not like a corn snake or anything less than deadly—did not deter Peter. He wouldn't run.

Mr. Biggerstaffer, his lean body so well-defined in the expensive suit he wore, just turned Peter on in every way possible. Especially when he stuck out the tip of his tongue. A slight dip in the tip of it reminded Peter of a snake's tongue, as it should have done.

"Hello, Peter Ruiz," Mr. Biggerstaffer replied, his deep voice melodious, almost hypnotizing. That accent was another turn-on for sure, too.

Peter touched his name tag briefly, his smile broadening. "You seem quite—" *Less uptight, less ready to break, or strike* — "Content today. Have you had good news?" Peter was not out of line. They were encouraged to speak with guests, remember their names, and make them feel welcome.

Mr. Biggerstaffer approached the counter. Lucy made herself scarce. "You smell—" There went that tongue again. "Mm. Rabbit," he whispered.

"Jack," Peter added, then snorted and rolled his eyes at himself. "Jackrabbit," he replied just as quietly. "And you are…" Peter inhaled deeply, nose twitching madly. "Yummy." He slapped a hand over his mouth. "Sthorry!" he said through his fingers.

Oh, sweet Lord! Peter's legs quivered when Mr. Biggerstaffer gave him a predatory smile.

"As do you," Mr. Biggerstaffer replied. He raked Peter with a gaze that meant Peter would be walking around hard most of the day.

The scent of arousal not his own filled Peter's nostrils. Mr. Biggerstaffer wanted him, too.

"My reservation here is for the week," Mr. Biggerstaffer said, moving even closer. He leaned over the counter, and Peter went dizzy with the smell of him. "I won't mix business with pleasure, but when I have checked out, if you'd like to fuck then, I will make sure you are satisfied like no one has satisfied you before."

Peter gulped. He'd never been so hard in his life — or disappointed. "When you aren't staying here?" he asked, trying to keep the whine out of his voice.

"I feel very strongly about what lines should not be crossed," Mr. Biggerstaffer stated, leaning back, out of Peter's personal space. "You are an employee here and I am a customer. When those dynamics have changed, if you are still interested, then we can see about..." That smile went sly. "Other things." He took out his wallet, removed a business card from it, and slid it across the counter. "My cell is on there. Call me when and if you want to meet up."

Fuck. He means fuck. Hell yeah! Peter wanted to cheer but remained composed. "Yes, sir. Thank you. I hope you enjoy your stay at The Emma."

"I am certain I will." And with that, Mr. Biggerstaffer walked away, whistling a slightly hissish tune.

Peter admired the man from the top of his coppery hair to the heels of his no-doubt-expensive shoes. He wished the suit jacket didn't cover Mr. Biggerstaffer's butt.

Hopefully, he'd get to see that part up close and personal. Peter wasn't much of a top, but he did love ass play, giving and receiving. It'd be interesting learning what a snake shifter liked.

Peter picked up the card and looked at it. *Oliver Biggerstaffer, Advertising Executive.* The phone number had an unfamiliar area code. No surprise there, since the address above it was in Boston.

A week was a long time to wait for Peter. He pocketed the card. It would be a long time to wait, but he didn't have one second's doubt that it'd be worth it.

Peter heard and scented Lucy returning to the counter. He glanced at her and she fanned her face. "I thought you liked Mr. Blond Adonis?"

Lucy nodded. "Oh, I definitely do, but the pheromones were thicker than wet cement between you two."

"Thicker than—" Peter frowned.

"Hey, what can I say?" Lucy snapped. "I'm hungry and a little jealous. Mr. Blond probably wouldn't have any qualms about fucking me while staying here. The fact that Mr. Biggerstaffer does means he's not your usual loser."

"He's not a loser at all," Peter felt compelled to argue. "Don't say that."

"I didn't mean he was," Lucy replied. "Jeez, calm down. I just *said* he's *not* a loser."

That wasn't quite what she'd said, but Peter let it go. He was nit-picking when he knew she'd meant no insult. "Why don't you go take your lunch break? Jenner is supposed to be in soon. I can handle the front until then." It'd keep him too busy to have a hard-on, hopefully.

* * * *

When he finally got off work, Peter asked Lucy if she wanted a ride home.

"Nope, I'm going out," she informed him. "And not with the blond guy."

"With who?" Peter asked.

"Whom," Lucy corrected.

Peter shook a finger at her. "You're stalling. Cut it out."

"No, I'm trying to educate you," she retorted. "For your information, Jack called me. He wants to see if we can rekindle what we used to have back in high school."

Peter gawked at her. "He broke your heart! *And* he's named Jack!" Which was so not funny, considering he was a jackrabbit shifter, like Peter and Lucy. Then again, Peter was a hare, and there was the whole Peter Rabbit thing that he got teased about all the time. "He cheated on you," he added, pushing aside everything else. "With a guinea pig."

Lucy pushed back her bangs and avoided looking at him. "That's what everyone said. I didn't give Jack a chance to explain, and anyway, it's been eight years. I want to see him."

"How did you keep this secret from me all day?" Peter demanded, planting his fisted hands on his hips.

"Because I knew you'd argue with me, and he called me while I was at lunch. Look." She sighed heavily. "I want to meet up with him, okay?"

Peter hoped it wasn't the same kind of *meeting up* he'd be doing with Oliver Biggerstaffer in a few days. "Just, be careful, okay?"

"I will. We're going to The Bonham. Want to come?"

It was a rare thing for Peter to turn down such an offer. He loved going out and getting laid as much as the next horny person did.

But oddly enough, he wanted to hold out for one certain guy. Maybe he'd even stop masturbating—

"What are you laughing about?" Lucy asked with a hint of irritation.

"Not you, I promise. Just my own silly ideas, and, nah," he added. "I'm taking a pass on tonight. I have to do a few forum replies, anyway."

Lucy hummed. "How close are you to being finished?"

"Six more classes and I am *done!*" he exclaimed, excited at the prospect. "I'll have a Masters in Hospitality Management!" He'd always had goals, and wanted more out of life than to work an average nine-to-five job. "I hope they'll promote me here. I really love The Emma."

"I'm sure if there's any openings, they will," Lucy said. "Okay, I'm off. And Peter?"

Peter bit his bottom lip as he waited for whatever she was going to say.

"Please, don't be a dick about Jack," she pleaded. "This is between him and me, and if I'm accepting of him, then I want you to be, too."

He sighed as he released his lip. "Anything for you, Lucy. Always."

She smiled and gave him a kiss on the cheek, then she was darting out of the room.

Peter envied her that hope and happiness. Jack Culvers had grown up with them, too, though he was a couple of years older. He and Lucy had dated all through Lucy's high school years, then Jack had stood her up for prom, and word had gotten around that he'd had a guinea pig shifter on the side. Then Jack had done a vanishing act.

If he broke Lucy's heart this time, Peter was going to lop off one of Jack's back feet and make it into a keychain. Preferably while Jack was shifted, but Peter wouldn't be too choosey. He'd take whatever he could get, and he was certain Lucy's brothers would help.

He was amused at his imagined violent protection of Lucy. Chances were good that she'd castrate Jack if he broke her heart. Or at least punch his lights out. She was fierce now, not timid like she'd been in high school.

Peter changed out of his uniform into jeans and a T-shirt. It was hot outside still, but he was used to it. "Wouldn't be Texas without the heat," he muttered as he left the employee room, his duffle over one shoulder.

A sensuous chill went down his spine when he neared the exit doors.

"I don't suppose you'd know where to get the best Mexican food around here?"

Peter turned and looked Oliver over from head to toe, then up again. The man was dressed in his trousers still, but had ditched the jacket and tie. The collar of his white shirt was open, and Peter could see a few golden-red hairs peeking out of it.

"Peter?" Oliver asked, sounding amused.

Peter gave himself a shake. He grinned abashedly. "Sorry, got distracted. Best Mexican food, huh? Well." Peter scratched the underside of his chin. "That depends on your taste. Do you like things mild, medium or spicy?" He couldn't quite keep the flirtiness from his voice as he cocked his right hip. "Americanized Mexican food, Tex-Mex, true Mexican food?"

Oliver raised both hands up in the classic 'stop' position. "Whoa, whoa. See, that's why I had a problem deciding. I looked on Yelp, but there's so many reviews and suggestions, I just gave up."

"We have an excellent menu here," Peter offered.

"I can vouch for the veracity of your statement, having eaten three meals here, but I'd like to try something different." He took a step closer to Peter and tipped his chin toward the doors. "Care to step outside for a moment?"

"I'm off work, so no problem." Peter had moved the duffle bag around to cover his erection. But by the way Oliver sniffed and licked his lips, Peter was certain the man could smell his arousal.

Oliver walked a few feet away, then turned to Peter. "I'd like to take you to dinner, nothing more."

Peter was confused. "But I thought you said you didn't do stuff like that? Date someone working where you're staying."

"Well." Oliver huffed and shuffled his feet, watching them before looking at Peter again. "I don't, so I was thinking this would be a meal between possible friends. I'll be moving here, and I don't know anyone."

"You got the job?" Peter asked, pleased for Oliver. "And you don't want to just fuck me?"

"I would never *just* fuck you," Oliver replied in a way that made Peter shiver with need. "You strike me as an intelligent, interesting man, as well as a sexy one. So I would like to have dinner with you, get to know you and let you get to know me. Maybe by the time my stay here at The Emma is over, we'll be able to decide if we're interested in more than fucking."

Peter was shocked. Most men looked at him like a cute fuck, and nothing else. "You think I'm worth more than…than—"

Oliver touched his cheek, just briefly, but Peter could have sworn his skin would bear a warm mark there forever. "I think there's more to you than meets the eye."

"I've almost got my Masters in Hospitality Management," Peter blurted out, wanting, perhaps even *needing*, to prove Oliver true. "Just six more classes to go."

"Really? That is amazing," Oliver replied. "It also proves my point. You are a sexy, handsome man who exudes sensuality. That isn't the whole of you, however. It's just a part that most people glom onto. I'm at an age where I'm interested in…more."

"How old are you?" Peter asked, his toes and fingers tingling. He was hopeful, horny, and happy—his favorite three h's. "I'm twenty-six."

"Thirty-nine," Oliver said. "Is that out of your range?"

"Not at all, and—" Peter rolled his lips in between his teeth then released them. Was he ready for more than just sex and bad boys? Yeah, he thought he was tired of that game. Oliver and he might not work out, but Peter was through being used and having sex on the fly just so he wasn't alone. "And I think I'd like to get to know you."

That did not rule out sex. Peter could wait the week if he had to, wait until Oliver's stay at the hotel was up. But after that? He was going to have Oliver fuck him until they were both unable to move an inch.

"Spicy and authentic," Oliver said out of the blue.

Peter must have looked confused, because Oliver chuckled.

"The food. I'd like something spicy and authentic, and I'd like to share the meal with you. What do you say, Peter Ruiz?"

Oliver wasn't demanding, wasn't all over Peter, wasn't treating him like he was only worth fucking.

Peter was starting to see that he was worth more than that, too.

He winked at Oliver. "I know just the place. It doesn't look like much, but the food is to die for."

"If we can skip the dying part, you're on," Oliver joked.

Peter laughed. His snake had a sense of humor. He'd have never thought that would be the case. He'd only met rattlesnake shifters, and they could be touchy, to put it mildly. "Then follow me to my car and we'll get the best Mexican food in the state."

Chapter Four

There wasn't time for Oliver to search for a place to live. He had too much to do, helping Jagger set up the offices and decide who to hire, and which accounts they would transfer from Abilene until the new agency built up a steady clientele. Fortunately, he was lucky enough to find an excellent administrative assistant for himself, and she in turn, recommended a realtor who she promised was incredible at his job.

By the week's end, Oliver had a rental contract for a luxury apartment at one of the best complexes in San Antonio. That it was new and in the Pearl area was a bonus. He arranged to have his furnishings shipped to Texas immediately, and the only downside was that the apartment, and his furnishings, wouldn't be available until the middle of next week.

As busy as he was, Oliver knew one thing — waiting to have sex with Peter was a torturous thing. Peter flirted, but not overly so, and seemed very flattered when Oliver stressed that he wanted to get to know him better before taking things further. They'd been out on three dinners. Oliver didn't consider them dates. There'd been no kissing or groping.

But he and Peter had talked and laughed, and that was more stimulating than fucking would have been.

Almost. Oliver was certain that when he and Peter did finally have sex, it either would be explosive, or a horrible letdown. As often as he'd thought of stripping Peter naked, of slowly peeling the clothes from him, kissing every inch of bared skin, discovering what made Peter shiver and what made him cry out with need, the reality might not live up to the fantasy. In Oliver's experiences, fantasies almost always proved better than reality.

Even so, he couldn't imagine the sex being horrible, despite his worries. Peter was too sexy, too witty and energetic to be a bad lay. Oliver wasn't a slouch in the sack, either. They should do just fine.

Though he wanted better than fine.

"You look like your mind's a million miles away."

Oliver jolted, almost slipping out of his leather chair as he snapped his head up to find Jagger standing in the doorway. "Just thinking about strategies."

Jagger snorted. He came in and shut the door. "Sure, sure. I can scent things, you know. Don't worry about it. I'm about to go nuts without Kevin here. He's flying down this weekend and staying through Wednesday, then he has to get back to work. I'm sure I'll be distracted for a few days myself."

Jagger's wicked smile bordered on filthy, and Oliver grinned at him. "You can't take off from work?"

"Nope, but Kevin can come in and help out." Jagger's smile didn't falter.

Oliver could just bet Jagger and Kevin would be having some X-rated breaks. Not that he blamed them.

"But that's not what I'm in here for," Jagger said, pulling up the chair on the other side of the desk until he could plop into it and brace his elbows on the smooth surface. "I came in because I need you to sit in on the conference call with Mr. Renner, the head of our Abilene office and owner of the businesses."

Oliver knew who Mr. Renner was. The man was snooty and pretentious, and Oliver sincerely hoped Renner didn't decide to relocate to the San Antonio office.

"I can do that. When?" Oliver asked.

"In five minutes, my office." Jagger pushed the chair back and stood up. "Not much notice, but he just texted me about it. He's got some leads and a possibly big client for us already. If they come through, we'll never hear the end of how much of an advertising genius he is. FYI—" He stopped by the door and looked back over his shoulder. "He's really not, but he *does* have two assistants worth their weight in gold that are brilliant. Not as fabulous as Debbie is, but they're great."

Debbie was Jagger's assistant. She was efficient and sarcastic, and Oliver had liked her from the moment he'd met her. "Hopefully my assistant will be just as fabulous."

Jagger shook his head. "Nope, no out-assistanting Debbie allowed." He opened the door. "Three minutes to go."

Oliver got up and strolled after Jagger. It wasn't the first call he'd had to sit in with Jagger and Renner, and he agreed with Jagger. Renner was pompous, a bully, and rich enough to get away with it. It was people like him that had made Oliver want to be his own boss.

He'd failed at that, so this was what he had, and he'd make the most of it. He was truly excited to have a chance to get the new agency up and running, and to help make it successful.

And this time, he couldn't be blackmailed out of his position. Oliver had learned his lesson. He'd be very, very careful and never let his guard down.

* * * *

"Why did you just wail like your world is coming to an end?" Lucy asked.

Peter uncovered his face, having pressed his palms to his cheeks and fingers over his eyes. "Lucy, he can't move into his new apartment until *next week! Next. Week!* I'm going to burst! I've got a build-up of—"

"Ahem," Lucy said very loudly. "Good afternoon, ma'am. How may I help you?"

"I have a reservation for tonight through Tuesday." An older woman with thick, long gray hair stood at the counter. She cocked her head to the left and looked at Peter. "What, exactly, do you have a build-up of?"

Peter spluttered and stuttered, and the lady tutted.

"They have medications to clean you out," she whispered, except she was loud when she whispered, and a couple walking past tittered, pausing to watch the show.

"Er, ma'am, I don't—" Peter began. He looked pleadingly at Lucy. *Check her in, check her in!* Lucy didn't seem to get the telepathic memo or, more than likely, she knew just what Peter was thinking and was having fun at his expense. "I don't—" he began again.

"Oh, I know. Most of you men don't cleanse like you should, and do you know how that backs up your intestines?" the customer asked. "It can become toxic in there. Bacteria, germs, all sorts of things in the intestinal tract along with the fecal—"

"Ack!" Peter couldn't stop himself from making the sound. His cheeks were so hot with his blush of embarrassment, he should have combusted on the spot. "No, no, no, ma'am, that's not what I was talking about!"

"Mrs. Hughes, correct?" Lucy said, finally intervening.

"Yes, yes," Mrs. Hughes replied, clearly distracted as she studied Peter. "Is it a urethral blockage?"

"Oh my God, no." Peter looked up at the ceiling. Maybe God would just strike him dead now and spare him anymore humiliation. But he doubted it. God was probably laughing His ass off.

"He meant he has a mental build-up—stress, you know," Lucy said, possibly saving him from death by mortification. "He uses an all-natural cleanser that I suggest," Lucy added. "Weekly. He's as clean as a whistle inside."

Peter was going to kill her.

"That's good then. If you've got mental build-up— whatever that means—perhaps you need some physical activity to help," Mrs. Hughes suggested. She smoothed her hair down. "You know. Get out and play ball or jog. Yoga! Yoga is excellent, too."

For a minute there, he'd thought Mrs. Hughes was coming onto him. Peter almost whimpered in relief. "Yes, ma'am. I'll do that. There's a yoga studio right around the corner."

"Oh, excellent," she practically purred. "Can you give me the name and number of it? I'd love a place to go practice at while I'm here."

Peter looked up the information while Lucy resumed checking Mrs. Hughes in. He didn't know when Oliver showed up exactly, but he knew when Oliver was watching him. That sensual tickle down his spine made

Peter clench his ass while he wrote out the yoga studio's name and number. He should have had it memorized, since one of his numerous relatives owned the place.

Peter's breath hitched when he looked up and met Oliver's gaze. Most of his blood shot down south. He was always erect around Oliver, or almost always. Not jacking off while he waited for Oliver was making Peter crazy. He was going to come if he so much as sneezed right then.

Oliver's eyes darkened and his lips thinned. He didn't look displeased, but rather like he was struggling for control. Then he did that thing, the one that made him look harsh and likely to bite. The calm came over Oliver from one second to the next. He was in utter control of himself, and Peter was more turned on by that than ever. He loved that stern, cold look. It was Oliver's snake nature, and it scared Peter's hare even as it made him horny.

"Now if you decide you need to change your cleansing product, let me know, and I'll give you the name of mine," Mrs. Hughes said loudly. "It'll clear out your intestines and leave you five to ten pounds lighter. That goes for both of you." She shook her finger at Lucy. "Ladies should always be clean."

Lucy nodded. "Oh, yes, ma'am, I agree. If I ever become unhappy with what I use, I'll let you know." She smiled brightly. "Now, Steven will take your luggage to your suite. I hope you enjoy your stay, and if there's anything you need, please don't hesitate to let us know."

"I won't," Mrs. Hughes replied before leaving the counter.

Oliver walked over, gaze still locked with Peter's. "Cleansing?"

Peter halfway expected his body to collapse from confusion as he felt the blood rush to his face since he was embarrassed all over again.

"His insides," Lucy chimed. "Mine, too. You know, gotta clean out the ol' —"

"Don't say it," Peter warned. "Customers."

Not that any were close by now, but it was worth a shot.

Lucy nodded. "Right. Wouldn't want them to hear me say anything about butt stuff."

"Lucy," Peter groaned.

Oliver grunted. "It *is* inappropriate work conversation."

Lucy glared at him. "When you aren't a customer here anymore, I'll be flipping you off, *Mr. Biggerstaffer*."

"Until then, you have to smile and act like you like me," Oliver informed her. "Even while you're off the clock."

"I can still like you and flip you off, believe me," she mumbled.

Peter could vouch for that, and did. "It's true. She gives me the finger all the time."

"Wow, that sounds kinda dirty." Lucy snickered when Oliver gave her a stern look. "I'm going back to being a mature professional now."

"In all fairness, the customer started that whole conversation," Peter said just loud enough for Oliver to hear. "We would never have brought up that topic. She just overheard part of something I said and took it wrong."

"Oh?" Oliver quirked one eyebrow at him.

Damn it! I'm going to end up telling him! Peter looked at the time. "I'm off in five more minutes. We can discuss it then, if that's good with you?"

Oliver pulled something from his suit pocket, and put it on the counter. "After you check me out, please."

"Check you—" Wow, Peter hadn't known his voice could squeak like that! "Out?" he finished in a less mouse-like manner.

"Check me out," Oliver agreed. "I did only arrange to stay a week. I've decided not to extend my stay here until my apartment is ready."

Peter's mouth and throat were so dry, he could hardly swallow. "Was...was everything not to your liking, sir?"

"It's a lovely hotel, with very efficient staff," Oliver observed, "but there is one particular thing, or rather, one particular person, who is very much to my liking. It is for that reason that I've booked a suite at the hotel across the street a few blocks down."

The heat in Oliver's eyes should have liquefied Peter. As it was, despite being at work, he had to reach down and pinch his cock before he shot off in his trousers. At least the counter hid his actions, though Oliver's slow, smug smile seemed to imply that he knew exactly what Peter was doing.

He probably does. Peter's hand shook as he reached for Oliver's room card. "Your things—"

"Have been packed and a valet has them waiting." Oliver gestured to Vanessa and the luggage rack she was standing by. "I could call a taxi, but I was wondering if I might catch a ride from you instead? Since you're getting off work and all."

He wants me. He wants me, bad. Oh, God, I'm going to have to make sure he knows how us hare shifters work when it comes to sex. He didn't want to freak Oliver out by coming and coming and coming...and coming even more.

"I can do that," Peter forced himself to say as he took care of checking Oliver out. "I just need to change out of my uniform before we leave. It'd look really bad for me to show up at another hotel in this." He tapped his shirt.

"Understandable. I'll be happy to wait for you here." Oliver's hand brushed his when Peter handed him his receipt.

Peter shivered.

Oliver hissed, and there was nothing human about the sound. His snake was close to the surface, which meant his control was slipping.

It was good to know Peter wasn't the only one ready — more than ready — for sex.

He had a minute to go. Oliver moved to stand by his luggage cart.

A minute had never passed so slowly. As soon as it was time to clock out, Peter bolted from the lobby and to the employees' room. He stripped out of his uniform, said a silent prayer of gratitude that he was off work the next day, then he sniffed himself. All he could smell was pre-cum and horniness. It wasn't a bad mix.

The skinny jeans almost did him in. Peter had to wiggle and squirm and push and stuff to get his dick in them and zip the pants up. He put a silky blue T-shirt on, slid his feet into his Vans and he was ready to go.

As he walked out of the room, all he could think was, *Finally. I'm finally going to get to kiss Oliver.* It surprised him that kissing was the first thing that came to mind.

Surprised him, and intrigued him. Peter had never been huge on kissing. It'd always been wham, bam, thanks, sir. Most of the time he'd fucked around with other hare shifters. A few humans here and there. In his experience, neither species did much more than the basics before fucking him.

But he'd never been with another breed of shifter. He'd certainly never been with anyone who'd spent so much time getting to know him first—and that was a sad reality, considering that he and Oliver had only known each other for less than a week.

It still felt right, different from the possibility of sex with anyone else ever had. Peter had always picked guys, or been picked up by guys, intent on simply using him. Sometimes they hooked up with him several times, and Peter hoped they had come to care for him. That hadn't ever been the case.

This time was different. It was, and nothing was going to convince him otherwise.

Chapter Five

There was no other choice but for Oliver to change hotels. He couldn't wait another day to at least kiss Peter.

Though there would be more than kissing tonight. Oliver thoroughly intended to have sex with Peter all night long, to learn everything possible about his compact, sexy body.

His stamina was much greater than a human's, and part of his nature — the inhuman part of it, his snake — liked sex slow and deep, meaningful and very intense. That didn't mean there wasn't hard, fast fucking, but there was more to a night of sex than that.

And when Oliver wanted a night of sex, he wanted *a whole night* of sex. Tomorrow was a Saturday, and even though Jagger wouldn't be coming into the office, Oliver would need to go check on things later in the morning. He could function well on a couple of hours sleep.

Peter looked like sex incarnate as he appeared, his jeans so tight Oliver could see the outline of his dick.

Pink tinted Peter's cheeks, and his pupils were wide, both signs of arousal that went with his scent.

"I'll just pull my car around," Peter rasped. He had a duffle bag over one shoulder. "Be right back."

"He's leaving with you?" Vanessa, the valet assisting Oliver, sounded scandalized.

Oliver answered for Peter, "Mr. Ruiz is driving me to my new accommodations. All the staff here have been extremely friendly and helpful, going out of their way to see to it that any issue I have is taken care of. I will make sure to let the manager know how pleased I am with the services rendered."

And he'd give Vanessa a big tip. Peter wasn't breaking any rules by giving him a ride, and Oliver wouldn't feel guilty or doubt why Peter was going out with him, not that he believed Peter was just seeking to make a guest happy. But, other people could view it as such, like Peter's manager, and Oliver didn't want that. The potential problem was dissolved now that Oliver was no longer a guest at the hotel.

"Yes, sir." Vanessa smiled and gestured to the doors. "Thank you in advance for the good review to my manager."

Someone has goals, good for her. Vanessa was smart and knew what a good review could do for her there at the hotel. "You're quite welcome, Vanessa. You've been very patient and discrete." As soon as Oliver said that last word, he wondered if he'd screwed up, if he'd made it appear that he and Peter were up to something unseemly.

They weren't, he reminded himself. Everything was ethical and above-board. He wanted Peter. Peter wanted him. Peter wasn't having sex with him because he was a customer at the hotel. No one could make such a claim.

Peter pulled up outside in his little blue car. He hopped out as the trunk opened. "Let me help," he said to Vanessa as she brought the luggage rack over.

Oliver would have offered to help as well, but he let Vanessa do her job, and Peter help to perhaps make sure she didn't want to spread gossip about him.

He tipped more than he usually would have, then he was finally alone with Peter. "Are you sure?" he asked.

Peter bobbed his head almost violently in assent. "Yes. More than. Oh, my God, so much more than ready!"

Oliver's ego was stroked and he got in the car. Peter joined him.

"I should tell you something though," Peter said as he began to drive. "Because I don't want to freak you out."

"Okay." Oliver noted Peter's serious tone. "What is it you need to tell me?"

Peter cleared his throat. "Uh, well. I come a lot. Like, a lot *lot*. And fast. Refractory time isn't an issue for me the first four or five times, at least."

Oliver's shaft hardened. "So you have several orgasms, and you come and stay hard, at least four or five times? In what time span?"

"Uh." Peter blushed. "Usually really quick. Minutes. Then after that it takes me about half hour per orgasm or so. The whole fucking like hares thing, you know. Most of us have a whole crap-ton of siblings because of that. I don't. It's just me, and a lot of cousins and aunts and uncles. We're not very close, though. I'm closer to Lucy than I am to anyone else. But, anyway. I'll probably come before I even get naked."

Oliver knew there was a story inside of Peter, one about his family, but he didn't press. Now wasn't the time. Oliver didn't want to talk about his family, either.

Instead, as soon as Peter stopped at a red light, Oliver asked, "So if I were to reach over and touch your cock right now, even through your jeans, if I were to stroke and caress…" He trailed off as Peter shuddered, moaned, and the scent of cum filled the car.

The light turned green, and someone honked. Peter started driving again.

"I can make you come just from talking?" Oliver asked.

Peter slanted him a look. "Well, no one else ever has. Then again, you're the sexiest man I've ever seen, and I haven't masturbated since the first time I spotted you in the hotel. I've been holding out for the real thing, instead of my hand."

Oliver almost shot in his trousers himself. He pressed a palm to his stiff cock. "You masturbated at work?"

"I was off the clock, on break," Peter clarified. "I jacked off four times before I could get myself under control. I wanted you so bad."

Oliver was tempted to ask why, but he didn't need to have his ego stroked any further. He was still flying from Peter's eagerness for him.

"This place?" Peter asked, pointing to the hotel Oliver had reserved his suite at.

"Yes, this one. I'm actually already checked in, so as soon as the valet gets my bags, unless you'd like to eat—"

"Room service later," Peter interrupted. "This place has pretty good food, but that's not what I want." He turned his gaze to Oliver, his dark eyes so full of need. "I want you."

"You'll have me." Oliver pointed. "Valet parking."

"Oh, yeah." Peter zipped his little car right up to the valet stand. "Shoot! I've got cum—"

"Carry your duffle," Oliver suggested.

"Good idea." They got out, and Peter raced to the trunk to grab his duffle bag. "I'll carry this," Peter said to the valet. "Please just get the rest."

"We're in the Ambassador suite," Oliver informed the valet gathering his bags. "Please have the car parked, as well."

"Yes, sir," the valet replied.

Oliver was more turned on than he'd ever been in his life, yet he felt calm, his snake close to the surface, wanting to mate. There was no desire for him to shift and have a hare for dinner. There never had been. He understood Jagger's proclamation about not wanting to make a meal of his pronghorn husband. As a snake, Oliver had never eaten a rabbit—for which he was now going to be forever grateful—but it wasn't unheard of for snakes to eat smaller rabbits, usually babies. Even in his snake form, Oliver had abstained from eating baby anythings. He tried not to eat unless he was human. Even then, he tended to avoid mammalian meats, at the very least.

No, the things he wanted to do to Peter were all sensual. He could hardly wait to lick him, to learn his scent from the taste of his skin.

There was no hiding his own tented trousers now. Oliver gestured for Peter to walk in front of him. Peter's gaze dipped to his groin then his eyes went wide. He glanced back up at Oliver, and the need was apparent in his expression.

Oliver nodded. He would take care of Peter's need, soon.

As efficient as the staff were at the hotel, it still seemed to take too long for them to reach the suite. The elevators stopped at every floor then the valet gave a speech about the amenities in the room, which Oliver hadn't heard before because he'd checked in but not entered his suite. Oliver finally pulled some cash from his wallet, handed it to the valet, then ushered him to the door. "Thank you," Oliver said, opening the door. "Please leave."

The valet rushed out of the door, smirking.

Oliver shut the door, locked and bolted it, then turned just in time to catch Peter as he all but leaped onto Oliver.

Heat, so much heat, and the good kind. Peter felt like the bright Boston sun on a cool day, chasing off the cold and warming Oliver all the way through to his bones. He moaned as he parted his lips, Peter's mouth meeting his for a kiss that sizzled and ramped the heat up to new levels.

Oliver grasped Peter's ass and tugged. Peter raised up, his arms and legs wrapped around Oliver. The press of groin to groin was dizzying—Oliver thrust automatically and Peter threw his head back, whimpering as he came. The heady scent of spunk filled the room, filled Oliver's nose, his lungs, his being. He had never been an aggressive lover, but something snapped in him and he surged toward the bed, carrying Peter while he continued to come.

Seams ripped and material gave as Oliver stripped Peter. Never had he been so rough, but never had he needed so badly before, either.

Peter tugged and pulled at Oliver's clothes as well, and together they managed to get naked. "Finally," Oliver declared before framing Peter's face with his hands, then kissing him fiercely, teeth and tongue fully engaged. As happened when he was truly turned on, Oliver's tongue split, something he normally had to hide from sexual partners, and the main reason why he'd had so few. The snake in him always leaked out in that manner when sex was good.

And this time it was beyond good, skyrocketing past fantastic. Peter's groin and pubes were wet with his cum, and Oliver wanted to lick him clean.

He twined his tongue with Peter's, and knew the moment Peter felt the widened slit.

Peter stiffened, then went lax except for his grip on Oliver's hair. With both hands, he held Oliver in place and sucked on his tongue until Oliver used one knee to shove Peter's legs apart so he could lie between them and thrust.

His skin was covered in goosebumps despite the warmth. Need coiled in his gut and his balls and his dick dripped with pre-cum. Oliver nipped Peter's tongue, then moaned as Peter did the same to him.

All Oliver's plans to go slow went up in flames. He grabbed a handful of Peter's hair and used his grip to tug, forcing Peter to arch his neck and break the kiss. "Too much?" he asked, surprised at the huskiness of his own voice.

"No. More," Peter demanded. "Fuck me."

"Condoms?" They weren't necessary, but Oliver knew some men didn't like the mess of spunk everywhere. Though, considering Peter's sexual stamina, he wasn't surprised when Peter snorted.

"No way. Fuck me." It seemed as if Peter was trying to top from the bottom, but Oliver wouldn't have it. He dipped his head instead and bit Peter right below his chin, then below each ear.

Oliver left marks, hickies and bites, as he pulled moan after moan from Peter. He touched Peter everywhere — his face, head, neck, shoulders, chest — taking time out to play with his nipples, tugging and nipping, twisting and pinching.

Peter tasted like heaven, salty and sweet in all the right places. Oliver had never been free to taste and touch as he wanted to. Even though his dick ached to be inside Peter, Oliver made himself slow down. He didn't want to miss anything, any part of Peter.

Peter's belly was soft, not chiseled. He was stout, and Oliver liked that. He didn't want what some people considered the perfect body in a lover—rippling abs and such. He wanted a real man, someone who ate and played and fucked.

And he wanted things he hadn't let himself hope for in the past, when he'd been focused so intently on building his business. "You taste so good," he murmured, getting his mind back to where it should be. "So good."

"That tongue." Peter squirmed. "Oh, God, I want it…I want it everywhere. I want it in me. Please, please tell me you—"

"I'll eat your ass until you scream," Oliver promised.

Peter thrust his hips up and came again.

Oliver hissed and grabbed his biceps, holding Peter down. Then he began a sinuous, slithering move, his cock sliding in the copious amount of cum Peter had released.

Despite all of his orgasms, Peter's shaft was still hard, like he hadn't come at all.

"Going to have so much fun with you," Oliver added, though he hadn't ever been so talkative during sex before. Peter brought out a side of him that Oliver had never known, but he liked it. "Lick you, suck you, fuck you…" He hissed again, free to be himself. "Make you mine." *Wait. What?* That was a bit more possessive than he was prepared to be.

Luckily, Peter had been moaning again, and Oliver didn't think he'd heard that last bit. Oliver sucked on Peter's left nipple—the tip hard, hot, swollen—while he plucked at the other. Peter writhed non-stop, thrusting, grinding, gripping on to Oliver where he could manage with Oliver still holding him down with one hand.

Oliver had to let go of Peter's biceps to slide down, licking a path to Peter's belly button. He flicked his tongue in and out of it, then bit below it, and Peter shouted, more cum spurting from his cock.

The thick shaft was uncircumcised, probably average length, but thick, almost as thick as Oliver's. For all that Oliver was thin, his dick was not.

He kept moving down until he got his first taste of Peter's semen. Not salty, which was a surprise, but earthier instead of briny, and less strong in taste overall. It even had a sweet hint to it that Oliver enjoyed as he lapped at more of the jizz.

Peter rested his hands in Oliver's hair, caressing. His legs were up, spread in a wide vee, such an invitation that Oliver could hardly hold back.

But he waited until he'd licked up every trace of cum, then he gripped Peter's dick, opened his mouth and slipped his tongue into Peter's slit while taking the cockhead into his mouth.

Peter howled. He dropped his legs down and kicked at the bed, then thrust up, pushing his shaft into Oliver's throat. The first jet of cum didn't surprise Oliver. He knew his lover now, at least enough to know he'd come again.

Oliver cupped Peter's balls, the sac tight, wrinkled. He pressed on it as he sucked hard, then he pulled up and used just part of his tongue on Peter's slit again.

"Oh, my God, oh, my God!" Peter shouted, every part of him moving, as if the pleasure was more than he could bear. "Fuck my slit! Fuck it," he bellowed. "I never— Oh! Oh!"

Oliver slipped his hands under Peter's ass and squeezed each cheek. He began to knead and spread them apart, further and further, exposing Peter's hole.

When he left off teasing Peter's dick, Oliver sat up and rolled Peter onto his stomach.

"Oliver, please," Peter begged, arching his back, pushing his ass up.

Oliver slapped one buttock then the other as Peter moaned. "Like that, do you?"

"Didn't know it before," Peter rasped, "but fuck yeah!"

Spanking wasn't something Oliver had ever suspected he'd enjoy doing, but as he slapped Peter's ass again and again, turning the tan skin a dark pink, leaving his handprint over and over, Oliver discovered another side of himself. He hissed as he shoved Peter's ass down, then he covered Peter completely, lying on top of him, dragging his shaft up and down Peter's crack.

As Peter begged Oliver to fuck him, Oliver kissed and nibbled on his nape. He needed to come, needed to slide his cock deep into Peter's hole, yet he also needed this, the kisses, the touches. It took him several minutes to make sure he'd tasted every part of Peter's back, then Oliver finally spread his hot ass cheeks and ran his tongue from the top of Peter's crack to his asshole.

The first flick of his tongue over that puckered skin struck Oliver to his soul. He moaned and pushed Peter's cheeks even further apart, opening his ass, his hole gaping. Then Oliver licked into him, twirled his tongue around the inside of his rim, and Peter screamed, surprise and pleasure in the sound.

Oh, yes, Oliver could have *so* much fun with his tongue! And Peter was certainly enjoying it. Oliver closed his eyes and lost himself in his lover's scent, his taste, the sounds Peter made and the feel of him, buttocks clenching, legs moving, hands curling in Oliver's hair.

Every furl of skin, every spot that made Peter moan, Oliver memorized. He'd know the aroma of Peter anywhere, would be able to pick him out of a crowd blindfolded. For all that Oliver had had sex before, had fucked, this was nothing like any of those times.

He was going to die, and, oh, what a way to go! Peter could pass cheerfully from this world under the waves of pleasure Oliver kept him awash in. This wasn't like all the times Peter had let a guy fuck him, or whatever. He'd certainly never trusted anyone enough to let go and admit that he thought he'd like to be spanked. The difference was that he *did* trust Oliver. Why him, why not one of the other men Peter had been with? *Because he's Oliver. He's sexy and deep, he looked at me and saw a person, not a fuck hole.*

Oliver curled his tongue inside of Peter and he gave up on doing anything other than feeling. Over and over, Oliver licked him, pushed tongue and fingers into him, sucked the delicate skin of Peter's hole, laved the soft spot above it, behind his balls.

All the while, Oliver kept touching him, either kneading his ass or caressing his legs, calves, ankles, then up to his hips, belly and chest. It was like being worshiped, treasured, and Peter was never going to be able to settle being treated with any less care again.

When Oliver pushed two slick fingers into him, Peter wiggled his butt. He'd seen how thick Oliver's cock was, how long. It was going to fill him perfectly.

Oliver licked under Peter's left butt cheek, then the right. It sure seemed like there wasn't a spot on his body that Oliver hadn't touched in some manner.

"Roll over," Oliver said, his voice a raw whisper as he removed his fingers from Peter's ass. "I want to see you when I slide my cock into you."

Peter shivered, a delicious curl of pleasure swathing him. He rolled to his back, and Oliver immediately parted his legs, pushing his knees to his chest.

Oliver shook his head. "Like this." He grabbed two pillows and gestured for Peter to raise his hips up.

Peter held himself up while Oliver put the pillows in place. Then Oliver grasped each of Peter's ankles and pulled his legs up and open, toes toward the walls. "Hold on for just—" Oliver let go of Peter's left ankle, then there was the press of something big, warm and slick against Peter's hole.

Peter tried to keep his eyes open, but they rolled back as the thick length of Oliver's cock penetrated him. The broad rim of the crown stretched him *so* good, he could have wept from the pleasure.

Oliver grabbed his ankle again. "God, Peter, you feel so—" He pushed more of his length into Peter. "*Ah!* So hot and tight—" He broke off on a grunt, hands clenching around Peter's ankles. "Fuck, so amazing. I can't— Sss—"

That hiss was incredibly arousing. It reminded Peter of the way Oliver's tongue felt all over him, inside of him. Tipping his head back, Peter closed his eyes and clenched his ass, trying to pull all of Oliver's dick into him.

Which got him another long, drawn-out hiss as Oliver pushed fully inside.

Peter gasped, clawing at the blankets, at Oliver, at anything he could grip. He needed something or someone to ground him.

Oliver moved his hips and Peter came, that brush of cockhead over his prostate too much pleasure to resist.

Oliver froze, and held still as Peter's orgasm rippled through him. When it ebbed, he opened his eyes and Oliver gave him a concerned look.

"Do I need to stop? I know after coming, it can be uncomfortable—" Oliver started.

"Don't you dare fucking stop," Peter growled. "Or don't you dare stop fucking me. I told you before, I'm not your average guy. I'm a rabbit shifter. I can come and—" He lost his breath as Oliver pulled out then pushed back in. "Ungh! More!" He could at least get one intelligible word out.

Oliver gave him more, fucking slow and hard, driving Peter out of his mind with the need for *faster faster faster!*

"Turn over," Oliver ordered, withdrawing all the way and releasing Peter's ankles.

Peter went ass-up in record time. "Get it."

Oliver slapped one butt cheek then before the sting could truly register, he thrust his cock fully into Peter's opening.

Peter howled like a coyote rather than making the honking sound most rabbits did while aroused. He couldn't help it—he'd never felt such sheer perfection when being fucked before.

"Yess," Oliver murmured, still moving slowly—in, out, in, out—grinding his hips against Peter's buttocks, gripping him hard at the shoulders.

Peter wiggled and tried his best to shove himself backwards, to get more, faster, deeper.

Then Oliver gave him all that and more. He cursed softly and began hammering into Peter, the sounds of their bodies meeting, the slap of groin to ass loud in the room.

Oliver ran his hands down from Peter's shoulders to his hips, then to his butt. He kneaded and pinched and

Peter lost his mind and control. The orgasm hit him harder than any prior, and he might have shrieked — it was hard to tell, his ears were ringing — as he came.

He felt the sharp prick of teeth at his nape and shuddered as another violent wave of release rolled through him. Oliver's cum pumped into him, the spunk cooler than Peter's, and copious in its amount. He felt it leaking from his hole even as Oliver continued to ejaculate.

Peter floated on a cloud of bliss, sore and sensual, sated as he had never been before, and just plain happy.

And tired. Oliver had worn him out.

He shivered as Oliver left off biting him and whispered, "Better rest now, little hare. I'll be fucking you again in a few minutes."

Peter's eyes popped wide open. His heart raced. *Holy shit! I might have just found the perfect man!* At least when it came to sex. Peter didn't have much faith in Oliver being The One for him, and he tried to bury the little voice in his head that kept arguing, *but what if he is?*

Chapter Six

Waking up with someone else in the bed with him was unusual enough that, for one moment, Oliver almost panicked. Then it came back to him in a flash. Peter, legs in the air, on his knees, crying out, clinging, scratching –

Oliver opened his eyes and smiled at Peter, who had one arm over Oliver's chest and his head on Oliver's shoulder. The hotel suite smelled like sex, as it should, considering how many times Oliver had taken Peter, and not just in the bed. He'd vowed to last all night, and they both had, falling asleep after they'd watched the sun begin to rise.

Now the sunlight was streaming through the window. It warmed Oliver's skin, and the urge to curl up closer to the glass was strong. He closed his eyes again and thought about lying on a warm rock, or even a warm beach, letting the chill leave his body as the sun's heat entered it. The suite was actually cold, the AC apparently having been set to 'Freeze Balls'. Somehow the covers had come off them.

Oliver peeked at Peter. No, Peter had all but rolled himself in them, and had an arm and one foot poking out, besides his head.

Blanket hog. Oliver couldn't be irritated, just cold. Although, the longer he peered at Peter, the warmer he got.

And harder.

Almost as if he sensed Oliver's burgeoning arousal, Peter moaned softly and pressed closer. Oliver opened his eyes wider, no longer sleepy at all.

Then Peter surprised him with a quick move, darting down and dragging the covers with him. Oliver grabbed at them and managed to get a fistful of blankets — and immediately after he did so, he felt Peter's hot, wet mouth sucking on the tip of his dick.

Oliver had no need for the bedding after that. Heat suffused him as he bent his legs, digging his heels against the bed. He tried not to thrust, but Peter tapped his hip, and Oliver took that to mean he could move.

Peter used his tongue to drive Oliver mad with lust. He tickled and teased, laving the sensitive underside of Oliver's crown. Oliver buried his hands in Peter's dark hair and held him in place, thrusting slowly lest he come in the next two seconds. He pushed in an inch or two then pulled back, letting Peter tongue and suck on his tip before sinking in a little deeper.

Over and over Oliver fought back his orgasm, letting the pleasure build and build. When his cock was engulfed in Peter's mouth fully, the head in his throat, and Peter swallowed, that tight constriction of muscles was too much to resist.

His climax was wrenched from him, his entire body held rigid as he came. Peter pulled back and sucked on the head, moaning as if Oliver's cum was the tastiest treat in the world.

Oliver could smell Peter's release along with his own. He loved the way their scents mingled, the combination of them. As he came back down from his orgasm, Oliver opened eyes he hadn't realized he'd shut and glanced down at Peter. "Do you need me to take care of you?" he asked.

Peter grinned as he wiped at a drop of spunk on his lips. "Nope. I came plenty just from getting you off. You taste divine, by the way." He winked.

"Divine?" Oliver asked, skeptical despite being pleased.

Peter nodded. "Yup. I get to decide what you taste like to me. Divine seems to fit." He bounced up off the bed. "You mentioned having to go into the office today, and I've got classwork to do. Want to shower and get breakfast before we head our separate ways?"

Peter sounded as if he were just going about any other day — as if his entire world hadn't been rocked by the incredible sex he and Oliver had shared.

Oliver narrowed his eyes at Peter's back. Then he lowered his gaze and saw that Peter was walking gingerly. "Are you okay? Did I hurt you?"

Peter glanced back over his shoulder with a smirk. "Only in the best way. I'd love to meet up again when you have time for me."

Something about that sentence irked Oliver, as if Peter didn't think he was important. *No, like he doesn't think what we did, what we might be able to have, is important — or possible.* Oliver kept the observation to himself. He didn't know Peter very well, despite their shared meals, but if Peter thought all Oliver wanted was sex, he was about to be in for a surprise.

Because Oliver had reached a point where he wanted more. His business had made him happy, but it'd been an angry, kind of revenge-type happiness that hadn't been healthy. Now he'd been forced to give up his company, and he wasn't going to get tied up in proving anything to anyone ever again.

Unless he decided to prove to Peter that he wanted him for more than fucking. Oliver was definitely going to think on it.

"How about dinner tonight, then?" Oliver offered before Peter made it to the bathroom. "We don't have to have sex—"

Peter spun around, one hand planted on his cocked hip as he glared. "The hell we don't! I'd better get to ride you until you scream at least once!"

"I didn't want to presume, but I would never dream of offending you by refusing such a thing." Oliver lit up inside when Peter smiled brightly.

"All right then, it's a date," Peter replied, blushing before he turned and darted into the bathroom.

* * * *

The files on his desk were a good thing, and rather than dread going over them, Oliver had looked forward to the task. He picked up another one and began reading it. He wanted to know which accounts were good prospects and which weren't. They were almost all potential transfers from the Abilene branch, and none of them were spectacular. The new branch needed to land a few big accounts, ones they could make a name for themselves with.

A few more hours of reading files, and Oliver sighed in frustration. He set the mess of them aside, and instead turned in his chair to look out of the window at the cityscape. He wasn't familiar enough with the area or economy to know where to start looking for big accounts, but that could be fixed. He could find out a lot of that on the Internet—and he could talk to Peter tonight at dinner, see if he had any ideas on prospective businesses in need of excellent advertising.

After checking the time, Oliver forced himself to focus on work again. He had hours to go before meeting Peter for dinner, and those hours would pass quicker if he kept himself busy.

By the time six o'clock in the evening rolled around, Oliver was feeling optimistic. He'd done quite a lot of research, and felt that he had the start of a list of potential clients. He tucked the folder with their info in it into his briefcase. Once he'd tidied his desk and made certain everything was put up as it should have been, Oliver was ready to leave.

With his briefcase in hand, Oliver made certain to say goodbye to the security guard at the desk before walking out. Security performed a thankless job as far as Oliver concerned. People got mad at having to show ID and wait to be approved to enter the rest of the building, but in today's society, unfortunately, such precautions were necessary.

The heat outside didn't hit him quite as hard this time. Perhaps he was already adjusting to it. A few steps later, he was sweaty and bordering on grumpy. He'd thought about walking to his hotel—it wasn't all that far—but he'd reek by the time he got there.

Eh. He needed a shower, anyway, before meeting up with Peter. He might as well just keep walking.

When he reached the street corner, he caught the right to walk, the sign flashing that he had ten seconds left to get to the other side. He stepped off the curb just as a shiver ran down his spine. Oliver jerked his head to the left and saw the black sedan coming around the corner at high speed. His snake-like reflexes kicked in and he shot backward, stumbling but managing to keep upright as the sedan zoomed past. Had he stepped fully off the curb, and not been a shifter, he'd likely have been dead.

"Geez, fuckin' crazy-ass drivers!" a woman said, touching his arm. "Are you okay? He almost splattered you all over."

Oliver wasn't comforted by her description of what could have been, but held back his criticism. "Yes, I'm fine. Did you happen to see the man driving?"

The woman shook her head. "No, I just saw short hair and guessed it was a man. Could have been one of those butch women, you know, lesbians. Had a bulky form, not soft like a woman. Like them dykes, or a kinda pudgy man."

Oliver bit his tongue until his eyes watered. He wasn't going to correct this stranger on her assumptions about anyone or anything. He'd learned not to waste his time on those uninterested in moving beyond their bigotry.

"Well, thank you, none the less," he murmured, looking around to see if there were any other potential witnesses. Though several people were out walking around the neighborhood, none appeared to have noticed him or what had happened. Or, if they had, they pretended not to.

Oliver gave himself a shake. There was no point in making a big deal of it anyway. Someone had run a red light, or maybe they had the right to turn on red, he didn't know. They most certainly hadn't been paying attention. He'd have to make sure to do so more ardently himself if he didn't want to get hit by a car.

"Got someone out to kill you?" the lady asked, her hazel eyes bright with interest. "Maybe there's a contract on your life!"

"No, no," Oliver protested. Maybe he'd just run across the street and hope for the best in order to get away from this woman. "I'm sure it was just carelessness on the driver's part. Now, if you'll excuse me, I must go. I hope you have a pleasant evening."

"Snooty manners," she muttered. "That's an annoying accent you got."

Oliver didn't even look at her. "Back at you, ma'am." He wasn't feeling particularly nice, either. Sometimes the snake got the better of him and he said something mean.

He crossed the street against the advice of the signal, jogging to beat the cars coming from both directions. Once he made it to the other side, he walked as fast as he could back to the hotel. He was meeting Peter at seven at a restaurant in the Pearl area. He had the name of it and directions already downloaded to his phone.

La Gloria was supposed to have excellent Mexican food. Oliver's mouth watered as he thought about the menu he'd pulled up for the place. Between the food and the company he'd have, it should be a fabulous evening.

Rather than dress in a suit after he showered, Oliver put on a comfortable pair of jeans he had rarely worn outside his apartment in Boston. There, he'd been very concerned with always appearing to be a successful businessman. Now he was learning to unwind, and that doing so wasn't going to make him appear weak. He wore his favorite designer T-shirt and a pair of loafers. After checking his appearance in the mirror, Oliver decided he looked good enough. He tucked his wallet and phone, along with his hotel key card, into his pockets, then left the suite.

Peter met him in the lobby. Oliver was delightfully surprised. "Peter! I thought we were meeting at La Gloria?" Oliver asked. "You look amazing."

Peter blushed and gave him a smile that made Oliver's heart tingly. "Yeah? Thanks. You look pretty hot yourself. I didn't want to wait alone at La Gloria, so I thought I'd meet you here and we could ride together?"

"Sounds good to me." Oliver really wanted to kiss Peter, and judging by the way Peter's gaze kept going to Oliver's mouth, he felt the same way. "Do you think we could — ?"

"Not here," Peter said quietly, giving the barest shake of his head. "You're in an open carry state now, and there are some people..." He didn't finish, but he didn't have to.

Oliver got it. Physical affection between two men was still a dangerous thing to do in public in most places. He hated it, but it was the truth.

"Well, then we'll save it for after dinner, if you're in the mood to accompany me back to my room," Oliver offered, hoping he didn't sound desperate. He sure felt desperate for Peter's touch, his kiss.

"I was hoping that was the plan," Peter murmured, eyes hot with desire. "I meant what I said about riding you, mmm."

Oh, God. Oliver was going to wind up with a hard-on right there in the lobby.

Peter wiggled his nose, reminding Oliver very much of the shifter he was. "I can smell you," Peter whispered. "Yum."

"Behave." Oliver leaned close, his lips against Peter's ear. "Or else I won't spank your ass tonight."

"Oh." Peter shivered, rubbing his hands over his biceps. "You win. Let's go eat."

Oliver willed his erection to chill, and it did, though he had to keep from ogling Peter's ass when he turned around. Oliver moved to walk beside him. "So, how'd the college work go?"

"Ugh," Peter grunted. "I hate the forums. Online, at least where I take classes from, you have to post at least three times a week in a forum for each class, and you have to comment at least three times each on someone else's post there. We're given topics to choose from, but damn. You can't criticize, or correct grammar. You just have to converse, via the Internet. Do you know how hard that is when some people are posting political stuff I totally disagree with? I might have to take up booze to get through those things."

"You don't drink?" Oliver asked, wincing at the sunlight. It didn't get dark until well after eight at night this time of year in Texas.

"Eh, you know alcohol and our kind don't mix," Peter pointed out. "I get very irrational when I drink. That's the way my dad was when he was drunk, and it's why I'm an only child." He stopped at his car and opened the door for Oliver.

Oliver was confused by the confession. "You got drunk and did something to your dad?" That didn't sound like Peter at all.

Peter snorted. "No way. Get in."

Oliver got in and buckled up while Peter joined him in the car.

"No," Peter said after he'd pulled out of the parking lot. "I didn't do anything to my parents. My folks had me as a human, you know, less red tape that way. I have a birth certificate and Social Security card, all that. So they had me all legit-like. One evening, Mom and Dad got in a fight. He started drinking, then he shifted and hopped out of the house. Mom tried to stop him." Peter gulped.

"You don't have to continue." Oliver already knew this wasn't going to have a happy ending. "It's okay."

Peter huffed, exhaling hard enough that his breath fogged the windshield for a brief moment. He wiped at it quickly. "Nah, I don't even remember him. I was two. I just hate it that Mom was so broken-hearted over him she never married or bred again. Not that I want to think about her doing…*that*. Anyway, not long after he went out, she heard a coyote howl. Some of the herd got together the next day to try to find my dad, but all they found were some, er, bits and pieces."

"I'm so sorry," Oliver murmured, placing one hand on Peter's right knee. "I truly am."

Peter shrugged. "I mean, yeah, I wish I'd had a dad around when I was growing up, and even now, but I didn't and don't. I had a lot of men from the herd helping Mom with me, though. I think I turned out okay. And after getting drunk exactly twice, one time of which resulted in my running butt-naked down the Espada Aqueduct and ending up covered in slime when I fell in, well, I learned my lesson."

"I bet." Oliver could picture a slightly younger, naked Peter loud and boisterous, running— "What's the Espada Aqueduct?"

"It's part of an irrigation system the Spanish used to water crops and such when they came here," Peter explained. "I'll have to take you on a tour of all of the Missions."

"Including the Alamo?" Oliver asked. "I have to see that, right?"

"Sure," Peter agreed. "Personally, though, I love Mission San José best. It's got some cool stuff, and the chapel there is really…I don't know. It gives me chills in there."

"Huh. I'll have to look into the Missions," Oliver said.

"If you're going to live here, you have to do the tourist thing first!" Peter exclaimed. "That means, after we eat, I'm taking you to the River Walk. We'll stroll for a while before I drag you into bed and blow your…mind." He waggled his eyebrows as he turned the car off.

Oliver hadn't even realized they'd reached their destination. "We could skip the River Walk, or you could show me it online." He *really* wanted to get Peter naked, soon.

"It just wouldn't be the same. And besides" — Peter leered at him — "anticipation is a great thing." Then he unbuckled his seatbelt and, smirking at Oliver, got out of the car.

Chapter Seven

The River Walk and boat tour had entertained Oliver, Peter had been able to tell. He was glad to have gotten the chance to spend time with Oliver just having fun. Although, maybe he should be more cautious. Peter was beginning to worry that his heart might be getting involved. He wasn't in love with Oliver, but he *did* like the man a lot.

Was fear of being hurt a good reason to walk away after tonight? Peter scowled to himself as he pulled up to the valet parking. "You sure this is okay?" he asked, glancing at Oliver.

"Of course. Want to tell me why you looked so pissed off just now?" Oliver inquired. "That was a pretty fierce glower you had going. You don't have to come to the suite with me —"

"Uh, excuse me," Peter interrupted, his fear all but forgotten as horniness took over. "Don't think you're getting out of letting me ride you."

"Never, as long as you're sure."

"I am a hundred percent certain and more," Peter assured him, and he was. "I want you. Very, very much."

"You can have me," Oliver said with a beatific smile.

Peter would worry about his heart later. For now, he would go with the flow and enjoy his time with Oliver. Besides, it was silly to be worrying about getting his heart broken when he hadn't even given it away.

The valet took the keys and Peter insisted on tipping this time. He and Oliver were lucky enough to catch an elevator instead of having to wait for one, then they were striding to the suite, exchanging such heated glances that Peter knew he'd probably be coming as soon as they got past the door.

Oliver opened the suite and surprised Peter by taking holding his hand. "Thank you for taking me out and showing me the River Walk."

"You're welcome," Peter whispered, though he didn't know why he was so quiet. There was no one else in the hall.

Oliver brought him into the suite then closed the door. He flipped the locks and tossed his key card onto an end table. All the while, he kept his gaze on Peter.

Peter wanted to squirm. He was used to being looked at like a piece of meat—in a sexual manner *and* when he shifted and ended up fleeing from something wanting to eat him.

But that wasn't how Oliver was looking at him. No, there was affection and gratitude in his stare, and lust, yes, that, too. It wasn't the predominant thing, though, and Peter grew warm inside. Odd tingling sensations zipped along from nerve to nerve, and hope began to bloom in Peter's heart, hope that there might be more than sex, more than the physical between him and Oliver.

He didn't have it in him to try to squash that hope, either. How could he, when Oliver was so clearly looking at him like that?

"What's happening here?" he heard himself ask.

Oliver cupped his jaw, then eased closer. "I don't know, but it's...it's got the potential to be big. I feel it, in my chest."

"Me, too," Peter managed before he closed his eyes, parting his lips for Oliver's.

Peter whimpered and clutched at Oliver as their tongues touched then slid alongside one another. Oliver pulled him closer as well, and the kiss went from sweet to scorching in an instant. Cock rubbed against hard cock as Peter went up on his toes.

Oliver's moan—the sound spilling into Peter's mouth—fired his arousal to even greater heights. He tugged at Oliver's clothes while Oliver was trying to remove his as well. They tangled arms and hands, jammed their fingers, both grunting at the slight pain. Oliver finally stepped back. "You do you, I'll strip me," he offered.

"Deal," Peter agreed, whipping off his shirt. He got undressed in record time and raced for the bed.

"Your ass is so fucking perfect," Oliver said, his footsteps sounding even, unhurried.

Oliver hit the bed on his hands and knees, then looked over his shoulder at Oliver. "Perfect for fucking, you mean."

"That, too." Peter stopped at the edge of the bed. "Back up for me." He rubbed his hands together.

Peter gave Oliver's long, lean figure, and especially that thick, gorgeous dick, one more look, then he turned his head back around and scooted to the edge of the bed, his knees on it, but his calves and feet not.

The first spank was so good, the second made him come, and the third made sure his dick stayed hard. Peter got a few more swats, all of which made him hornier than ever. He finally raised up onto his knees, twisted around, grabbed Oliver and pulled him down onto the bed.

Oliver's startled expression was cute. His shaft bobbed as he bounced once. Peter straddled him, rubbing his balls over Oliver's length repeatedly, smearing his own spunk between them.

"Feels incredible." Oliver grabbed his ass with both hands, urging Peter to move faster. "So good. Everything with you feels so much better —" He bit his bottom lip and thrust up, hard.

As much as Peter would have loved to say he felt the same way, he was breathless, speechless, the need to come building up in his balls. He wanted Oliver in him every time he came tonight, though. It was difficult to make himself stop, but Peter did. He rose up onto his knees and used some of his own jizz to wet his hole. Oliver's cock was dripping pre-cum. It would be enough to ease the way in.

Oliver had stopped biting his lip and opened his mouth instead.

"I'm gonna ride you now," Peter said. He maneuvered around until his ass faced Oliver. "First, I'm gonna stretch my hole." He pushed two fingers in.

"Wait," Oliver rasped.

Peter couldn't stop. His fingers weren't enough. He was dimly aware of Oliver moving, but that was about it — other than the feel-good sensations coming from his ass — until cold, wet lube hit his crack. He yelped in surprise, but soon was humming in bliss as Oliver smeared the lube in, warming it, and Peter, in the process.

When Oliver slipped a finger in alongside Peter's, the stretch was *so* good. Peter shoved back onto their fingers several times, until the press of another to his rim slowed him down.

"Can I?" Oliver asked.

"Have at it," Peter said huskily. "Put your fingers in me." He withdrew his own, the awkward angle too much to keep up any longer.

"Sweet. Sweet ass. Sweet man." Oliver filled him immediately.

Peter didn't know how many fingers were in him, but the burn and tug sent him soaring. He fought back his climax for several minutes, then finally came with a shout.

Oliver kept pushing those digits in, pulling them out, turning them, rubbing Peter's gland and keeping him hard.

"Ever been fisted?" Oliver surprised him by asking.

Peter clenched his hole around Oliver's fingers. "No. Is that—uhn—is that something you're into?"

"I don't know, honestly, but the way you feel around my fingers, the rippling of your muscles, almost like you're trying to tug my hand in—it makes me curious, and hard as fuck," Oliver admitted.

"Hard as fuck, eh?" Peter leaned forward, until Oliver's fingers slipped free. "Sounds like a plan." He reached under him and fisted Oliver's dick. Without a moment's hesitation, Peter lined up and slid down that thick, thick length. "Oh, oh, God," he moaned. He was good and stretched, and *still* Oliver's cock felt like almost too much. Peter was determined to get it all in at once. He kept going down until his ass was pressed to the curly hairs at Oliver's groin. "Yessss!" Oliver wasn't the only one who could hiss.

Oliver rumbled and spread his hands on Peter's ass. Reverse cowboy was one of Peter's favorite positions, but after five or six minutes, he needed to see Oliver's face.

"Hold still," he requested before turning around. Oliver's pale cheeks were dotted with red, a flush of arousal spreading down to his neck and chest.

Peter pinched both of Oliver's nipples. Oliver grabbed Peter's hips and thrust up harder than before.

Then Peter did his best to stay astride while Oliver fucked him, driving up with great power, pulling Peter down and snarling fiercely every time he went in deep.

Peter kept his hands on Oliver's chest, grazing his fingers over those taut nipples, scratching them and pinching.

It seemed to be driving Oliver wild. His forked tongue flicked out as he narrowed his eyes, then Oliver pulled out.

Before Peter could complain, Oliver flipped him over.

Peter would have purred from the sheer pleasure of Oliver pushing his cock into him again, but his breath was gone on a gasp. Oliver began fucking him, that dick so hard and wide, filling Peter's ass until he couldn't take anymore. Peter gripped his own shaft and came and came and came, not in the same way he usually did, but as one long, extended orgasm.

Weak and sweaty, dazed and out of it, he heard Oliver whisper something unintelligible, then Oliver went stiff and his cum spurted into Peter.

Peter tried to keep his eyes open. He wanted to say he was ready for another round, but his body betrayed him and sleep took him away.

* * * *

A noise woke Oliver up. He wasn't certain what he'd heard, but the memory of a noise was there in his head. His heart raced, and his senses were screeching *Danger! Danger!* Peter lay asleep on him, much as he had the morning before, head on Oliver's shoulder, one arm across his chest.

Flicking his tongue out, Oliver tested the air. No one else was in the suite. Some of his fear eased. He must have had a bad dream he couldn't remember.

Now that he was awake, his bladder let him know there was a need for him to attend to. Oliver carefully slid out from under Peter then took a moment to appreciate the handsome man in the bed before trotting off to the bathroom.

He stopped on his way out of it and cocked his head. Something just felt *off*. Peter was still asleep in bed. The suite hadn't been broken into. It smelled clean, except for his and Peter's scents.

Which is odd, because I should at least pick up housekeeping's odor. I know they came in and made the bed after we left yesterday. There's not a hint of anyone, anyone, but me and Peter.

It was a puzzle—Oliver didn't pick up harsh chemical smells or anything. It was as if the place had been deodorized completely. There was no good reason for anyone to do that. There were few things that could completely remove scents, for that matter.

To take a scent away, or scents... Did that mean someone knew he was a shifter, and they'd been in his suite before he and Peter had gotten back? That made no sense at all. Oliver didn't have any enemies. Granted, he wasn't welcome in any of the snake pits, but that didn't mean they'd seek him out. He'd never been harassed in Boston, only banned. Ellis had gotten what he wanted. Who would have bothered with breaking in?

Oliver couldn't figure it out. He had to be wrong, and somehow, someone had used a chemical he'd never heard of to remove all scent. There were products coming out all the time that promised to fight odor or erase it. Perhaps someone had finally made one for human sale that actually worked.

Even with that explanation, Oliver still felt uneasy. He went to the closet and took out one of the white fluffy robes there. After he put it on, he walked to the door and looked out of the peephole. There was no one in sight through it. As quietly as possible, he unfastened the bolts, then opened the door a few inches. It didn't make a sound.

Oliver checked the air again. The hallway was rife with odors, too many to sort out. If he knew what he was searching for, that would make it easier. He opened the door wider and stuck his head out.

And screeched like a cat whose tail had just gotten stepped on when someone popped him on the butt.

"Sorry," Peter said, but he started laughing as Oliver spun around and glared. "What? I couldn't help myself."

"You most certainly could have helped yourself," Oliver groused, though he wasn't angry now that he knew he wasn't being attacked. "You *did* help yourself. Right to my ass."

Peter giggled then chuckled. "You jumped like three feet high!"

"You startled me," Oliver retorted.

"And you screeched," Peter pointed out.

That was just too much for Oliver. He locked the door, feeling behind him for the knobs and switches.

"And now, my sexy little hare, you're about to do some screeching of your own."

Chapter Eight

"So, when are you moving in with Mr. Slithers and making beeee-yooo-ti-ful babies together?" Lucy asked, smirking at Peter. "Do you think they'll have features of both species?"

Peter threw a wadded-up paper towel at Lucy, his housemate and, at the moment, his major pain in the ass. "Shut up. Besides the fact that *duh*, we're guys, we can't give birth, Oliver and I have only been dating a month."

"That's *eons* in hare years," she pointed out.

"We're human, not hare, most of the time," he retorted. "And you smell like Jack, so what gives?"

Lucy stuck her tongue out at him. "We're having a purely sexual relationship since I wouldn't put out in school and always regretted that. He's a pretty good fuck."

She seemed to be telling the truth. Peter knew Lucy better than she knew herself — maybe — and he knew when she fibbed, she developed a tic at the corner of her left eye.

"So he's cool with being used for sex?"

Lucy laughed. "What guy wouldn't be?"

Peter flopped down into the recliner. "Not all guys are whores, Lucy. Not that there's anything wrong with fucking everyone willing, but not all men are that way. Stop being a misandrist."

She propped herself up on one elbow and frowned. "A what?"

"Contemptuous of men, like misogynists are of women," Peter explained.

"Eh. Maybe it's just the guys I know. You were never serious with anyone until Mr. Slithers came along," Lucy said.

"For the billionth time, stop calling him that! He hates it as much as I do." Peter glared at Lucy. "Why can't you be nice to him?"

Lucy sat all the way up. "I'm not mean. I just tease him with that name, and at least I do it to his face, not behind his back, like you do with Jack."

Peter blushed. "Jack looks like he could snap me in half. Of course I won't call him Jackhole to his face. I'm not stupid or crazy."

"You need to let go of the past, Peter," Lucy advised, resuming her supine position on the couch. "Jack was a dumb kid back then, and so was I. He can fuck whoever he wants to now, and so can I. That shouldn't offend you."

"It doesn't," Peter argued. "What offends me is that I still remember how wrecked you were over him. You cried for weeks—*weeks*!"

"And it's in the past," Lucy reiterated. "If he vanishes tonight, oh well. The sex was good while it lasted."

"He really doesn't want more than that?" Peter asked.

"I told him up front what I wanted, and he agreed, so I'm going with no, he doesn't, which is good, because I'd be annoyed if he fell for me now." Lucy yawned and her jaw popped. "Ow. Fucking TMJ. Why was I born with a defective jaw joint or whatever the hell causes this crap?"

The more Lucy cussed, the more annoyed or in pain she was. "You want me to get you something for it? We have enteric-coated aspirins." Which was about all they could take for mild pain anyway.

"Sure." She looked at him and batted her lashes at him. "And a chocolate shake and fries with gravy from Whataburger? Pretty please?"

"The day before yesterday, it was a three-pound cinnamon roll from Lulu's for lunch," Peter complained. "What am I, your delivery guy?"

"My favoritest cousin *ever*," Lucy countered.

"Aw, fuck. Let me get my keys." Peter was at least glad to escape the drilling about him and Oliver. Lucy sure seemed intent on pushing him off into blissful coupledom.

Truthfully, Peter would have been at Oliver's tonight had they both not had to work late. Oliver was still at his office, going over some big presentation for an account he said he really needed to bring in.

Being a grown-up sucked sometimes, Peter thought, then quickly vetoed that. If he wasn't an adult, he wouldn't be able to be with Oliver, so adulthood was great. Jobs were sucky.

He picked up his keys and slid on his flip-flops. He'd showered after work and his hair was still damp, tousled, and would be a frizzball by the time he got back. Tomorrow morning he'd tame it down into something less fluffy.

"I'll be back in a few," he said to Lucy as he walked past her. "Do you want a drink, too?"

"Ohh, sweet tea, extra-large, whatasized, whatever!" She made a shooing motion. "Go on, hurry up and get back."

Peter left the house, distracted as he walked to his car. He didn't see the figure until it lunged at him. "What the fu— Oomph!"

As a hare, Peter's tendency was flight when danger was near. It wasn't much different when he was human, but as he hit the ground, he knew he was caught, for some reason. Peter opened his mouth and screamed at the top of his lungs before a leather-clad hand slapped over his lips. He tasted blood, and that pissed him off. He fought, trying to kick and claw, then suddenly he wasn't being squashed by a bigger body as the man—and he knew it was a man—leaped up and took off running.

"That's right, motherfucker," Lucy shouted. "I'll blow your damn balls off!" She held her pistol in her hands.

"Don't shoot," Peter rasped, sitting up. "It's dark, you might hurt someone else."

"I have excellent night vision," she argued, but she lowered the weapon. "I already called the police. If I'd have shot that asshole, I'd have done them a favor."

"Uh, I think they frown on vigilantism," Peter said. "Jesus, what the hell happened?"

"You tell me," Lucy countered as the sounds of sirens began to wail in the distance.

"I don't know. I was just walking to my car, then, *whammo*! Some big guy tackled me. I have no idea who or why or anything," Peter concluded.

"Your mouth is bloody." Lucy cursed again. "Damn it, I should have shot him in the 'nads at least."

Peter's balls were never ever coming down around Lucy again. "Er, can you stop talking about that? Or at least shooting and genitals?"

"Fine," Lucy snapped. "I wish I'd shot him in the big toe."

Peter couldn't help it. Maybe it was the adrenaline, but he started giggling and couldn't seem to stop.

"That's it. I'm calling Oliver," he heard Lucy say under her breath.

Peter could have protested, but he didn't. The truth was, he wanted Oliver there. He needed comfort, and Oliver's arms around him.

The police arrived quickly, and Peter found himself recounting his attack, over and over again. He understood the need for the police to be thorough, but he was ready to tear his hair out by the time Oliver arrived in a taxi.

"Are you okay?" was Oliver's first question as he cupped Peter's face. Then he scowled. "He busted your lips."

"Sir, how do you know it was a man that attacked Mr. Ruiz?" Officer Barker asked.

"Because I told him when I texted him what Peter said," Lucy answered. "I can show you the text, too. I thought Peter's boyfriend should know what happened."

Peter's boyfriend. My boyfriend? Is Oliver my boyfriend? Peter couldn't quite bring himself to look Oliver in the eyes.

Until Oliver nudged his chin up, and Peter couldn't resist looking at him.

"You are," Oliver said very quietly, so softly that human ears wouldn't have been able to hear it. "Mine, my boyfriend."

Peter's heart felt like it was going to thump right out of his chest. "Yeah?"

"Most definitely," Oliver informed him.

Then, seemingly not worried about what the police or anyone else might think, Oliver kissed him, tenderly, hands still cradling Peter's face with care, as if Peter were precious.

Peter began to understand that to Oliver, he really *was* important. Their month of dating had included a lot of sex, but it had also included conversations, laughing and getting to know one another better.

And Oliver was special to him, too.

Oliver eased back, and touched Peter's lips with one finger. "I'm sorry you were hurt."

"Just my lips," Peter said.

"He wouldn't let me shoot the perpetrator in the balls," Lucy complained loud enough that half the neighborhood must have heard.

The police officers glanced at each other, then at Lucy. "Are you licensed?" Officer Ortega asked.

"Of course I am," Lucy replied tartly. "I've got the papers in my pocket. Wanna see 'em?" She pulled them out. "My pink baby and I are good to go." She patted her twenty-two in its holster on her hip.

Officer Ortega took the papers, looked them over then handed them back. "Thank you, ma'am." He returned his attention to Peter. "Now, sir, is there any reason you can think of that someone would want to hurt you?"

Peter thought about it for a moment. "No. I don't have anyone hating on me that I know of. No angry exes, nothing like that. I've never had a customer complaint from anyone at the hotel."

"Everyone loves Peter," Lucy added. "Not in the stalkerish way, either. He's just that guy who is everyone's friend."

"And that doesn't bother you, Mr....?" Officer Ortega looked at Oliver.

"Oliver Biggerstaffer," Oliver said, "And, no, it does not. I am secure in my relationship with Peter, and secure in myself, as well. I can't blame anyone for liking Peter. He's amazing."

After more questions that seemed to take an interminable amount of time, the police finally left, saying they suspected it had just been a random robbery attempt. *Lucky me.* Peter was going to have to call in sick for a couple of days since his lips looked pretty swollen and cracked.

"Come home with me and I'll take care of you," Oliver offered. "Tomorrow's Friday, and I have that presentation, but you can relax and have Lucy come over."

"I'm off, so that should work," Lucy said. "They may want me to work, but, nope, not when my favorite person in the whole world just got attacked. I don't care what those cops say, I don't think it was random."

"But you said—"

"I know." Lucy cut Peter off. "I think maybe it was someone watching the place, who knows I get you to go out on late-night food runs every few days. He probably figured he'd get your money and car."

"Why didn't you tell the police that?" Oliver demanded.

Lucy glared at him. "Because they need to do their fucking jobs, and if I'm wrong, but all they do is work my theory, then what? If they don't come up with the same conclusion in a day or two, I'll tell Jack. He can get them to put their noses to the grindstone."

"What's Jack got to do with any of this?" Peter had lost the whole train of conversation somewhere along the way.

Lucy gave him a crooked grin. "Guess I forgot to tell you that Jack is a detective with SAPD. My bad."

"Asshole." Peter knew she had kept that a secret on purpose. For whatever reason. That was just how Lucy was.

"Twunt," Lucy retaliated.

"Children," Oliver growled. "Stop."

"You are no fun, snake-man." Lucy held out her hand to Peter. "Give me the keys. I'll make the food run, y'all wait here. Once we've eaten and you've cleaned up your face, y'all can split."

"Deal," Peter agreed. Lucy hardly ever made the late-night runs. "Get Oliver a number thirteen, Whatasized, with two gravies and a sweet tea. And can you turn off the porch before you leave?"

"Will do." Lucy took the keys, shut off the porch light, then went to the car.

"What am I getting to eat?" Oliver asked, sliding an arm around Peter's shoulders.

"Fried chicken strips, French fries, Texas toast and gravy," Peter told him. "And a cold sweet tea."

"Okay. Sounds decent. Now." Oliver licked his lips, then frowned and licked again. "Would it bother you if I shift after we get you inside?"

"Smell something?" Peter asked.

"Not sure. My senses aren't as accurate in human form. Are yours?"

Peter shook his head. "Nope. I can shift, too, and—"

"Peter." Oliver took him by both hands. "I'm a snake. I don't know what will happen if…if you shift around me."

"You told me about that guy Jagger and his husband. They're predator and prey," Peter argued. "Have you ever eaten rabbits?"

"No." Oliver's distaste at the very idea was evident on his face. "I'm more in control of my snake than it is of me."

"Okay, then. That's settled." Peter kicked off his shoes.

Oliver glanced around and let go of his hands. "What are you doing? Go inside before—"

"Nah, there's the shrubs here just for that reason." Peter jogged past the shrubs, shuddering when he thought of the man who'd been hiding there. "No one will see us between that and the privacy fence running around the sides and back of the house. Let me just open the gate."

"Peter, wait, just a sec," Oliver called out, running to catch up to Peter. "Please, I'd rather you go inside."

Peter stopped, Oliver stopping beside him. Peter canted his head so he could study Oliver's expression. "If we're going to ever be together for more than a few months, we need to be able to trust each other."

Oliver gulped and tipped his chin up, pressed his lips together then sighed, bowing his head as his shoulders slumped. "I'm not...normal."

Peter frowned. "Well, of course not. You're a shifter."

"No, but—" Oliver swiped a hand over his face. "I wasn't accepted by the pits in Boston because my parents were of differing species. Different types of snakes. That's not... It's unacceptable in our world."

"Yeah, I know some people shit bricks over stuff like that," Peter agreed, wondering what mix Oliver was. "It shouldn't matter, though. I mean, some species might have trouble breeding except in human form. I can't imagine say, a horse and a guinea pig. But an

Arabian horse and a Quarter horse? Why not? Jackrabbits and other rabbits and hares? It happens sometimes."

"But I'm a freak because when I shift, I…I—" Oliver touched his copper hair. "I'm a copperhead with a…with a rattle. It's one of the reasons—the main reason—I felt the need to build my own successful business. To prove that I wasn't worthless. The pit elders weren't impressed."

Peter knew his eyebrows were arching up but he couldn't help it. "That's it? That's the reason the snake pits wouldn't accept you? That's beyond stupid!" He threw his hands up in disgust. "I thought you were going to tell me you had three heads or turned into the male version of Medusa or something. A copperhead with a rattle tail, that sounds cool." Peter's lips were beginning to really ache. "Please, Oliver. Trust me, trust us, trust yourself."

Oliver was quiet for so long, Peter expected a 'no' out of him, so when Oliver begin to quietly undress, Peter was surprised and very proud of his boyfriend.

Chapter Nine

As he began to undress, Oliver wondered if he was becoming paranoid. Odd things had been happening around him. He'd almost been run over again when someone in the crowd behind him had pushed him into a busy street. Fortunately, several Good Samaritans had grabbed him and pulled him back before he'd been hit.

There'd been the rock thrown from an overpass that had narrowly missed the taxi he'd been in, and there'd been the night he'd decided to go for a walk while Peter had been at work, and Oliver had been certain he'd been followed.

But there'd been no scent at all when he'd checked the air. That anomaly was bothering him. Twice he'd been unable to detect any scent. He was beginning to think he wasn't paranoid, that someone was out to cause him trouble. Now, maybe they were even going after the man he cared for.

Which might not matter once Peter saw him in shifted form. Oliver had been told plenty of times by pit members that he was a freak. Not thinking of himself in such a way was impossible at times.

The moonlight was dim, but Oliver could still make out Peter's nude form. It was as if what light there was reflected off the perfect places to most accentuate Peter's build.

Then Peter smiled at him. "Trust me, Oliver. I trust you." He shifted, the act so quickly done that if Oliver had blinked, he'd have missed it.

There was a cute black and brown hare in front of him, its—Peter's—nose twitching rapidly. He wasn't as small as Oliver would have thought, which perhaps was one of the differences between rabbits and hares.

Or it could have been a shifter thing. Oliver took a deep breath, closed his eyes, and let his shift come over him. He'd only been relaxing in his reptile form in the privacy of his own home, so it felt exceptionally good to do it outside, even if it was dark instead of sunny.

He opened his eyes, the world looking different—his vision was shitty as a snake, which was normal for his type. When he flicked his tongue out, tasting the air, Oliver also rattled his tail, another issue he had. He'd never learned to control that end of himself, and tended to shake his rattle at inopportune times.

Peter hopped closer to him and sniffed, long whiskers tickling Oliver's scales. Being tickled was an entirely new experience to Oliver in his reptile form. He wiggled and slithered, his tail rattling a mile a minute, tongue flicking out the other end.

There was no scent, not even that of the garbage cans nor the cops who'd been there earlier, or of Peter himself. Peter must have realized the same thing—he sat up on his hind legs, sniffing, sniffing, sniffing, his nose twitching faster and faster. Every direction he turned in, Oliver scented as well. There was nothing, not even the aroma of them there, together, at that moment.

Someone has found a way to completely mask or erode scent. That could be dangerous, or a blessing, depending on the use of it. Since Oliver had barely escaped being killed a couple of times, and someone had tried to harm Peter, Oliver was inclined to believe the scent destroyer was not a good thing. It was too thorough. He couldn't catch even the slightest whiff of anything, not the grass he slithered on or the bushes beside him, much less Peter or even himself.

There should have been *some* scent in the air.

Without it, he didn't know if the man who'd attacked Peter was still around or not, if it was someone he knew…and no matter how hard he tried, he couldn't think of a reason for anyone to be stalking him, or attacking his boyfriend.

Peter hopped past him and Oliver moved faster. He couldn't catch up to Peter in a race, not in his current form, at least. Peter slowed down and waited for him.

Oliver hissed at him. *Don't run off! Hop off, whatever! Let me lead. I have the venom.*

Peter either sneezed or blew off Oliver's hissy fit. Away Peter went, and Oliver, unwilling to be left behind, shifted into his human form and ran. He managed to surprise Peter, to scoop him up, but that was a mistake. Peter panicked, and his back feet were deadly weapons, or at least really painful ones, with his powerful kicks and sharp nails.

"Peter," Oliver snapped, pain burning along his forearms.

Peter stopped fighting and turned those pretty eyes on him.

Oliver sighed and caressed Peter's soft coat. "I'm not mad. I understand that I surprised you and you didn't know it was me. I'm glad to have learned that you have some wicked defense available. Those back legs of yours are powerful, and those nails, man, you could sever an artery if you hit the right spot. But, honey…"

Peter's ears twitched and he blinked.

Oliver might have been blushing, or his cheeks might have been hot from the sprint…or it could have been that he let the endearment escape. He didn't regret it, though. In fact, he was going to say it again. "Honey, I have venom that can kill most other creatures, or at least cause them significant harm. It's not just copperhead venom—it's rattlesnake, too. The combination is quite…toxic. We found that out when I fought back against some bullies at the pit when I was younger." It was a memory Oliver preferred not to relive. "I almost killed three others. One boy, Thomas, was left with serious scarring and muscle loss from where my venom destroyed his tissue. He was the first one I bit, so he got the worst of it. The other two were less damaged, but my venom shouldn't have done more than sting them, as theirs did me." He shook his head. "The point is, I should go first if there's ever a chance of danger."

Holding a hare that suddenly shifted into a human was disconcerting and impossible. At least it was for Oliver. He had to let go of Peter, and he stumbled back, his heel striking a stone. If Peter hadn't grabbed his arm, Oliver would have landed flat on his ass.

Peter glared while he gave Oliver's arm a shake. "I am not some delicate flower that needs sheltering."

"I know that," Oliver protested, scowling in return. "You're a man, capable of taking care of yourself. But when you're shifted—"

"Stop right there," Peter warned, his voice dropping low. "Before you say something you regret."

Oliver gulped. "I just want to keep you safe. I'm not trying to insult you."

"You're not trying, but you *are*," Peter countered. "I get that you have the venom, but I am not helpless. Now…" Peter let go of him and rubbed the back of his own nape. "Okay, I should have waited for you, moved with you, instead of hopping ahead. I suppose I was doing what you're trying to do now, or talking about doing — protecting the man I care about. My boyfriend."

"That's why you took off in front of me?" Oliver asked.

Peter huffed as he flung his hands up. "Well, yeah, so now I'm a hypocrite because I just got mad at you for wanting to do the same thing. Shit."

Oliver couldn't help it. He chuckled then reached for Peter, catching him by the wrists and gently tugging him close again. "I think it's natural to want to protect each other. Instead of either of us being mad, maybe we should just accept that urge, and try to work on our communication."

Peter licked his lips, still swollen, though not as much as they had been before his shift. "I thought we were communicating well. Was I wrong?"

Oliver shook his head. His arms were stinging, bleeding, and he'd need to shift to speed the healing up, but first things first. "Not at all. I was, though." *Oh, God, this is hard, but it's coming out, anyway.* Oliver felt like a stone comprised of fear and hope was lodged in his gut. "I was because I haven't told you that I'm falling for you, Peter. I'm falling hard, and I think…I *hope* that you're feeling more affection for me, too, that you want to have a…" His throat was so dry, Oliver coughed then tried again. "Have a long-term relationship, in some form or another, possibly. That you'd consider it after we've dated longer."

"Oh." Peter touched Oliver's cheek. "Oh. That's what you—I thought—I don't know what I thought, but it wasn't that you'd be the first one to confess to feeling like we have more than just an affair going on."

"It's never been *just* an affair to me," Oliver whispered. "From the moment we met, you struck a spark in me that I didn't know was there."

"You are such a romantic man," Peter said, brushing his fingertips over Oliver's lips. "And, yes, I want that, to see what happens between us. You mean more to me than anyone ever has. I've never had this intimacy with someone else before. I want to believe we can have more."

"We can," Oliver promised. He knew then he had to be completely honest with Peter. "We will. That means I need to talk to you about some things that have happened, things that make me suspect this wasn't a random attack."

"Oh, really?" Peter's left eyebrow went up in a high arch. "So you have some 'splaining to do, Oliver?"

"I do, indeed, right after I shift to take care of these." He let go of Peter and held up his bleeding arms. "Then, we're going to talk."

* * * *

Chills ran down Peter's spine after Oliver finished telling him about almost being run over twice and feeling like he was being followed. "You didn't call the police?"

"What would I have said, Peter?" Oliver lay back on the bed, folding his almost-healed arms behind his head. The bleeding had stopped, and scabs were forming over the scratches.

Likewise, Peter's lips were healed, though slightly tender. "That someone tried to run over you and someone else tried to push you into traffic?"

"They'd have thought I was off or something," Oliver protested. "There was no proof. Even the people who pulled me back the second time I was almost hit thought I'd just stumbled forward."

Peter considered that for a moment, then shivered. "That means the person that pushed you may have also been one of the ones pulling you back."

"So as not to look like the guilty party if I said I'd been shoved." Oliver closed his eyes. "I suppose you're right. There was no scent then, either. Somehow, someone's blocked scents." Then his eyes popped open. "Oh, shit! Or they've found a way to inhibit my — possibly all shifters' — sense of smell. They don't vaporize odor. They block our scenting ability."

"That's not possible, is it?" Peter didn't want to believe it was. The idea of anyone tampering with his body that way was well past creepy.

"Anything's possible now days," Oliver replied. "It might just be some sort of odor blocking spray, though."

"I couldn't smell you outside," Peter said.

Oliver opened his eyes and scented the air. He frowned darkly. "I can barely smell you now."

Peter sniffed and sniffed. He leaped up off the bed. "Be right back!"

"Okay." Oliver didn't question him as Peter ran to the door. He opened it and barreled down the hallway.

"Lucy!" Peter called out. She had the TV cranked up, probably thinking they'd be having loud, fun sex —

which they would do, later, and hopefully at Oliver's place.

Lucy was reclined on the couch, eating popcorn and watching some gory film that, just then, appeared to consist mostly of blood and guts.

"What?" Lucy asked distractedly, around a mouthful of popcorn.

Peter sniffed. He could barely detect the aroma of the popcorn. "Lucy, this is important. Can you smell anything? Or smell it as well as you usually do?"

"Huh?" Lucy finally looked at him after she paused the movie. "Smell what?" She scowled at him. "Is this some lame fart joke? Because you know I only like the not-lame ones."

"No!" God, sometimes his cousin was incorrigible. Peter tried again. "There was no scent at *all* outside where I was attacked, or around the front and side of the house. I can barely smell your popcorn, and Oliver said his scenting ability is hampered or something's been sprayed or...or...or whatever, but something might have been done around here, something that cloaks odors."

By now, Lucy was wide-eyed and slack-jawed, and Peter didn't particularly enjoy the view of semi-masticated food. "Close your mouth or you'll swallow flies."

Lucy snapped her mouth shut, twisted around to grab her soda then chugged the bottle of it to wash down her food. Then she turned back to him. "Oh my God! I hadn't realized it, but yeah, I can't—" She sniffed. "Wow. That's so fuckin' weird. Is it because our scenting ability is being screwed with? Is it hurting *us* somehow? Will we be able to smell again—?"

"Yes," said Oliver, coming down the hallway. "Every time this has happened, the sensation has passed after a few hours. I wish I had answers to whether or not it's going after our sense of smell or just blocking odors, period, but I don't, just as I can't answer whether or not there'll be long-term damage to us if this keeps up."

"Shit." Lucy pushed her bowl of popcorn away from her. "I'm going to call Jack."

"You're going to call your fuck-buddy for something important?" Peter teased.

Lucy flipped him off. "He's more than just a talented dick. And, no, I am *not* falling for him."

Peter wasn't going to argue with her. "Okay, well then I think we're going to Oliver's in a little while."

"We can stay here," Oliver said. "So Lucy won't be alone."

Lucy gave them a broad smile. "Oh, don't worry. I'll have company."

Peter hoped his cousin didn't end up broken-hearted again, but he feared very much that she would.

An hour and a half later, he had shifted that fear over to Jack instead. Peter had been prepared to hate him for hurting Lucy in the past, but it was clear that, while Lucy seemed very blasé about her relationship with Jack, Jack, on the other hand, was besotted with her. Peter could practically see the stars and hearts in his eyes when he looked at Lucy, which was most of the time.

Lucy had to know Jack was in love with her. She wasn't stupid. But she probably *was* afraid to trust Jack again, and Peter could understand that. As he sat and listened to Oliver explain the goings-on to Jack, Peter mused over his cousin's relationship. He'd never known her to get serious with any guy after her heart had been broken back in high school. Somehow, he thought Jack might stand a chance at winning her over again.

And if he hurt Lucy, Peter would do what he'd wanted to last time, and beat the shit out of the man, no matter who or what he was.

"I want you to come in and—"

"No," Oliver cut in, his tone quite blunt. "I will not come in and file a complaint or whatever. If this is shifter related, we don't need more police interference."

Jack looked like he wanted to argue, but Oliver was pushing up out of his seat. He held a hand out to Peter. "All packed and ready to go?"

"Yes." Peter had his duffle by his chair. He stood, picking his bag up as he rose. "Lucy, you call us if there's anything that seems off."

"I'll stay with her tomorrow," Jack offered. "I'm off the next two days."

Lucy gave him an arch look. "We'll have to discuss this."

"We'll leave you to it." Peter gave his cousin a loud, wet kiss on her cheek, then darted for the door as she swatted at him. "Don't do anything I wouldn't do!" he said as he made his escape.

"That leaves my options wide open," Lucy shouted back at him.

Peter couldn't even argue with her about that.

Chapter Ten

"Don't you think you should have told Jack about what happened at the pit in Boston?"

Oliver glanced at Peter, who was driving. Oliver didn't have a license — he'd never driven a car in his life. In Boston, he'd gotten around by cab or public transit. More often by cab, however.

"Oliver?" Peter pressed, "Don't you think so?"

"No, I don't," Oliver replied, trying to make certain he didn't sound mad, though his words were blunt. "Had I wanted him to know, I'd have told him. I do not for one second believe that has anything to do with what's going on now. It was decades ago — twenty plus years. I'd have expected any revenge to have been taken on me ages ago, but the pit masters *did* ban action and revenge against me. At least they were fair in that, since I had tried and tried to evade a fight with my bullies. This has to be something and someone else."

"A competitor?" Peter guessed. "Even though you just started your job?"

"It *is* a cutthroat business, although this seems extreme."

"People do worse for less," Peter said. "Kill over a dollar or getting cut off on the road. For no reason at all."

"I'll start checking into the advertising firms here." Oliver had already been studying the competition, but perhaps he hadn't been thorough enough in his research.

"What about your business? The one you sold? Maybe the new owner doesn't want you in the game anymore," Peter suggested.

"No, Ellis has no reason to come after me." Oliver had given the jerk what he'd wanted, after all.

"Why *did* you sell your business to that Ellis guy? I've never thought to ask before, mainly because I don't care in a way. You sold it and ended up here, which is great." Peter's smile held so much warmth and caring, which made it easier for Oliver to speak about what had happened.

"I had to." Oliver's gut clenched. "He blackmailed me into it. I trusted him with one of my biggest accounts, and he stole from them. Before you ask why didn't I have him arrested, it was because he told me about it himself, and he showed me how he'd set up an overseas bank account with my name on it, and the money in it. He wanted the business in exchange for returning the money and wiping out the account. Ellis is a fox shifter. He was pretty sly and immoral like everyone says foxes are, though I thought that was stereotyping of his species. Now I know."

"You still could have found a way to prosecute him, maybe," Peter argued. "That's bullshit!"

"Turned out the company he 'stole' from was run by his great-uncle, who was in on it. At some point, you have to walk away. I wasn't up for a fight," Oliver explained. "I was hated by all the Boston pits for being a mixed snake, my parents were gone, I had no family or close friends around. I just thought it was time to give up. All the fight in me was gone."

"How do you know he won't still say you embezzled money and stuff?" Peter turned onto the street Oliver's apartment was on.

"I watched him delete all the records and move the money back," Oliver said. "Then I hired a forensic accountant to make certain the books were correct. Once she said they were, I gave Ellis what he wanted — the company I'd built from nothing. I didn't make much on the sale, of course, and had to use my savings to live on. When I got a call about a job here, it seemed like a sign." He patted Peter's knee. "And here I am."

"But couldn't the forensic accountant have found proof of what Ellis did?"

Well, Peter obviously wasn't going to drop the subject.

Oliver bit back a sigh. "I don't know. My funds were limited, and Ellis said he had a professional do the whole thing, so if that was the case, there might not have been any proof. I guess I was just tired of fighting and being scared. We lost our biggest client because I was too busy freaking out over what Ellis had done to pay attention. Our biggest client, gone, like that." He snapped. "All because I was too panicked to come through with a good proposal for their new line of yoga shoes. Letting them down was worse than having Ellis betray me, honestly. I was afraid I wouldn't get another job in advertising because of it. I did insist on Ellis signing a confidentiality agreement, which benefitted him, as well. So I can't very well go to the cops about it now. And he has no reason to come after me."

Peter pulled up to the parking garage. Oliver handed over his key card and the bar raised, allowing Peter to enter the garage.

Oliver continued explaining, "Add in that Ellis is a shifter, and not a mix of two different kinds of fox, but a full-blooded red fox with the support of his den and all of their allies, it was time for me to leave. I was tired of fighting everyone, trying to prove that I'm not lacking because of what I am."

He had unbuckled, as Peter had also done, and they got out of the car. Peter tucked his hand in Oliver's. "I'm sorry you went through all that, but I'm very glad you ended up here. You've helped me, you know."

"Hm?" Oliver inquired, casting a sideways glance at his boyfriend.

"Yeah." Peter nodded. "I figured I was never going to find a guy I was attracted to who didn't treat me like I was just an orifice to fuck. Now I understand that I let myself be treated that way. I could have turned down guys, could have said 'treat me better or get the fuck out', but I didn't. There was a distinct lack of confidence on my side, and I'm not sure why, but I'm learning that I deserve better, and am capable of giving a lot to someone I care about." He looked at Oliver coyly. "You helped me to see that."

Oliver didn't know why Peter would have ever had low self-esteem, but he didn't question him on it. People were allowed their feelings, and sometimes no explanation could clarify emotions. "Thank you for telling me that."

"It's only the truth." Peter bumped hips with him. "You make me want to be a better, more confident man."

"I know exactly what you mean. That how you make me feel, too." Oliver was about to say something else when he noticed the lack of odor around them. "Peter, do you smell anything?"

Peter grabbed his hand and started running. "No."

Oliver had no choice but to follow. Fortunately, he lived in an apartment complex with security and keyed entries.

Unfortunately, he wasn't quite fast enough to reach the elevators which would get him to the doors, and the security guard was nowhere in sight. It registered to him that the lights out front had flickered off a second before a buzzing sound filled the air, then Peter yelped, and Oliver tried to see what had happened to him, but hundreds of sparks of pain shot through him and darkness swamped him.

Peter screamed at the top of his lungs. The Taser had mostly hit Oliver, but a few tendrils or wires — whatever the damn things were — had smacked Peter as well. Not enough to render him unconscious or even make him fall to his knees, which was a blessing because he needed to catch Oliver as he fell.

With Oliver unconscious in his arms, Peter knew two things immediately — whoever was fucking with Oliver was a shifter, and he or she wanted Oliver to suffer. The Taser attack had occurred in the dark. The parking garage lights had flicked out just as Peter had felt pain. That meant a shifter, someone who could see well in the dark. He supposed it could be someone wearing night goggles, but his gut didn't buy it.

Oliver groaned and Peter began shoving the remains of the Taser away from him. "Hey, I'm right here. We're okay."

The lights flickered on all around them. Peter used all his senses to see if there was anyone around them, but his scenting ability was ineffective — blocked or whatever it was the attacker did to make smelling anything impossible. He heard the light patter of footsteps, a squeal of tires and a rev of an engine.

But he didn't see anyone, and the sound of the vehicle made him very nervous.

"Upsy daisy," he muttered as he tried to get Oliver to his feet. "Come on, wake up, baby."

Oliver's lashes fluttered, and he jerked awake, arms and legs flailing.

Peter almost dropped him.

"What happened?" Oliver slurred, reaching for his head.

Peter steadied him. "Can you stand? You were Tasered. I don't want us to get run over in the parking garage."

"There's…cameras," Oliver said.

Peter noticed one nearby. "Oh. Well fat lot of good that will do us if we're dead."

"But I meant the attack won't be on camera because the lights went out, didn't they?" Oliver asked, rubbing his temples with both hands now. "Or was it just my lights that went out?"

"Ha. Ha. No, all the lights went out." Peter steered Oliver in between two large luxury SUVs. "They came back on quickly, though. I have to tell you, I think this is another shifter, and they want to make you miserable before killing you."

Oliver grunted at that, still rubbing, his eyes closed and a frown etched in his expression. "What if they don't want me dead?"

"What do you mean?" Peter looked around as if to find the answer floating around him. "They tried to kill you!"

"Or scare me away," Oliver said. "Maybe someone just doesn't want me here."

"But…" Peter shook his head. "But who? No one knows you except the people you work with and me, and Lucy. Well, and Jack, I guess. None of us wants you gone. Or is there someone at your job coveting your position?"

"No, I have a great team here at the San Antonio office, and none of them are shifters," Oliver replied.

"Then who and why?" Peter slipped an arm around Oliver. They freed themselves from the remaining parts of the Taser, then Peter began to guide Oliver to the elevators.

"I don't know. My grandmother was from the South, you know. Texas, in fact. Can't remember her saying what part. Her and my dad came up to Boston when Dad met Mom online. They didn't care that they were different breeds of snakes, they just…they just fell in love." Oliver sighed as the elevator dinged, announcing its arrival. "Grandma supported them, and she loved me. She left her pit to live with my dad and mom, and me, in a state far away from her home."

"So maybe someone hates you for that," Peter suggested, stepping into the elevator with Oliver. Peter glared at a man who gave them a disgusted look.

The man rolled his eyes and turned away.

Peter wished he could gnaw on the jerk's ankle, but that wasn't possible.

Oliver must have caught the exchange as he turned a scorching look the man's way before ignoring him and leaning against Peter. They remained quiet until they arrived at Oliver's floor. They left the elevator and Peter was relieved that the guy still on it hadn't yelled out anything rude.

He was tired and scared, worried for Oliver. Something very weird was happening, and he thought they weren't anywhere close to figuring it out.

Chapter Eleven

"How is everything going there?" Jagger asked via conference call.

Oliver tapped the folders on his desk. "All new accounts. We've got an amazing team here. Have you talked to the Jen over in the Media department?"

"Not today, but we had a conference call Tuesday." Jagger looked a little uncomfortable for a moment, then he cleared his throat. "I wanted to let you know that I put in my notice Monday. I'll be leaving on the twelfth."

"You're quitting? Why?" Oliver asked before he could think better of it. He liked Jagger and hated to see him go.

Jagger shrugged. "I have other priorities now. My sister has recently married and doesn't need my financial help anymore. Kevin wants us to go into business together so we aren't spending so much time apart. I'm just…I'm done with all the stress in this biz."

Oliver could understand. While he didn't particularly consider it stressful—he thrived on challenges—many people in the industry burned out after a few years.

"Well, I hope you'll stay in touch, and if you and Kevin ever get to San Antonio, give me a call. You can meet my boyfriend, Peter."

Jagger gave him a thumbs up. "Sounds like a deal to me. I didn't get to do the tourist thing when I was there. Didn't want to without my husband, and when he came down to visit we, err, we had other things to do. Maybe we'll come down in winter when it's not nine hundred degrees outside."

Oliver could just bet they *had* been too busy to go out, or even get dressed, though he made no such comment. Instead, he picked on Jagger about something else. "You exaggerate," Oliver protested. "It's only eight hundred and three out now."

Jagger laughed. "Aw, man, that's about right. Texas is just hot all over. Anyway, back to those files you've got there…"

Oliver went over them with Jagger, explaining the proposals and giving credit where it was due. By the time the conference call ended, it was time for lunch. Oliver was over the Taser incident. He'd shifted twice until he felt like he wasn't about to pass out, then he'd slept for a solid twelve hours. In the past three days, nothing untoward or weird had happened.

He worried about Peter, though. Lucy promised that Jack was keeping an eye on them while they were at work, and according to Peter, Jack had all but moved in since the night Peter had been attacked. Peter was hardly ever alone. Still, no one could be with him all the time.

And Oliver hadn't deduced why anyone was coming after him *and* his boyfriend. The events were all related—that lack of smell tied them together, otherwise he might think the attack on Peter was a coincidence.

Not that he'd be comforted if it was. The idea of Peter being hurt *hurt* Oliver, a pain in his chest that almost made him double over. For a moment, he feared he was having a heart attack, then it occurred to him that the pain wasn't actually physical, but more of a mental ache. It was strange how the body reacted to fear of losing someone.

Especially when it was someone Oliver was falling in love with. He knew that it wouldn't be much longer before he was head over heels, irrevocably in love with Peter. The idea both thrilled and terrified him. There was a tiny bit of doubt that Peter might not love him back in time, but for the most part, Oliver believed he would.

Which meant an unexpected future, one Oliver hadn't ever thought to have. He'd assumed he'd always be the shifter outcast. The pits hadn't wanted him. As far as he knew, snake shifters kept to their own kind. For him to take up with a hare shifter would be another sin, on top of his other ones of being born a mixed-breed and having deadlier venom than any of the other snakes. The elders in particular hadn't cared for that.

What he did with his life was none of their concern now. It hadn't been in a very long time.

His cell buzzed and Oliver was jolted out of his thoughts. He pulled his phone from his pocket and checked the text. Reading the lunch invitation from Peter made Oliver happier than he'd been since he'd woken up with Peter lying on him that morning.

Oliver replied that he'd meet Peter at The Emma. From there, they'd go to Pearl Plaza then walk to their favorite vegetarian restaurant. Neither of them were vegetarians, though, Peter did eat less meat then Oliver.

However, the restaurant had very good food and an excellent selection on its lunch menu.

Oliver decided to walk the two blocks rather than call for a cab. He left his suit jacket and tie in his office, and waved at his assistant on the way out. He also greeted the security guard at the front desk, Elizabeth, aware as always of the importance of their job.

Outside, the heat him like a tsunami of humidity and hell. He was getting used to it, though, and merely rolled his sleeves up as he started walking. Every few steps, he tasted the air, relieved to find numerous scents in it.

Spotting Peter, Oliver waved and noticed the happiness that filled him as Peter strolled over. He was definitely hung up on Peter, and he was glad. Peter was witty, sexy, determined and open-minded. Oliver was lucky to have met him.

Peter's smile was bordering on brilliant. "Hey, babe. How's work going?"

Oliver was still getting used to being called 'babe', as it was what Peter called him more and more. It had always seemed like a cheesy word in the context of a boyfriend before, but coming from Peter, Oliver liked it.

"It's going," Oliver replied. "How's your day?"

Peter glanced around, then darted forward and up, brushing a quick kiss across Oliver's cheek. "Good. My manager talked to me about a possible promotion in the near future. She knows I'm working on my degree, and the position opening up requires one, but she'd be willing to work with me and make an exception since I'm so close to finishing college."

"That's wonderful news!" Oliver exclaimed. "We'll have to celebrate."

Peter's wicked expression sent heat straight to Oliver's cock. "I get to pick how we celebrate."

"Of course." Oliver was no fool. Peter would pick a very sensual celebration. Oliver was all for sensual celebrations with his boyfriend.

"Tomorrow night, since I'm off the day after," Peter said, "and I plan on being very sore and well-loved—er, I mean well-fucked the next day."

"Well! I never!" said a woman walking past them.

Oliver noted how darkly Peter blushed. Was it over the slip 'well-loved' or because he'd been overheard by someone obviously not pleased about his wording?

Whichever it was, Oliver would try to help with both of them. "If you've never, you really *should*, because it's amazing," he said to the lady. "Really."

The woman looked scandalized as she rushed away.

"I like the idea of you being well-loved," Oliver informed Peter, who was still blushing. "We do more than fuck. We're more than that. We're a...a couple. Boyfriends. Lovers. Friends. Not fuck buddies."

"I was afraid you'd think I meant, you know," Peter mumbled. "That I was saying the 'L'-word. I didn't mean it like that."

"I know you didn't," Oliver assured him, "but it would have been fine if you *had* meant it that way."

Peter's blush faded somewhat. "It would have? Would be?"

"Yes, because I know how I feel about you. We haven't been together long, but you are very, very important to me," Oliver said. "I meant it when I said I wanted more with you. I..." Well, he hadn't expected to be saying this now. "I want forever, I want to love you, and for you to love me, and I think we can have that."

Peter grabbed his hand and held it tightly. "I think we're halfway there."

"Halfway?" Oliver asked, heart racing. He didn't even care if someone saw them holding hands and got offended. Nothing was more important than Peter and what his answer would be.

"I love you," Peter replied, with so much openness and honesty that Oliver's eyes teared up. "I know, it's early in our relationship, but it feels right and I've been afraid I'd slip up and say it and you'd freak out. You're not, right? Not freaking out?"

"Not freaking out at all." Oliver wished they were alone, somewhere he could kiss Peter, hold him, make love to him. Though they were holding hands, even that was daring for the area. He would just have to restrain himself until he got Peter alone. "Not at all, because that's how I feel. I mean, I love you, and being with you makes me feel whole, like I've been living a half-life until I met you."

"The things you say," Peter whispered. "Can you take off work?"

Oliver thought of the files on his desk, his responsibilities. He was caught up on everything, ahead of his projections, so he could take the afternoon off, surely. He'd been working a minimum of six days a week since he'd started. "I can."

"Me, too. Take me back to your place?" Peter asked.

"Well, you'll have to do the driving, so if you'll take us back to my place?" Oliver grinned.

"Damn right I will." Peter took out his phone, letting go of Oliver's hand as he did so. "Let me just call my boss. She'll be cool with it. She was telling me I needed to use my vacation days soon."

"And I'll call my assistant." Oliver and Peter began walking toward The Emma, where Peter's car was parked. At the street corner, Oliver spotted a dark sedan stopped across from them at the red light. He finished his call, and when the crossing signal switched to Walk, Oliver found himself hesitating. He licked his lips.

Peter sniffed. "I smell people. Cars. Food."

"So do I, but something about that sedan is creeping me out." Oliver shook himself. Other people were crossing, however, so he took a step off the curb.

"You think it's him?" Peter was staring at the sedan. "I can't see his face. He's got on big sunglasses and a ball cap, and his head is tipped down."

Almost like he's hiding? Oliver wondered. He and Peter crossed the street without any issues. It could have been because they were in a crowd, or because the driver of the sedan had nothing to do with the attempts on Oliver's life or the attack on Peter.

"The longer we go without anything happening, the more nervous I get," Oliver admitted.

"I think that's his or her game plan. Make you worry until you're so on edge, you can't relax." Peter glanced over his shoulder for a moment then grunted and faced forward. "The guy in the sedan looked this way. Still couldn't make out his features, but as soon as he saw me staring he turned his head away. Seems sketchy as hell to me."

"Did he have any scars?" Oliver winced. He'd permanently disfigured the first boy he'd bitten.

"Not that I saw," Peter answered. "We'll see if he shows up on the next block."

The sedan didn't appear again before Peter and Oliver made it to Peter's car.

"I don't think him not showing up again rules him out," Oliver said.

"Oh, me either." Peter unlocked the car. "In fact, I feel like that was him, and he was a little unnerved at us spotting him."

"Except I didn't see him, or what I *did* see of him didn't look familiar." Which was frustrating to Oliver. "I suppose someone could have hired him to harass me. Maybe killing me isn't the goal."

"Maybe it's not," Peter agreed. "This is an open-carry state. He could get a permit and shoot you if he wanted you dead. And on that note, I don't want you outside and you need to wear Kevlar."

The idea that he could be shot, taken out by a sniper at a distance or even someone closer to him was terrifying, but Oliver also believed it unlikely. "Seems like I'd be dead already. I suppose if it was someone who didn't live in Texas, however, it might be more difficult to get a gun?"

"Honestly, I don't know. I haven't read up on the law," Peter said. He started the car after they got in and buckled up. "Still, I'm not sure they want you dead. But what do they get out of fucking with you?" He backed out of his slot.

"Just making my life hell?" Oliver guessed. "They're not, though. You make me happy, and I love my job. It's not the same as having my own business, but in some ways, that's better. I feel less pressure, but still have the drive to succeed. So if they're trying to make my life hell, they're failing."

"Are they?" Peter countered. "You're fearful now. You've been hurt. I've been jumped. How safe do you feel? How much time do you spend worrying about you or me?"

"Point taken." Oliver wouldn't feel safe, or feel that Peter was safe, until this mystery was solved and the culprits had been dealt with. Though just how that'd be done, he didn't know. If it was another shifter, as both he and Peter suspected, then Oliver really didn't want the police involved. That included Jack, because Oliver didn't know where his loyalties lay, other than with Lucy.

"So, we put an end to this stalking and harassing crap," Peter said. "Security cameras in your place and mine, inside and out. Your apartment complex has them outside and in the halls, but you don't have anything inside your place. If he managed to break in somehow, and we can't dismiss that, not after the garage parking lot attack, then you'd need video, something that doesn't run on electricity, either. Also, a dash cam for the car, and maybe some kind of tracking chip we could each carry hidden somewhere."

"You've really thought this out," Oliver observed, impressed with Peter.

Peter nodded. "I have. I've actually got a list I was going to go over with you, and I will. After."

"After." One word, and Oliver's dick went hard as stone. He was glad he didn't live far away at all.

Peter pulled into the apartment complex and drove to the parking garage. He used Oliver's keycard to get in, rolled both front windows down a few inches, then went all the way to the top level to park. They had a method now, one that would hopefully keep them from being attacked and Tasered. Oliver and Peter both checked the parking garage, every level of it, as they drove.

"All clear," Peter declared as he parked.

"All clear," Oliver agreed. They rolled the windows up, unbuckled, then got out of the car.

Peter locked it, and together they headed for the elevator. After a couple of minutes, during which Oliver considered just what he was going to do to Peter when he got him naked, the elevator doors opened. A man stood in the back, looking down at his phone. Oliver stepped onto the elevator, with Peter right beside him.

Then it hit him, just as a sharp pinch registered to his neck. Oliver blinked slowly, eyelids suddenly too heavy to hold open for long. There was no scent in the elevator. None at all.

Chapter Twelve

Peter didn't have time to dodge the projectile coming at him. He saw Oliver collapse, and was thrown off balance by it since Oliver was right beside him. The projectile turned out to be a dart that hit Peter in the right biceps. The needle pierced his skin but not his muscle. It went through, the sharp end protruding as he let himself drop to the floor of the elevator.

Some of the drug in the dart must have gotten in his system, or fear was making him light-headed and on the verge of passing out. He kept his eyes almost closed, hoping his thick lashes would disguise the fact that he was trying to watch the attacker.

The man didn't look familiar at all. Then again, why would he, if he was an enemy of Oliver's? Peter noted the stranger's worn tennis shoes, dark jeans, black T-shirt and sleek build. He wasn't tall, maybe five-eight or so, and his long black hair hung in a braid over one shoulder, his red ball cap covering the top of his head. Large sunglasses were hooked on the collar of his t-shirt. He stared down at Oliver and Peter with dark brown eyes, no expression on his face at all.

After a moment, the elevator began to move, and the stranger took his phone from his jeans pocket and sent off a text.

When the elevator stopped, it must have only gone down three or four floors, not the entirety of the parking garage. The doors swished open.

"Good, you got the motherfucker," a second man rasped. "And his fuck toy."

The black haired man hissed, not like a snake. He sounded like an angry possum or cat. "What you got against this one?" He nudged Peter with one foot. "He ain't the one that did anything to you."

"Doesn't matter. Hurting him will hurt Oliver. Now, come on and help me get them loaded while the cameras are disabled." The second man was tall like Oliver, thin, and he licked his lips often.

Snake. He's a snake. But why — ? Peter barely repressed a gasp when the man turned his head. The right side of his face was terribly scarred, as if all the flesh under the skin had rotted away and numerous attempts had been made to graft skin in places where perhaps the original had been destroyed.

And Peter knew why he and Oliver were being kidnapped. And he also knew nothing good was going to come of it.

"Keep that snake unconscious," said the one who had to be Thomas, the now-grown boy Oliver had left scarred. "His bite will kill you if you're lucky, or leave you like me if you aren't."

"What about the rabbit?" asked the black-haired man.

"Hare," Thomas corrected, "and fuck if I know, Benny. I guess he could wake up and fuck you to death. You know what they say about bunnies."

"Is it the same for hares?" Benny asked with a hint of snark.

"Fuck you. Help me with these so we can get them back to the room before Ellis gets there." Thomas grabbed at Oliver's arms.

Peter noted the way Thomas' hands shook. And he remembered the name Ellis—the bastard who'd screwed Oliver out of his business. It seemed that the two people in the world who hated Oliver—Ellis, for some unknown reason, and the man who'd been a boy left scarred by Oliver's venom—had colluded to do something to him.

And to me. They aren't going to be letting me hop away. Which was true. Peter closed his eyes a little more as Benny hefted him up.

"Look," Benny said, "I don't know what's going on here, but this guy didn't do anything to you."

"Oh, please," Thomas sneered. "You know exactly what's going on. We hired you to find Oliver, to stalk him and make his life hell."

"Hired me?" Benny snapped.

"Just shut the fuck up and do what I tell you!" Thomas' voice reached an eardrum-piercing screech. "Now!"

Oliver was dumped in the back of a van, one of the creepy kind with no windows except for the windshield and the two for the driver and passenger seat sides.

Thomas jabbed Oliver with a second dart. "Stay asleep, fucker." He pulled the dart out and slammed the van doors closed.

A minute later, the van was moving. Peter didn't know who was driving, but he certainly knew one thing—they were both idiots, Thomas and Benny. Neither had bothered to check for cell phones.

Their mistake. Peter made sure his phone was on silent once he got it out. Then he sent Lucy a text, telling her what had happened. He added a plea for her to not call the police, because explaining how Thomas got the scar and why he wanted revenge would expose shifters to the world.

Then there was Ellis, the sneaky fox shifter. What was his role in this?

Peter couldn't figure it out. He kept a close eye on Oliver, making sure he was breathing, that he hadn't overdosed on whatever drug he'd been given. His chest rose steadily, almost like he was asleep rather than knocked out by some unknown substance.

Peter checked his phone and saw a text pop up. Lucy had sent a flurry of them, actually, with lots of exclamation points, curse words, and threats of demise for their kidnappers. She also said Jack was on his way to the parking garage.

The next text Peter sent had descriptions of Thomas and Benny, and he asked Lucy to Google Ellis, because Peter didn't know what he looked like. He didn't have a last name, either, but surely it wouldn't be difficult to find a guy named Ellis who owned an advertising agency in Boston.

She sent him a pic not a minute later. Peter had always thought foxes were cute, but he was going to have to revise his opinion on them after this. At least on shifter foxes.

Another message popped up. Peter almost giggled when he read Lucy's claim that Ellis looked like a bitter man with a small dick. Peter didn't see any such things in the photo and knew she was trying to keep him from going into full-blown panic.

He wasn't going to do that. He had Oliver to take care of, to guard. Peter opened his eyes wider and sat up, which made his head spin. A little woozy, but not too much so. He pulled the dart out of his arm and examined it. Whatever chemical it had held was gone. There went his plan to stab one of the kidnappers with it.

Although it'd still hurt like a motherfucker if he stabbed them in the right place.

Lucy sent him more texts, asking if he had any clue where he was, what speed they were going, anything. He could only tell her when they turned, and that the van held no scent at all.

There was something about the black-haired man that made Peter think he had something to do with the scent issue. Peter frowned as he tried to remember every detail of Benny, and when he pictured the long braid, he saw bits of white in it. Had that been white hair, or something else?

Peter wrinkled his nose. He only knew of one kind of shifter with black and white hair, and while they could be quite nice, there was usually a lingering odor that nothing could disguise, even when they were in human form. Those tended to be the people that doused themselves with perfumes and colognes—because a skunk shifter carried their scent on some level at all times. Maybe the human nose couldn't detect it, but other shifters could.

Except if Benny was a skunk, he'd had no odor.

So maybe he's something else? Peter texted Lucy and asked her about the possibilities of what Benny could be.

Her answer surprised him.

Maybe he's a descented skunk? I've heard of that happening to some skunk shifters, if they get caught while little and kept for pets. Eeeee. He could be neutered, too!

Peter's balls and cock tried to shrink up. Getting caught in animal form and kept as a pet was every shifter's worst nightmare. Many times, if they couldn't escape quickly, they ended up spayed or neutered. The females could still have sex, though not reproduce — but the males were pretty much impotent for the rest of their lives. Then there were the shots and being kept in a cage, or anywhere that wasn't a shifter's home.

The best thing a shifter could do in such scenarios was to get out of sight somehow, shift back into human form, and haul ass out of the situation without being seen.

He wondered if he and Oliver were going to end up as pets.

He wondered if Benny was a de-scented skunk, and if so, what that meant for him when he was human.

If it meant he had no scent at all.

And it there was some way he could spread his scentlessness.

All of those questions, he texted to Lucy. She didn't have answers, but at least she could try to find some.

Oliver's breathing was still steady, deep. Peter touched his neck, felt his pulse, then leaned over and kissed Oliver. "I do love you," Peter whispered, "and we aren't letting these motherfuckers steal our happy ending, babe. It just isn't happening."

He needed a plan. Peter had the dart, but a search of the back of the van left him with nothing additional to use. He could shift, fast. When the back doors were opened, maybe he should stab whoever he could in the eye or neck, and shift forms, because he could haul ass as a hare. That would mean leaving Oliver alone, but if Peter could just get his bearings, and somehow manage to run and hop with his phone — no, he couldn't manage that.

Playing it by ear was his only option. If he had to leave Oliver in order to get help, he would. He'd just have to hope they wouldn't kill Oliver. He didn't think that was their plan, otherwise they could have killed Oliver and Peter in the elevator. Yes, there'd been cameras in it, but he'd bet they'd been disabled.

Lucy texted him again, informing him that Jack and some other shifter police officers were unofficially looking for them.

God, Peter hoped they found them before it was too late.

Then he imagined a shoot-out with him and Oliver being killed in the crossfire.

Maybe he didn't want an off-duty police rescue after all.

Peter went back to trying to figure out how to escape with Oliver instead of leaving him behind.

Wherever they were going was likely to be someplace isolated. It wasn't like Benny and Thomas could just carry two unconscious men — or one unconscious man and one faking it — into a hotel, or anywhere there were other people. He texted that thought to Lucy.

It sucked that he couldn't get a scent at all. If he could, even a hint, he might have some idea of where they were.

Peter pressed his nose to the back doors, the seam where they met. *Nothing.* Then he shifted, and his senses sharpened. He sniffed and sniffed at the doors, and there, in one corner by a hinge, he smelled exhaust fumes, heard the sounds of other vehicles. They weren't on an extremely busy road. There was traffic, but not too much. There were also stoplights. A few whiffs of fast food places. Peter registered them — *Luby's, Bill Miller's, Sonic Drive-In, ooh, ick, a gas station — Death. Death, I smell chemicals and death and water —*

Peter knew where they were. At least, he thought he did. The San Antonio River ran down to the south side of town, and the city had recently restored an area of it, making it into a nicer place to go than it had been. There were bike paths and such, but there were also still bodies found there. If he didn't think quick, there might be two more.

Not happening. Peter shifted back and texted Lucy with his newfound hunch. He didn't bother putting his clothes on—he'd hopped out of them. Instead, he focused on trying to get Oliver to wake up. Peter shook him and tried tickling him. Normally, Oliver couldn't stand to have the soles of his feet touched. He'd squeal and giggle and squirm. Peter tickled and poked, pinched and finally, though he hated to, slapped Oliver, all to no avail. The man slept on.

Peter put his underwear back on, then his pants and shoes. He left his shirt off. Maybe he'd draw more attention if he ran screaming, half-dressed. *If* there was anyone hanging around Espada Park. And *if* that was where they were going. He might have just sent everyone looking for them off in the wrong direction.

He couldn't hear any conversation between Benny and Thomas. Peter went back to the doors and examined them. There were no inside handles, no way that he could see to open them from where he was. He traced over the seams and wondered if a credit card would unlock the latch. If so, he couldn't figure it out. Five minutes of frustration and he was cursing as he put his credit card, now warped, back into his wallet.

Then Lucy sent him a huge smiling GIF.

What? he sent back, irritated and scared.

You have Find Your Phone on. I can see where you are, and you were right. Espada it is.

Peter wanted to bang his head against the side of the van. He hadn't even thought about that app!

Well, at least Lucy had, and now he knew someone would be coming to help them, soon, hopefully.

Chapter Thirteen

Oliver groaned as sunlight so bright it should have burned his eyes clean out of his head breached his eyelids.

"Wake up, you son of a bitch."

Someone slapped him jarringly hard. He tasted blood from his split cheek.

"Wake." Another slap. "Up."

"Hey, stop hitting him!" That was Peter, and the slap following his outburst had Oliver trying to sit up with a roar, eyes snapping open, fury coursing through him.

"Ah, that's how we get to you, just like I thought."

Thomas. That's Thomas! The scars were still terrible.

"Look, Thomas, I am sorry you were scarred. I've told you that before. If you hadn't attacked me with those other boys—"

"Shut the fuck up, you freak," Thomas yelled. "You are a freak and you had that coming! We don't need your fucked-up kind in our pits, or in our world."

"What world is that?" Oliver dared to ask, spotting Peter, who was lying behind Thomas. Another man,

273

this one with black hair, and perhaps some white in it, stood behind Peter, glowering.

"The shifter world." Thomas hissed. "I'm gonna fix you, asshole. You're gonna shift, and I'm getting me a rattle."

Oliver hated being half rattler and half copperhead. That rattle had been the bane of his existence, but he wasn't keen on having it chopped off. Pain was not something he wanted any part of.

"You're gonna shift, or I'll hurt your little boyfriend here. Or hare." Thomas snickered at his own joke. "I won't even wait for him to shift before I neuter him."

Peter blanched and anger made Oliver's head pound.

The man behind Peter glared at the back of Thomas' head. "This is not anything I want a part of. I told you—"

"And I told you, you would do as I ordered, skunk, or I'd have your whole family put down. Rabies is such a horrible thing, and everyone knows skunks carry it."

Oliver knew that voice. "Ellis."

Ellis came around the side of a white van. His beady eyes narrowed at Oliver. "Yes, and unfortunately, I've decided that I can't trust you with the knowledge you have. Granted, I fixed what was done, and it was all part of getting your business, but still. You're a loose end."

Oliver shook his head, more to clear it than in denial. "What have you got against me?"

Ellis gestured at Thomas. "Did you know that Thomas and I were lovers from the time we were boys up until now? We still are, of course. I have to look at those scars. I have to see them. I can't leave, can't find someone else, because I have always loved him, and you *ruined* his beauty."

Thomas was cringing, shoulders slumping more and more as Ellis spoke.

"That's how you talk about the man you claim to love?" Peter queried. "Shouldn't you love him regardless, and think he's beautiful no matter what?"

Ellis' laugh was uglier than sin. "Grow up, you stupid hare. Beauty isn't more than skin deep. If you think Oliver would still want you if you looked like Thomas…well, maybe we should see if that's the case."

"That's enough." The skunk shifter strode forward. "This stops now."

"Fuck off, Benny." Ellis smiled, all sharp little teeth, and he lunged forward. Benny's eyes went wide and he gasped, looking down at the knife protruding from his chest.

"Sorry you won't get to say goodbye to your family," Ellis said. "I'll have the vet put them down in a week or two, once they've had time to suffer." Ellis shoved Benny, and he went down hard, head hitting the ground with a thud that made Oliver almost throw up.

Ellis wiped his hands together. "Well, that's done. Now, Oliver." Ellis approached him. "Time for you to make your precious lover look like mine." He removed a pistol from his jacket and aimed it at Peter. "By all means, he can be scarred for life, or I can leave his brains all over this very nicely paved lot."

"I've apologized," Oliver said, just as he'd done to Thomas. "I didn't know. No one knew my venom was so toxic."

"Don't give a fuck," Thomas rumbled. "I want your rattle. Think it'll leave you deformed in some way? Maybe you and your boyfriend will be a matching pair of ugly motherfuckers."

"You think Ellis is going to stay with you?" Oliver asked. "Did you *hear* how he talked about you?"

Thomas scowled. "He's right. I'm ugly as fuck. I'm a kid's nightmare, all 'cause of you."

No, all because you and your friends decided to jump me one day. Pointing that out didn't seem wise. "I wouldn't have bit you had I known. Don't make a mistake just because I did."

"Ain't gonna be a mistake," Thomas snarled. "Now shift or Ellis is gonna blow hare brains all over."

"It's okay, Oliver." Peter smiled bravely at him. "Bite me. Scar me. I know you'll still love me."

"I will always love you," Oliver declared.

"Sweet," Ellis said sarcastically. "Are you two going to start singing and dancing now?"

"Hard to do under the circumstances," Peter replied.

Ellis shoved the pistol against Peter's temple. "Shut up, asshole."

Thomas gestured to Oliver. "Shift."

Oliver took a breath, then he let himself shift and hoped he wasn't making the biggest mistake of his life. Before he'd even finished his shift, he was diving at Ellis.

Peter knocked Ellis' hand away and Thomas roared, jumping onto Oliver's back.

But Oliver had gotten close enough. He sank his fangs into Ellis' neck, the first place he reached. He released his venom and Ellis screamed.

Thomas grabbed Oliver by the tail, knife in hand. "No!"

Peter slammed into Thomas. They both grunted, and Peter grasped Thomas' wrist with both hands, shoving the knife up and away.

Thomas shifted. Oliver pulled his fangs out of Ellis.

Ellis writhed and shifted into his fox form, perhaps seeking to heal the bite.

It had been a long time since Oliver had released any venom. He hadn't thought about that when he'd leaped onto Ellis, but now, he feared the man wouldn't survive.

Then the skunk shifter rolled over, the bloody knife he'd been stabbed with in hand, and he nearly decapitated Ellis. Before Oliver could do more than gag — very painful in his snake form — Benny threw the same knife and sliced Thomas' head right off, as well. "That's done then," Benny rasped before falling over.

At that moment, the sound of multiple engines rang out in the air. Peter shifted into hare form and hopped behind some shrubs. Oliver joined him, and they both sighed in relief when Jack arrived with a half dozen other shifters.

"What a goddamn mess," Jack said. "Hey, this guy's alive. Better call an ambulance." He leaned down. "He has no scent. Not even his blood."

"Not really a scent to this area," another man pointed out.

"Huh. That's weird." Jack looked right at the bush where Peter and Oliver were. "Skedaddle. No one is going to be looking for a hare and a snake."

Maybe not, but they couldn't make it all the way to Oliver's place in their animal forms.

"Lucy's parked a mile up the road," Jack added.

That's better. Oliver coiled around Peter because he just had to hug him.

Peter rubbed his soft, furry cheek against Oliver's head in return. It felt good and safe, the two of them together. Oliver didn't like what had happened, but he couldn't change it. What he could do was let go of his past completely, and concentrate on the here and now with his lover.

E p i l o g u e

Peter wasn't certain that Oliver would be up to any sexy times. They'd had a pretty traumatic and violent day.

But they'd also had a deeply emotional day, so when Oliver came out of the bathroom, gloriously naked, and told Peter to get down on his knees and suck, Peter bounced over — in human form — and happily did as Oliver demanded. He liked it when Oliver was so commanding.

Peter palmed Oliver's balls and gave them a good, soothing rub. He looked up at Oliver as he licked from the base of his dick all the way to the tip. Pre-cum was already gathered there, and Peter smeared it over his lips before sucking on that little opening, seeking more of the sweetness there.

Oliver gave it to him, more pre-cum welling up.

Peter moaned and fisted his own dick. As soon as he sucked Oliver down to the base, as soon as he had the fat, hot tip of Peter's cock in his throat, Peter came.

Oliver grunted and held Peter's head still as he began fucking Peter's face. It made Peter hard, or kept him hard. It didn't matter which. He would come again soon.

Oliver's balls slapped Peter's chin repeatedly as Oliver moved faster, then faster still. The roughness was arousing, and Peter was completely caught off-guard by it when Oliver went stiff and spunk jetted into Peter's mouth. Usually, Oliver could go for hours without coming.

Peter swallowed Oliver's release, then nuzzled his balls and his still-hard erection. "Everything okay?" he asked after Oliver quit panting.

"Yes," Oliver said, his voice very rough. "I just started thinking about something and it— I couldn't hold back."

"Oh, yeah?" Peter looked up through his lashes at Oliver. "And what was that?"

"Your cock, in my ass," Oliver replied.

Peter plopped back on his butt in shock. "Y-you want m-me to—"

"Not if you don't want to. It's okay. It was just a fantasy," Oliver babbled. "I never let anyone even touch my hole and I just let my mind run away with—"

"Oliver," Peter interrupted, rising to his feet. He looked Oliver in the eyes. "I'm a bottom, it's true, but I have topped before a few times, and I would love to slide my cock into that lean, tight ass of yours."

"You would?" Oliver's face had reached a new shade of red. "I mean it. You don't have to."

Peter pointed to the bed. "Lie down, on your back. I'm going to love you like you've never been loved."

Oliver knew he meant it, too.

Once on the bed, Oliver felt oddly exposed, and didn't know where to put his arms and legs, where to look. Then it didn't matter, because Peter was lying on him, kissing, nibbling, making love to him.

Never had Oliver trusted anyone enough to give himself to them. Peter was special — Peter was loving, loyal and his. And now, Oliver would belong to Peter, would give him this, and would receive from Peter something only he would ever give Oliver.

Peter kissed a trail down to Oliver's cock. Since Oliver wasn't big on having his nipples played with, or on ass play for himself, he didn't know how he was going to feel when Peter finally touched him there.

Peter sucked Oliver's cock down in one smooth move. At the same time, he ran slick fingers over around Oliver's balls.

Oliver didn't know when Peter had gotten the lube, but he clearly had. He ghosted over his fingers over Oliver's asshole, and fiery tendrils of need burst out from that area, quickly spreading through Oliver's body.

"Please," he found himself saying over and over again as Peter teased his hole.

Then there was pressure, a burn, a very odd sensation of something in his ass. Oliver clenched, and Peter wiggled that digit until he found Oliver's gland.

Oliver relaxed a lot faster after that. He moaned and soon started to thrust, wanting, needing more in his ass. Peter fingered and licked him, pushed his tongue alongside his thumb, and he took the time to tell Oliver every dirty thing he was about to do.

"Both thumbs, babe," Peter said, mouth and chin slick from licking Oliver and from the lube. "Both thumbs," he repeated, pushing them in. "Then I'm gonna fuck and stretch you with them like this."

Oliver couldn't see what he was doing, but it felt magnificent. Panting, writhing, Oliver was burning up inside, needing more, needing something he hadn't thought to need.

"Yeah, you love it," Peter said. "I love doing it. We both learned something new from each other again."

Oliver tried to reply, but the gurgling sound he made was unintelligible.

There was a bigger stretch at his hole, more fingers, more burn. Oliver rubbed his gland over and over, until his dick was dripping pre-cum steadily and Oliver just had to reach for his shaft.

"That's it," Peter urged, "because I won't last long, but I'll come more than once, I guarantee it." He withdrew his fingers. "Ready for me?"

"Always," Oliver managed to say.

Hot, hard, thick, unyielding — the pressure at Oliver's hole was almost too much.

"Push," Peter advised. "Let me in."

Oliver looked into Peter's eyes, and it was easy then. He trusted this man with everything.

Peter moaned as his cock sank in deep. He didn't move fast, but he was steady, and it wasn't until his balls were pressed to Oliver's ass that he held still.

Eyes shining brightly, Peter moved just a little. "Oh, oh, God. Tell me when I can move more. Tell me when I can pull out and drive in."

"Soon?" Oliver guessed. He had no idea what he could handle.

But he learned, arching into every thrust, loving the tug of the underside of Peter's cock against the inner rim of Oliver's hole.

Peter came fast, a few strokes in, his cum hot and plentiful in Oliver. "More?" Peter rasped. "Can I?"

Oliver nodded.

Peter didn't slow down until he'd come two more times, then he pulled out and beat off until he came on Oliver's stomach.

Peter moaned and fell over onto his back. "Can't. Move."

Oliver knew how he felt. His hole was tender, but he felt…good. Whole. Loved.

It was a feeling he would do everything to retain, and as he looked as his lover, he saw his own silent vow reflected in Peter's eyes.

Two strangers, now two partners, and hopefully in the future, husbands. Oliver hadn't expected any of this.

But he'd take it, and he'd treasure it, and Peter, every day of their lives.

About the Author

A native Texan, Bailey spends her days spinning stories around in her head, which has contributed to more than one incident of tripping over her own feet. Evenings are reserved for pounding away at the keyboard, as are early morning hours. Sleep? Doesn't happen much. Writing is too much fun, and there are too many characters bouncing about, tapping on Bailey's brain demanding to be let out.

Caffeine and chocolate are permanent fixtures in Bailey's office and are never far from hand at any given time. Removing either of those necessities from Bailey's presence can result in what is known as A Very, Very Scary Bailey and is not advised under any circumstances.

Bailey loves to hear from readers. You can find their contact information, website details and author profile page at http://www.pride-publishing.com.